D1148697

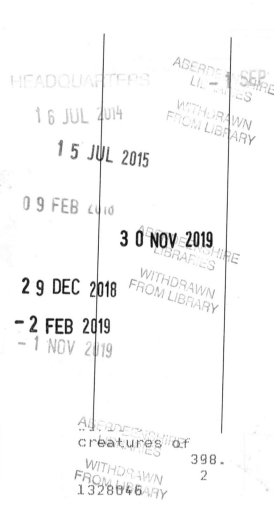

NOT OF THIS WORLD

Creatures of the Supernatural in Scotland

MAURICE FLEMING

Illustrated by
Alan McGowan

mercatpress
www.mercatpress.com

First published in 2002 by Mercat Press Ltd.
10 Coates Crescent, Edinburgh EH3 7AL
www.mercatpress.com

ISBN: 184183 0402

398·2
1328046

Set in Tiepolo Book and Ehrhardt at Mercat Press

Printed and bound in Great Britain by Bell & Bain Ltd

Contents

v

Illustrations

Introduction

'The sea eagle is back!' read the headline a few years ago. The report told how this beautiful bird, long absent from Scotland, had been re-introduced. Now, several years later, we read that a number of breeding pairs are once again established round our coasts. Other species have also been brought back and, as I write, Scottish Natural Heritage is planning to re-introduce the beaver and possibly the wolf.

No conservation body, however hard it tried, could bring back any of the creatures described in these pages. Would one want to see them return? Some might be welcome. Little Puddlefoot, for instance, who paddled happily in a Perthshire burn all day. The mermaids turning somersaults as they sported in the sea. The domestic brownie, who slept through the day and bustled out at night to clean the kitchen and sweep the floors. The mysterious Finn men who came out of nowhere in their tiny kayaks. Ghillie Dhu, the bright spirit of the Gairloch woods. I would even put in a personal plea for the urisk, the lonely, shambling grey man of the mountains.

Of course not all have gone. Of the whole strange ragged army, there are, here and there, a few survivors. Ghosts are not dealt with here—the term is too general—but ghostly green ladies are included for they are still being sighted, as are grey ladies and phantom black dogs. Somehow these linger on in this increasingly unbelieving world.

The vast majority of supernatural beings or creatures, however, seem to have departed as surely as the fairies did when they rode up from Eathie Glen and vowed they would never more be seen in Scotland.

As far as many of the creatures are concerned, we may well say 'good riddance!' Nobody would want to come on the bean-nighe bending at her melancholy task, washing shrouds in the river, nor hear the ominous three barks of the green fairy dogs or the hoarse roar of the giant winged boobrie. Our roads are dangerous enough without the risk of meeting Coluinn the Headless in Morar or the Black Walker in Rannoch.

Our lochs and rivers are a lot safer without the wily water horse, our seas a better and happier place without the merciless blue men, the seefer, the giant worms, and the appalling nuckelavee which so terrified poor Tammas.

And yet, in losing sight of all these, the kindly as well as the malevolent, the tender with the cruel, are we not turning our backs on something precious? If we want to get to know our ancestors, learning to know what they believed in is as good a way as any. Understand the creatures and we may come to know why minds were so gripped by them.

For gripped they were. Every family then had its own fears and taboos, every community its own tales, its own shared knowledge of how to deal with the visible and the invisible.

The history books are little help here. This is an area that is largely ignored. Even the social historians tend to have little to say about it. Yet it was all so real to people living on the land two centuries and more ago. For them this was not the stuff of fairy tales but the stuff of life. There were wee folk under the ground, witches in the sky, there was a glaistig or a gruagach amongst the cattle, a kelpie in the burn, a water bull in the lochan, while that black cat or hare might well be Satan himself.

In *The Folklore of the Scottish Highlands* Dr Anne Ross quotes this *cri de coeur*:

> From every gruagach and banshee,
> From every evil wish and sorrow,
> From every glaistig and bean-nighe,
> From every fairy-mouse and grass-mouse,
> From every fuath amongst the hills,
> From every siren hard pressing me,
> From every urisk within the glens,
> Oh! save me till the end of my day,
> Oh! save me till the end of my day!

Appeals such as this were commonplace in devout areas of the country. The God-fearing Gael of those times would be astonished to learn that we see no need to raise such a prayer now. He would be horrified that we no longer safeguard newborn babies against abduction by the fairies, that we don't understand the protective properties of the rowan, cold steel or a crowing cockerel.

What was everyday essential knowledge in pastoral Scotland is all but gone. Fortunately men and women, here and there, were writing it down. It is thanks to them that we know something of what was happening, what was being said, in kitchen and byre, in the fields and on the hills, and out at sea. Through the stories they recorded we can see the creatures which loomed so large in peoples' imaginations.

And the tales and beliefs take us even further back in time, for as we meet and inspect these weird and wonderful creatures, we can often glimpse behind them even older presences, the gods and goddesses of an earlier set of beliefs, ancient deities that ruled the minds of men long before the coming of the saints with their Christian crosses and creeds.

All that aside, I hope many readers will simply enjoy the stories told in this book. Scotland has one of the richest collections of traditional tales in Europe, so vast a number that many lie still unpublished. I have found room for as many as possible and some, told only briefly, can be found in my earlier books. If appetites are whetted for more, the list of works consulted points the way. And if demand increases, perhaps it will speed the availability of material still locked from sight in archives.

Many of our best writers and artists have drawn inspiration from traditional sources. In art John Duncan and Jessie M. King are outstanding examples. Novelists, poets and playwrights have all found themes from folklore. I have tried to reflect this with quotations and references.

When I was writing the book I thought long and hard about the order in which the subjects should best appear. In folklore terms the creatures discussed are nearly all fairy types. I could have divided them into groups, such as Tutelary Fairies and Nature Fairies.

Tutelary Fairies would include such creatures as the brownie, glaistig, gruagach, gunna, killmoulis and old man of the barn. These are all solitaries which attach themselves to a house, castle, farm, mill etc. They take on duties which may consist of domestic chores, herding cattle, threshing corn or other work.

Nature Fairies would cover a wide range: mermaids, water horses and kelpies, king otters, bean-nighes, selkies, trows and individuals such as the Cailleach Bheur, Ghillie Dhu, the Gyre-carline and Habetrot.

A third section of Monsters would be filled with giants, sea serpents, worms, blue men, the bochdan, boobrie, wild shackle, Great-hand, and It, the beast too terrible to name.

Fairies I could have put in a section with the boys said to have consorted with them. Fairy changelings would sit nicely alongside these, as would the trows and harmless little characters such as Wag-at-the-Wa.

Another possibility was to group my 'cast list' according to where they were found—in buildings, under the ground, in the countryside, in fresh water or in the sea.

Instead of any of these, I have chosen to put them in alphabetical order, letting Fatlips, for instance, rub shoulders with fairy dogs and the Fearsome Man. This, I hope, makes for easy reference and an enjoyable and varied read.

I will welcome further information from readers on any of the creatures mentioned and any that are not. The hunt to track them to their lairs continues!

The Collectors

A list of sources consulted in the writing of this book appears at the back. It ranges from the nineteenth century to the present day.

If folklore is not recorded in some way it can be quickly lost to future generations. It is a sad fact that many otherwise useful local histories written in the last two centuries contain very little folklore. In some, if it is dealt with at all, it is in a cursory and dismissive manner. In many cases, the writer has been unaware of the rich folk culture around him. In others, he or she has seen it as of scant interest or value.

There is nothing more frustrating for the folklorist than to come on a bald reference or brief summary of what sounds like a fine legend. Many parish histories are littered with these.

Fortunately, things have improved greatly in recent years and there are now examples of new local histories which devote at least some space to the accurate recording of tales, rhymes, customs etc.

Writers concentrating exclusively on the folklore of an area have, until more recent times, been few and far between, and are all the more appreciated for their rarity. It is to these that we owe much of our knowledge today. Readers will find, in the pages that follow, frequent references to some of the great collectors on whom we have come to rely.

In the Highlands and Islands, three Campbells all produced classic works. John Francis Campbell of Islay, born in 1822, not only collected himself but he roped in his friends and sent them out into the field in their home districts. Having written it all down they passed it to him to deal with. The result was two volumes of *Popular Tales of the West Highlands* published in his lifetime and two more after his death.

John Gregorson Campbell, born 1836, became a minister on Tiree and Coll. His books, such as *Superstitions of the Highlands and Islands of Scotland*, are remarkable achievements at a time when his church frowned upon all superstitious beliefs.

The third of the trio, Lord Archibald Campbell, edited *Waifs and Strays of Celtic Tradition* (1891) inspired largely by Gregorson Campbell.

Alexander Carmichael, born on Lismore in 1832, compiled the amazing *Carmina Gadelica*, a huge collection of Gaelic prayers and invocations which also contains folklore in various forms, especially in his extensive notes.

Easter Ross lore was diligently written up by the redoubtable Hugh Miller, the Cromarty stone mason who became a leading geologist and, after his move to Edinburgh, editor of a Free Church newspaper. His books, *Scenes and Legends of the North of Scotland*, *The Old Red Sandstone* and *My Schools and Schoolmasters*, are filled with tales and character studies of strong interest.

Another Easter Ross writer, Donald A. Mackenzie, researched legends in his native county and across the Highlands and left us very readable books, of which *Scottish Folk Lore and Folk Life* is probably the best.

Sir Walter Scott's fascination with Border history and lore runs through many of his writings, and his major folklore works are *Letters on Demonology and Witchcraft*, *Minstrelsy of the Scottish Border*, and *The Border Antiquities of England and Scotland*.

James Hogg in the Borders, and Robert Chambers in Edinburgh, both recorded tales and customs which repay study.

Orkney and Shetland have been well served by native collectors W. Trail Dennison, Tom Henderson, Ernest Marwick, Tom Muir, James R. Nicolson and others.

Also, more recently, R. MacDonald Robertson roved Scotland, especially the Highland counties, coaxing tales and traditions from folk he encountered, as did another colourful character, Alasdair Alpin MacGregor.

When Edinburgh University formed the School of Scottish Studies in the 1950s, trained field collectors were dispatched with tape recorders to build up an archive of folk material of all kinds. Readers may be familiar with the names of Calum Maclean, Hamish Henderson, John McInnes and D. A. MacDonald. Their exemplary pioneering work is now being carried on by students and graduates of what has been renamed The School of Celtic and Scottish Studies.

Although her books deal with folklore all over the British Isles, Katharine Briggs knew Scotland well and always gave due place to Scottish material. Her four volume *Dictionary of British Folk-Tales* is a treasurehouse as is her single volume *Dictionary of Fairies*.

Among excellent local collectors and recorders I would like to mention J. L. Campbell (another one!) of Canna, A. D. Cunningham (Rannoch), Alan Temperley (Sutherland and Galloway) and Affleck Gray (the Cairngorms). To them, and all the others, I express my thanks. Beside their efforts my own collecting pales into insignificance.

I also wish to thank all those who have helped in a variety of ways, particularly the following: Laurence and Jennie Blair Oliphant, Alison Cook of *The Scots Magazine*, Catherine Emslie, James and Moira Ferguson, Archy and Chrissie Macpherson, Adam and Mollie Malcolm, Andrew Valentine, Joane Whitmore of Glengarry Visitor Centre, the School of Celtic and Scottish Studies, the staffs of the A. K. Bell Library, Perth, Wellgate Library, Dundee, Blairgowrie and Rattray Branch Library, my daughter Airlie for her expertise on the computer and Mercat Press for their patience and encouragement.

Maurice Fleming
Blairgowrie, 2002

Bauchans

These creatures seem to have been as puzzling as they were infuriating: picking fights with people one minute and doing them a good turn the next. They could be dangerous, like Coluinn the Headless in Morar. Although it had no head this bauchan was greatly feared, and with good reason. It haunted a stretch of road known as the Smooth Mile, between Morar House and the river Morar.

It bore a loyal attachment to the family at Morar House and would never harm any of them. Women and children too were safe from it. But any man venturing on the road at night was liable to meet a violent death. His mutilated body would be found by the roadside in the morning.

One night it killed a stranger to Morar, a friend and relative of the MacLeods of Raasay. When the news reached Raasay, Iain Garbh, son of the Chief, prepared at once to avenge his friend's death.

He crossed over to Morar and set out, at night, to walk along the Smooth Mile. As he expected, the bauchan sprang in front of him. The beast lunged at him but Iain was ready and, after a struggle, had the loathsome creature in his grip. He knew that, if he could hold it till day broke, the bauchan would lose its powers to harm him.

As dawn approached, Coluinn begged Iain Garbh to let him go free, promising that, if he did so, it would never be seen there again.

Iain Garbh insisted that it swear on its knees. The bauchan did so and, just as the sun rose, Iain released his hold. The bauchan slunk away.

There were no more deaths on the Smooth Mile. Coluinn the Headless, it was said, went to live on a hill in the north of Skye where it seems to have caused no one any trouble.

A bauchan that lived in Lochaber struck up a relationship with a crofter called Callum MacIntosh. Sometimes it was a help to Callum but other times it would turn nasty and goad him into a stand-up fight.

One of the occasions when Callum had cause to be grateful to the bauchan was when a snowstorm cut off his house and he could not get to the woods to fetch more wood for the fire. He and his wife faced a cold few days, but during the night they heard a great crash outside, and when Callum went to investigate, there was the bauchan grinning at him and a huge tree trunk lying on the ground ready to be sawn into logs.

If the bauchan had always been as helpful as that it would have been fine but often it would start fighting with Callum for no reason at all. Once, when Callum was returning from the market at Fort William, he met the bauchan who began to throw punches at him. Callum was glad to get safely inside his house.

Afterwards he discovered his handkerchief was missing. This was a very special handkerchief because it had been given to him by his priest who had blessed it. Callum valued it highly.

He rushed back to the scene of their tussle and there was the bauchan rubbing the handkerchief on a flat stone.

'Ah!' said the bauchan, 'You are back. It is well for you, for if I had rubbed a hole into this before your return you were a dead man. But you shall never have it back till you have won it in a fair fight.'

'Done!' said Callum, and he fought with the bauchan until he had won it back.

The day came when Callum and his wife, along with many other people from Lochaber, left their homes and made their way to Arisaig to board an emigration ship for New York.

On arrival in their new country they had to spend many days in quarantine. When at last Callum came out, the first face he saw was the bauchan.

'Ah, Callum,' he grinned, 'You see I am here before you!'

If Callum was dismayed to see his old adversary he was to be grateful later as the bauchan, with its great strength, was a huge help to him when it came to clearing the land for his new home and farm.

This is not the only account of one of Scotland's creatures crossing the Atlantic to surprise the person they had secretly followed.

Bean-nighes

This is one nobody wanted to meet. The bean-nighe was a washer-woman and what she washed were the shrouds of those about to die. Sometimes it was the shroud of the person who saw her.

She carried out her mournful work at a ford or by a river or loch, and as she toiled she sang a wailing lament. The traveller would hear this from a long distance and the slap-slap of the garments as she beat them on the rocks.

Bean-nighe
This is one nobody wanted to meet... what she washed
were the shrouds of those about to die...

In some parts of the Highlands—Skye, for instance—the bean-nighe was no bigger than a child; a mere waif. In Highland Perthshire, though still small, she was stoutly built and clad in fairy green.

In Mull and Tiree, according to J. G. Campbell, the bean-nighe was blessed with such big breasts that they were in the way when she stooped to her task. She would throw them over her shoulder so that they hung down at the back.

It was considered the right thing for a man to creep up behind her and take one of the breasts in his mouth, holding it there until she gave him an answer to any question he asked.

What he most wanted to know, of course, was who was the shroud for? If she said it was for one of his enemies, he would seal the person's doom by releasing her to finish her work. If the shroud was for himself or a friend, he would not let her continue, and death would be postponed.

Elsewhere in the Highlands, if a man captured a bean-nighe, he would sometimes refuse to let her go until she had granted him three wishes. Men who had been granted wishes by a bean-nighe were considered very fortunate. And so they were, for if a man was observed before he seized her, she would put a spell on his limbs that rendered them useless.

One of Scotland's finest short story writers of last century, Dorothy K. Haynes, wrote a spine-tingling tale about a little girl's encounter with a bean-nighe. Hurrying home at gloaming from a long day's work at the big house, she hears a 'splash-clap' from the river. Expecting to find her mother washing clothes, she goes over to the figure on the river bank 'bent double, dabbling with her hands, a dim white smudge of greyness.'

But when the figure straightens and looks over her shoulder at the intruder, it is not Mary's mother. 'This woman was short, with a withered mean face, and small horrible feet grappling the ground, bare, webbed like a duck's.'

Mary runs home in terror and tells her mother, who persuades her to return a few nights later to find out from the bean-nighe the name of the person who is to die. This time the woman looks pathetic rather than horrible, 'a tired sad body washing in the dark. There was a world of heartbreak in the way she lifted the linen.'

Mary creeps closer, but does not get a chance to ask the fearful question. The bean-nighe swings round: 'There was a whirl of wet cloth, the stinging smack, smack of wet cloth on bare legs.'

The little girl is left lying helpless on the ground, unable to walk. That is how her mother finds her and the story ends with Mary being carried home in pain and misery, to await the 'deeper tragedy still to come'.

Dorothy Haynes' description of the bean-nighe as having feet 'webbed like a duck's' is one given in several accounts of the creature. Some reports say she had a large protruding tooth and single nostril.

She could be said to be the Highland equivalent of the Irish banshee which foretells a death, and the name banshee is sometimes used in Scotland, as in this Highland poem:

> The banshee I with second sight,
> Singing in the cold starlight;
> I wash the death-clothes pure and white,
> For Fergus More must die tonight.

Some folk believed that the bean-nighe had the power to appear by day in the shape of a raven, hoodie crow or black dog.

The Big Grey Man

It was to be just another Annual General Meeting of the Cairngorm Club, its 27th. The year was 1925 and there was no reason to believe that it would be any more exciting than the previous AGMs.

The speaker who had been booked, Professor Norman Collie, was a good safe choice. Professor of Organic Chemistry at the University of London and a Fellow of the Royal Society, he was Aberdeenshire-born and he knew his hills. Indeed he was one of the great climbers of his generation. He was also a quiet man to the point of reticence. His manner has been described as 'dry as dust'. Members of the Cairngorm Club, gathered in Aberdeen, did not expect any fireworks.

But when he rose to address them, what he had to say sent shock waves round the room. It was to become a headline story in the Press, a talking point not just in this country but abroad. It brought fame, or, if you like, notoriety, to the Cairngorm Club and to the Cairngorm mountains themselves.

For this austere academic described how, climbing alone on Ben MacDhui, he had experienced blind terror. Something, he said, had been following him, something he could not see in the mist. He could hear it, hear its steps crunching in the snow behind him. It must, he said, have been huge, for it took one stride for every three or four of his.

He went on: 'I said to myself, "This is all nonsense." I listened and heard it again but could see nothing in the mist. As I walked on and the eerie crunch, crunch, sounded behind me, I was seized with terror and took to my heels, staggering blindly among the boulders for four or five miles nearly down to Rothiemurchus Forest.'

And he added, 'Whatever you make of it, I do not know, but there is something very queer about the top of Ben MacDhui and I will not go back there again by myself I know.'

Coming from such a respected and sober figure, that statement alone was pretty shattering. It unleashed a controversy which is running still.

There have been many who have scoffed at Collie and suggested it had all been a trick of an overheated imagination. Others have put forward scientific explanations for the sounds he heard. It was pointed out by sceptics that Collie had been talking about something that had happened many years earlier: why had he not mentioned it before?

In fact he had. He had spoken of it to friends in Scotland and in New Zealand where the story had reached the newspapers long before it surfaced in the British Press.

Did he make his speech deliberately to cause a sensation? From what we know of his character from his friends, this seems out of the question. It is far more likely that it simply did not occur to him how newsworthy his story was. If he had realised it, and had wanted publicity, he would surely have spoken publicly on the subject long before. It had, after all, happened in 1891, 34 years before he stood up at that meeting.

Obviously he had thought about his strange experience many times during those years. He must have given it a great deal of thought. Perhaps he was simply taking the chance to share the memory of it with friends and fellow members of the climbing fraternity. He may have thought that, since it was a private club occasion, what he said would not go beyond the walls of the function room. It is a mistake that has been made by many public figures since. Not a few politicians have thought the same thing and suffered the consequences.

Collie did not speak about a 'Big Grey Man'. He made it clear he saw nothing. The name is from the Gaelic, *Fear Liath Mor*, the name by which the Ben MacDhui phenomenon was known to natives of the area long before Collie's disclosure.

How often it has been seen is impossible to say. Many of the old families that provided shepherds and stalkers for the Cairngorms have died out or moved away. Of those that remain, few members, in past or recent years, have been willing to talk about it.

Most of the reported sightings have come from visitors to the mountain, climbers and walkers. Men like two brothers called Kellas, who were chipping for rock crystals one afternoon when they saw a tall figure coming down the slope towards them. It went out of sight behind a rise and never reappeared. This incident was described by a correspondent to the Aberdeen *Press and Journal* who had been a lifelong friend of one of the brothers.

Alex Tewnion, a well-known naturalist and writer in the 1950s, heard footsteps following him on an overcast afternoon in October 1943. Like the steps heard by Collie, they were interspersed with long intervals as if the stride was a huge one. He turned and saw a large shape, drew out a revolver and fired it three times. When the shape still came on he turned, like Collie, and ran.

An even better-known personality, Wendy Wood, also fled from MacDhui. Wendy was a writer, an artist and a lively figure on Scotland's political scene for many years. A doughty fighter, she was not the sort of person to be feart of anybody or anything. Yet the footsteps and the sense of something there sent her hurrying to safety.

Affleck Gray, an assiduous collector of Cairngorm folklore, spent many years contacting people who had stories to tell of their experiences on MacDhui. His book *The Big Grey Man of Ben MacDhui* contains the results of his extensive researches.

He traced people who had heard mysterious voices when there was nobody there, and strange music which seemed to come out of the ground. These phenomena do not concern us here. Nor do the theories that link the mountain with spaceships or the Great White Brotherhood which, some claim, are manning hi-tech equipment in a great bowl under MacDhui's summit.

Nor can I take seriously the testimony of Sir Hugh Rankin, a Scot who became a Buddhist and was, in the 1940s, a leading player in the World Buddhist Association. I knew Sir Hugh and a fine and sensible man he seemed—he shared my interest in birds—but I could not accept his story of how he and his wife encountered, in the Lairig Ghru, a Bodhisattva, one of the five 'Perfected Men', billions of years old, who rule the world. The one they met, said Sir Hugh, lived somewhere on or inside Ben MacDhui. He was well over six feet tall and broad to match, and was wearing a long flowing robe and sandals. Not ideal clothing for a cold day on the Cairngorms, but such beings are, of course, immune to heat or cold. The Rankins claimed that, after kneeling before the 'Perfected Man', they conversed with him before going their separate ways.

To return to the Big Grey Man. The most convincing scientific explanation for the audible footsteps that I have come across is that it is the sound of snow collapsing in the person's own footprints. This, I have been told, can happen under certain temperature conditions.

The mountain is also the setting, when conditions are right, for the occasional Brocken Spectre, a huge shadow cast when a person is standing between the sunlight and a cloud of mist.

Still, it is easier to offer explanations than to prove them. I find it fascinating that *Fear Liath Mor* behaves in the manner of the legendary urisk (see page 139). In our folklore, urisks are big grey lubberly creatures that live, most of the year, high in the hills. They lead solitary lives but sometimes are said to long for company, when they will sit and watch walkers from a distance. And sometimes they will slip down and dog their footsteps.

The Big Grey Man may be the last of the ancient tribe of our mountain urisks. Whatever he is, he has the honour of being probably the only one of our supernatural creatures to have a whole book devoted to him alone.

Billie Blin

Billie (or Billy) is an elusive little character with something of the brownie in him. He crops up in ballads such as 'Willie's Lady' and 'Young Bekie', in each of which he is shown as intensely loyal to his chosen family, giving them advice in times of trouble.

Lewis Spence sees him as possibly the spirit of a dead ancestor who has adopted the role of tutelary or guardian.

Billie, who wears a bandage over his eyes, does not seem to have survived outside the ballads and it is doubtful if any children now play 'Billie Blin', a Scots form of Blind Man's Buff.

Black Cats

The cat bore a bad character in every respect.
Walter Gregor, *Folk-lore of the North-east of Scotland.*

In traditional witch stories, there is often a sinister black cat watching in the background. Eve Blantyre Simpson, in *Folklore in Lowland*

Scotland, says, 'There was always a suspicion hanging about a cat of being an assistant at witchcraft, especially if black—a colour associated with the powers of evil, the Devil's livery.'

Many witches were adept in changing into a cat. The story of the Witch of Laggan has been retold many times but is worth repeating in brief here.

Murray, a Badenoch hunter, was well known for his fearless attitude towards witches. There was one in the Laggan district where he lived but no one knew who she was, only the trouble she caused.

One stormy night he took shelter in a bothy with his two dogs. As the wind raged outside he lit a fire and was sharing his bread with them when there was a scratching at the door. The dogs began to whimper and back away, but Murray went and opened the door. In slipped a wretched, wet-looking cat.

'There, you see,' he said to the dogs, 'It's only a poor wee cat looking for a bit of warmth like ourselves.'

But the dogs showed their teeth and began to bark, making such a commotion that Murray was tempted to throw the cat back out. The dogs' unease was explained when the cat spoke, telling him she was an old witch who had repented of her evil ways. She pleaded with him to let her stay the night, promising to do no more harm if he did so.

Murray was a kind-hearted man and he agreed, though the dogs were still growling and snarling.

The cat gave him a long hair. 'Please use this to tie them up,' she said, 'lest they tear me to bits.'

Murray took the hair, but he was on his guard and, instead of fastening the dogs, he tied it round a beam at the back of the bothy. He then sat down facing the cat on the other side of the fireplace.

As he sat there, he thought he noticed a change coming over the creature sitting opposite. Were his eyes deceiving him? No, it gradually changed shape until it was not a cat sitting there but an old woman whom everyone knew as the Good Wife of Laggan. She was loved and respected by all her neighbours but now she sat there with a cruel smile. 'Yes,' she breathed, 'I am a witch and you have long been an enemy, but now your time has come.'

Next moment she had flung herself at him like a tiger, and he would have been defenceless but for his faithful dogs which sprang at her, one gripping her face and the other her breast. She cried out to the hair to hold them back and it tightened its grip so much that the beam snapped in two.

She fought with the two dogs like the wild thing she was and the terrible struggle finished with her escaping through the door, leaving the dogs dying on the floor. Some said she turned into a raven and flew away, but others said it was just a wounded old woman who limped from the bothy leaving a trail of blood on the ground.

Later that night, two travellers met a bloodstained woman stumbling in the direction of Dalarossie graveyard and, a little further on, two great black dogs following her trail. Then along rode a tall, dark stranger, clad in black and riding a black horse.

In a deep voice he asked the travellers if they had seen a woman followed by two dogs and if they thought the dogs would catch up with her before she reached the graveyard. On being told the dogs were close on her heels, the stranger spurred his horse into a gallop.

Meantime, when Murray went home he found his wife and neighbours were at the cottage of the Good Wife of Laggan who had taken to her bed and was dying. She had told them she had caught a chill on the peat bog. The women were all in tears but he strode in and pulled the covers off her to reveal the wounds his dogs had inflicted.

Before she died she wept as she confessed her sins, admitting to many acts of witchcraft against her neighbours in Laggan.

What the travellers had seen on the road was her spirit desperately trying to reach Dalarossie followed by two of the Devil's servants. The man on horseback was, of course, Satan himself. If her spirit reached the hallowed ground before him it would be free from his power since neither he nor his dogs could enter its gates. She could then be absolved of her sins.

According to the version told by Affleck Gray, an authority on the folklore of the area, the tall dark man was seen later that night riding past with a woman's body slung on his horse in front of him. So it would seem she did not reach Dalarossie in time.

As with some of the tales in this book, 'The Witch of Laggan' has been repeated by countless storytellers and has appeared in numerous books of history and folklore. Details vary from one version to another. There is no 'right' version but after studying as many as possible I have followed fairly closely that given by Affleck Gray in *Legends of the Cairngorms*. He was a folklorist of standing who collected much of his material from living lips and I recommend his book to readers wishing to study this and other tales from the Cairngorm area.

In the chapter on witches, we will look at the distrust many people once felt for single old women. 'The Witch of Laggan' is a good illustration of this but it also demonstrates the deep-seated fear of cats that was common throughout Scotland. A black cat might be a witch's familiar or assistant; worse, it might be the witch herself.

Isobel Goudie confessed to many acts of witchcraft at the Auldearn witch trials of 1662. My spelling and language here is modern, but this is the incantation she said she used when transforming herself into a cat:

> I shall go into a cat,
> With sorrow and sighs and a black shat [pain];
> And I shall go in the Devil's name
> Aye, till I come back again.

In 1611, Edinburgh Council minutes record that Barbara Mylne had been observed entering the city by the Water Gate 'in the likeness of a cat, and did change her garments under her own stair and then enter her house.'

In Skye there is a story of not one but three black cats that once entered a house in the Vaternish district. They were three witches in disguise and they had come to plot their devilment. They knew the woman of the house was away at the peats and the only person at home was her son, asleep in the corner of the kitchen.

It was only after they had finished their plotting that they realised the boy was awake and had been listening to every word. They made terrible threats to him, forcing him to promise not to tell a soul what had taken place.

Some time later, when he thought he was no longer in danger, the boy told his mother and not long afterwards she said something to one of the witches that revealed to her the boy had not kept his promise.

That night the three witches waylaid the boy in the dark and killed him. A cairn was built to mark the murder spot, but I understand it has long disappeared.

Sometimes, as at Thurso in 1718, an unfortunate victim was plagued by a whole army of cats, of all shapes and sizes, led by a chief witch. Little wonder that people sought ways of protecting themselves against cats. Supernatural cats, it was said, could be recognised by the white spot on their breast.

No one ever dared shoot a cat, for that brought disaster, and people would go out of their way just to avoid meeting a black cat. If they were unlucky enough to do so they might throw an old iron nail at it, since iron had special powers.

If flitting from one house to another, it was not wise to leave the cat behind; better to take it with you, and if you threw it in as the first thing to enter the new home, it would protect the house against diseases.

Nowadays we are aware of the danger of a cat lying on a baby's face and smothering it. In the past they were kept away from the cradle lest they sucked the baby's breath.

Of an unpleasant and vindictive person it would be said, 'He/she is like the cats, never does guid but oot o' an ill intention.'

Two points in the cat's favour: if a strange one came into a house and was friendly towards someone, it was considered lucky. And when a cat died—which it had to do in its own home or an occupant would die as well—you were advised to bury it under a pear tree and so ensure good crops. (A mouse would be buried under an apple tree for the same reason).

These beliefs, of course, applied to real cats, not supernatural ones, but they were all part of the general dread with which they were regarded, a dread mingled with healthy respect.

They were, however, not always treated with kid gloves. There is a story from Mull of a strange ceremony last performed on the island at the beginning of the seventeenth century. This involved roasting live cats, one after another, on a spit, over four days and nights, in order to raise 'Big Ears', a giant demon cat. The purpose, apparently, was to put important questions to him.

Oddly enough, another tale from Mull tells how a powerful witch, the great Suil Ghorm Mor of Lochaber, once summoned a whole army of cats at the bidding of a Lady of Duart who had learned that her husband was being entertained by a beautiful Spanish princess aboard a galleon in Tobermory Bay.

The cats clawed their way on to the ship and attacked the terrified crew who threw themselves overboard, all except one man who slipped down into the magazine and hid among the powder kegs. The cats pursued him but the sparks that flew from their fur ignited the powder and the ship went down in a great explosion. Its famous wreck lies there still.

Duart managed to escape and row to the safety of the shore, from where he dragged himself home, a very contrite husband!

The crest of Clan Macpherson bears a splendid wildcat and the clan motto is a defiant 'Touch not the cat but a glove', which simply means 'Touch not an ungloved cat'. In other words, beware of its claws. According to clan tradition, the Macphersons are descended from the Catti or Cat People, who arrived in this country from overseas.

Black Dogs

The Black Dog's day will come yet.
Gaelic saying.

The chances are that many of my readers will know someone who has seen a mystery black or grey dog. They may even have seen one themselves. Black/grey dogs are still part of Scotland's supernatural landscape. They linger on where other creatures have departed.

Friends of mine, James and Moira Ferguson, are convinced they saw a supernatural dog one evening in the 1960s. They were living in Broughty Ferry at the time and had been up in Braemar. Now, as dusk closed in on a September night, they were motoring homeward down the A93. James was driving, Moira by his side, and their two daughters were in the back, Jane, 11, and Gillian, 7.

James takes up the story. 'We had just passed Bridge of Cally and were on the long steep rise from the hotel when, about 100 yards ahead we saw a large dog come out from the trees on the right and start slowly to cross the road.

'"Oh, look at the dog!" one of the girls cried.

'I switched on my headlights and saw it quite clearly. It seemed to be reddish-brown and its movements were jerky. It showed no signs of haste as it crossed in front of us.

'Then one of the girls said, "Its feet aren't touching the ground!"

'It was true, they weren't. It reached the other side of the road and disappeared into bushes and that was that, but I remember we all talked about it the whole way back to Broughty Ferry.'

James adds that, a few days later, Gillian described what she had seen for a school exercise and was commended by her teacher for her vivid imagination! (Which she has, for she is now a successful poet and journalist).

The late John Stewart of Blair Atholl, latterly of Rattray, used to compete in the piping competitions at Highland Gatherings across the country. In 1955, he told me how he often walked from one Games to another, travelling overnight to arrive in time for the events next day.

Once, on a bright moonlit night, he was making his way along a lonely road near Aboyne, Aberdeenshire. There was a broken-down drystane dyke on one side with a fence, and suddenly he was aware of a large dark-coloured dog coming over or through the fence.

'When it landit on the road it cam that close tae me, I pit oot my hand tae it and spoke tae it. An' ye ken this? My hand gaed richt through it. There was nithing there.'

He also told me that he and his wife had seen what he thought was the same dog on a night seven years earlier at Kenmore, Loch Tay. 'Its een were as big as pennies,' he recalled.

Another time, between Kirriemuir and Forfar, in broad daylight, he saw a black dog run in front of an approaching car. When the car had passed he expected to see the animal lying on the road. There was no sign of it and the driver carried on as if nothing had happened.

In his excellent book *When I Was Young: The Islands*, Timothy Neat quotes a woman describing an experience of her mother's in Sutherland. Jessie MacKay had been returning home at night over a hill from Sculaby. 'When she came to the smithy, a black dog rose beside her and walked close enough to be touching her leg. As she tried to push it away she suddenly realised none of its paws were touching the ground.' An echo there of the Ferguson family sighting.

These are examples of one-off encounters. Or are they? It may be that other people have seen a dog at the same spots.

'The Grey Dog of Morar' has been sighted a number of times on a small island on Loch Morar. It is seen running to and fro as if seeking a way off the island, but anyone who rows over to its rescue finds nothing there. Its history is said to date from the time when a local man, Donald Gillies, went off to serve in the Army. Somehow his dog got stranded on the islet. Whether Donald left it there deliberately or not is not clear, but when he returned home he hastened across to fetch it back.

What he did not know was that she had given birth to pups and they had grown up wild as wolves. So, although their mother gave Donald a great welcome, the young dogs sprang at him and tore him to pieces.

Since then a grey dog has appeared from time to time on the islet and its appearances used to be linked to the impending death of a member of one or other of two local families. Curiously a similar belief exists concerning appearances by 'Morag', the Loch Morar monster.

In this same area, dogs have been heard barking furiously inside a house known to be empty. The barking ceases as soon as anyone enters the building.

Mystery dogs have been reported from many places in Scotland, from Shetland down to Wigtownshire, and from Raasay to Islay. Many of them seem to be harmless enough, not seeking out humans and being sighted or heard only by accident. In this they are unlike the green fairy dogs which were said to hunt people down and devour them.

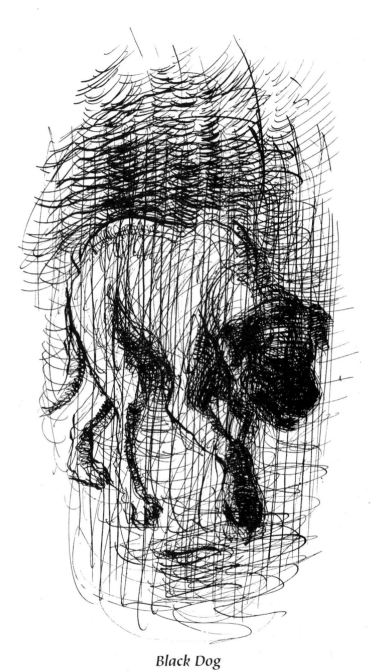

Black Dog

The dog is seen as the emissary of the Devil, perhaps even the Devil himself...

15

Some black or grey dogs, though, are best avoided. George MacDonald, a lobster fisherman who lived at Skerry, in Sutherland, was pursued one night by a big dog breathing fire. He said it was a fearsome looking beast with a chain around its neck and fierce red eyes.

He escaped by jumping over a burn which the dog, being supernatural, was unable to cross. It left its chain lying on the bank but when George ventured back later to examine it, the chain had gone. Hugh Miller told of a fire-breathing dog which confronted Donald Roy, a devout kirk elder, of Nigg, Easter Ross. Donald had not always trodden the straight and narrow but he had seen the error of his ways after the sudden deaths of three of his cows, which he took to be a divine warning.

Having repented of his previous slackness he had become a pillar of rectitude, but was backsliding on the night he saw the dog for, says Miller, 'walking after nightfall on a solitary road, he was distressed by a series of blasphemous thoughts…'

It was then the dog bounded in front of him, stopped, and bounded on again, sending a bright jet of flame which hissed and crackled beneath his feet.

Donald remained admirably calm. 'Na, na, it winna do,' he said. 'Ye first tried to loose my haud o' my Maister, and ye would now fain gie me a fleg [fright]. But I ken baith Him and you ower weel for that.'

He kept walking and when he reached the outer limits of his farm, the beast vanished.

The dog here is seen as an emissary of the Devil, perhaps even the Devil himself, and there are many stories in which this is the case. In other instances, the dog is a witch in temporary guise, or the ghost of someone departed this life. In Breadalbane it was firmly believed that there were ghosts which sometimes appeared as dogs, cattle, deer or one of several other animals. A James MacDiarmid who lived in the district claimed that a ghost from a farmhouse on Loch Tay's south shore used to wander forth at night as a dog.

That terrifying creature, the bochdan, may sometimes appear as a black or grey dog.

There are other roles played by dogs. One is as a guardian of treasure, usually underground, as at Murthly, Perthshire. The other is when some unfortunate soul is condemned to take the form of a dog as punishment for a crime.

I have written at length elsewhere (in *The Ghost o' Mause and Other Tales and Traditions of East Perthshire*) on the early eighteenth-century Perthshire case of the Ghost o' Mause which reputedly made a number

16

of appearances to a farmer near Blairgowrie. This black dog told the farmer it was the ghost of a murderer who had hidden his victim's body in a secret place in the vicinity. Not until the dead man's bones were given Christian burial would his spirit be released.

The bones were eventually dug up, placed in a coffin and interred in Blairgowrie's Hill Kirk graveyard.

The dog was never seen again, though I did have a strange report of a big dog glimpsed around 1940 at East Gormack farm, not far, as the crow flies, from Middle Mause where the events took place.

Then there is the sighting by the Fergusons a few years later even closer to the scene and, coincidentally, on the road above the low ground where the corpse was hidden.

We must hope, however, that the spirit of David Souter—he was the murderer—did indeed find peace after the funeral service of his victim's remains, and a release from his twilight existence as a dog.

Curiously the stretch of road on which the Fergusons had their sighting was also the scene a few years later of another strange report. A Blairgowrie woman has told me that she was driving along it with a friend when she saw a man in old-fashioned clothes cross in front of the car.

'What on earth was that?' she exclaimed, and was amazed when her friend said she had seen nothing.

Again it is tempting to speculate: could this have been one of the participants in the Ghost o' Mause mystery, the man who saw the dog and was given instructions by it, or the murderer, who suffered for his crime even beyond the grave? He could have been coming from the burial spot on the haugh below. Or is there another explanation?

A story with a similar theme to the Ghost o' Mause, also including a dog, is remembered in Banffshire. Here the phantom took the form of a green lady witnessed from time to time over a period of a year. At last she confided in a woman that she had been involved in robbing and killing a pedlar. His body, she said, was under an ash tree, while his gold was hidden elsewhere.

She appealed to the woman to find the gold and send it to the pedlar's widow in Leith. After making this plea the green lady hurried away and her witness saw 'a large black greyhound crossing the moor.'

The gold was uncovered and sent to Leith, after which neither green lady nor dog was seen again.

Andrew Valentine, a retired company director, told me of a strange experience from his boyhood. Every year his family spent a fishing holiday at Tomdoun Hotel, Glen Garry, in Lochaber. One day, in about 1956, he was with his father and mother in a boat on Inchlaggan at the head of Loch Garry. They were off Tornacarry, the Smithy's Knoll, and Andrew's mother was in the bow, his father was rowing, and he was in the stern.

'I guess we were about 30 yards offshore,' he says. 'The shoreline was clear and grassy for about ten yards, then there was thick heather and bracken. I saw a movement at the edge of that and said to my parents, "Look, there's a deer!" However, as it moved down to the water's edge, it became evident that it was a very large black dog.

'It stopped and looked straight at us, and my mother said, "I don't like the look of that." Meanwhile, my father, who had excellent long sight, asked us what we were looking at. The dog was only 20 to 30 yards away, totally in the open, and after a few minutes it turned and went back into the bracken, but my father never saw anything though he was looking straight at the spot where the dog was clearly visible to us.

'That evening in the hotel we told the owners, who we knew very well, what had happened and they immediately said "That's the Black Dog of Tornacarry!" Apparently it had been seen before but they gave us no details.'

It is not uncommon for one or more persons to see something—an apparition let us call it—that others can't. Only one man ever saw the ghost dog of Mause. On one occasion his brother was with him but saw nothing. The Ferguson family were unusual in that they all four saw a dog cross the road. The woman who saw the figure near the same spot was astonished that her friend, sitting beside her in the car, did not see it.

Andrew Valentine's father was evidently one of those people who are not 'tuned in' to what some call another dimension. A second incident would seem to be evidence for this.

The Valentine family home was an Adam house which had a circular central hall with all the rooms leading off it. There was no connection between them. Andrew told me, 'A couple of years after the Black Dog incident, my father was putting out the dogs at night and had closed the front door which had one of those old fashioned bell pulls that ring on a board downstairs.

'Just as my father locked the door, the bell rang and the dogs outside started barking. My mother came out of her room and I came out of mine, both asking who was there.

'He had never even heard the bell though we had done so from further away, and so, obviously, had the dogs. However, at our request he reopened the door and looked outside. There was no one there although there was a large open space in front of the house and nobody could have disappeared in that brief space of time.

'So, the same three people and the same result—two of us saw or heard, while the other did not.'

Not all supernatural dogs are black or grey. The Ferguson animal was described by them as 'reddish-brown' and one said to haunt Inchdrewer Castle, Banff, is small and white. Tradition says it is the spirit of a former mistress of the castle. The writer Nigel Tranter claimed that he and his wife saw it in broad daylight when they went to visit the ruin.

It is to be expected that dogs, which have been man's help and companion since early times, have become deeply imbedded in his folklore. If they do not fill as consistently sinister a role as the cat, this no doubt reflects the differing characteristics of the two species.

Nevertheless there are enough widely spread beliefs and traditions to illustrate that, after all, we do not altogether trust our canine friends. They retain, for all their 'doggyness', a certain mystery, an aura of faint threat, which keeps our suspicions simmering. 'Man's best friend' can have another side to him, especially if he is black or grey.

The Black Walker

A. D. Cunningham, who collected many of the traditions of Rannoch and published them in *Tales of Rannoch*, recorded how this 'threatening figure' attacked the miller of Aulich, announcing himself as the Black Walker of the Ford. The miller had two tussles with him but in the second one he must have dealt with him thoroughly for the Black Walker does not seem to have made a nuisance of himself again.

Blood-suckers

The four hunters had stayed out too long and gone too far. Night was falling and soon it would be too dark to find their way home. When they saw the empty shieling they made for it gratefully.

After they had got a fire going and eaten the food they carried, one of them broke into *puirt-a-beul*, the mouth music that is as good as any instrument. The others leaped to their feet and began to dance, their shadows grotesque in the firelight.

'Oh,' shouted one of the men, 'But if only we had partners to dance with!'

At that the door burst open and in ran four lovely young women. Three took a partner each while the fourth sat by the music-maker.

The men were delighted. They asked no questions but laughed and danced as the mouth music grew louder and faster.

Suddenly one of the dancers saw specks of red on the floor. It was blood, dripping from one of his friends. Horrified, he made for the door and rushed out into the night. Quick footsteps sounded behind him—the woman he had been dancing with was in pursuit.

He ran on and saw before him a group of horses in a walled enclosure. Leaping the wall, he slipped in among them. Looking back he saw that the woman had stopped at the wall. It was as though the horses were a protection against her.

He remained hidden until he was sure she had gone and then he scrambled over the wall and made his way home in the dark.

In the morning he led a party to the shieling. When they pushed open the door the place was empty except for the lifeless and bloodless bodies of his three friends.

The women had been *baobhan sith*, female demons who sucked the blood of their victims.

In a similar story, four hunters dance to the music of a jew's harp and are joined by four women. One of the men notices that his partner has deer's hooves, a characteristic of the *baobhan sith*. He escapes and when he ventures back to the scene he finds his companions with their 'throats cut and chests laid open.'

The *baobhan sith* were always beautiful, very hard for men to resist. They wore long trailing dresses to conceal their hooves. It is said they could turn themselves into hoodie crows or ravens at will.

A strange story of a male blood-drinker or cannibal is included in *Scottish Traditional Tales* edited by the distinguished folklorists A. S. Bruford and D. A. MacDonald, who describe it as the 'nearest approach to a vampire story in Scotland.'

It was told in Gaelic by a Duncan MacDonald of South Uist in 1953 and it tells how, some generations before, a family called MacPhail lived on the island. The family consisted of Mr and Mrs MacPhail, their married son and his wife and daughter. The daughter had been dumb from birth and was now nearly 13.

Mr McPhail died and his son went to the township to arrange the funeral, leaving the others with the corpse overnight.

In the early morning Mrs MacPhail was astonished to hear her granddaughter shout, 'Granny, Granny, my grandfather's getting up! He'll eat you and he won't touch me!'

Sure enough the dead man had risen up on the bed and when they slammed the door on him they could hear him begin to dig his way under it through the earth floor. His head and shoulders had appeared and the rest of him would have been through when a cock that roosted on the cross-beam crowed three times and he died instantly.

The editors explain that the man would not have eaten his granddaughter because she was of his own blood, but his wife and daughter-in-law did not have this protection. Other versions of this tale have been found in which the 'corpse' is a stranger to the island and so anyone is a potential victim.

From Annan, in Dumfriesshire, there comes the story of a stranger who once sought refuge in the town at the time of the plague. He was from Yorkshire and it was soon evident that he had brought the disease with him. He succumbed to it and was buried, but not long afterwards people reported seeing him in the streets accompanied by a pack of hideous hounds.

The plague was spreading through the town like wildfire and people were sure it was due to this walking corpse.

When the head of Annan's leading family, the Bruces, caught the disease and died, his relatives and friends decided something had to be done to stop this. The body of the Yorkshire man must be dug up and burned.

Two young men volunteered to do the deed. Under cover of darkness they went to the kirkyard and dug up the grave. The corpse, when they uncovered it, was swollen and the face not white but red.

One of the men was filled with rage when he saw it. He raised his spade and plunged it down on the cadaver's chest. A spurt of blood rose up soaking his legs and feet. With horror they realised it was far more blood than a single body should rightly contain.

They took the revolting monster from its grave and dragged it to the traditional place for bonfires. Crowds of townsfolk gathered to watch as a huge pyre was lit and they cheered as the bloated remains were flung into the flames. Some folk claimed they heard a great sigh as the body was consumed.

From that moment there were no more cases of the plague in Annan.

The story has suggestions of vampirism and in modern retellings these are even more explicit. It is also popular now to label Galloway's Sawney Bean and his family as drinkers of blood, although the original tradition depicts them as eaters of human flesh.

In the early 1920s a poacher benighted in a bothy in Glenfernate, Perthshire, claimed to have had his leg gripped by an unseen creature which sucked blood from it.

Blue Men of the Minch

When the tide is at the turning and the wind is fast asleep,
And not a wave is curling on the wide blue deep,
Oh, the waters will be churning in the stream that never smiles,
Where the Blue Men are a-splashing round the Shiant Isles.
Donald A. Mackenzie.

The Shiants lie in the Minch, off the south-east corner of Lewis, a tiny cluster of islets, Garbh Eilean, Eilean an Tighe and Eilean Mhuire. On my maps the passage between them and the Lewis coast is marked as the Sound of Shiant but it had an older Gaelic name, meaning 'The Stream of the Blue Men'.

The Minch, which divides Lewis and Harris from the Scottish mainland, is a stretch of water notorious for its treacherous currents and violent changes of mood. But it was never feared as much as the Sound of Shiant.

The reason was the Blue Men.

Even on days when the Minch is calm, the Sound can be in turmoil. Fishermen of old said this was the work of the Blue Men who, they believed, took fiendish pleasure in churning the waters in the narrow strait. Not only that, but they would rise from the waves and forcibly drag a boat under.

Little wonder that skippers avoided the channel even when it was a convenient shortcut to their destination. They said the only time it was safe to use the Sound of Shiant was when the Blue Men were sleeping in their caves. Even then it was still risky, for the Blue Men usually left a few of their number on lookout. When a boat approached they would go and rouse the others and then start, literally, to make waves.

Many of our supernatural creatures possess some redeeming features; the Blue Men seem to have had none. Their sole aim was destruction.

In appearance they were like men, powerful in build, bearded, with

Blue Men of the Minch
They would rise from the waves and forcibly drag a boat under…

long grey faces and blue bodies. A ship's crew would be filled with terror at the sight of them, plunging, rising waist-high from the sea, and plunging again. Often they would seize hold of a boat without warning and attempt to overturn it. On other occasions they would shout a rhyming couplet. If the skipper was sharp enough to shout back a rhyming answer, the Blue Men would swim away. If he was too slow or his answer was poor, he and his crew were almost certainly doomed to a watery grave.

John G. Campbell, in his *Superstitions*, tells of a boat that was passing through the Sound when the crew spotted a Blue Man floating on the waters, asleep. Greatly daring, they lifted him aboard, laid him on the deck and bound him tightly.

He slept through it all but suddenly two more Blue Men were seen swimming towards the boat. One was heard to say, 'Duncan will be one man,' while the other responded, 'Farquhar will be two.' At the sound of their voices, the prisoner woke up, 'broke his bonds like spider threads', and leaped overboard. He joined his friends and swam off with them.

Campbell offers no explanation for the story. I had surmised that Duncan and Farquhar were the names of two members of the crew and the Blue Men were planning their deaths. However, Donald Mackenzie tells a version of the story in which, before he leaves the boat, the Blue Man says:

> Duncan's voice I hear, Donald too is near,
> But no need of helpers has strong Ian More.

Thus he names his two rescuers and himself.

Mackenzie's first couplet is also slightly different to Campbell's:

> Duncan will be one, Donald will be two,
> Will you need another ere you reach the shore?

Which rhymes with the other couplet.

Blue Men were sometimes called storm kelpies but this is misleading. Although, like the kelpie of rivers and lochs, they enjoyed disturbing the water, their appearance was entirely different and I have no record of them coming ashore like kelpies.

In Gaelic lore of the Islands, the Blue Men were one of three groups of fallen angels expelled from Heaven. One group became the fairies who live under the earth, a second group became the Merry Dancers or Northern Lights in the sky. The third group landed in the sea and became the Blue Men.

However belief in them arose, it was genuinely held and the Blue

Men were blamed for countless wrecks. The Sound of Shiant was sometimes known as the Stream (or Current) of Destruction.

In contrast, the Shiant Isles themselves were regarded as a holy place. There is evidence of a religious community having lived there, and I can think of no more peaceful spot for contemplation despite lying so close to 'The Stream of the Blue Men'.

This is the final verse of the song at the head of this chapter:

> *Oh, weary on the Blue Men, their anger and their wiles!*
> *The whole day long, the whole night long, they're splashing*
>   *round the Isles;*
> *They'll follow every fisher—ah! They'll haunt the fisher's*
>   *dream—*
> *Where billows toss, oh, who would cross the Blue Men's Stream?*

Bochdans

It is impossible to describe this creature, as it seems to have been able to take on any form at will. A black dog was one of its guises but there were others more fearsome. 'The bochdan will get ye!' was a threat used by mothers, and was all the more potent because the children could only imagine, with dread, what it might look like: a headless man, maybe, a billy goat, even a man with one arm, one leg and one eye. A bochdan seen in Glen Etive had a hand coming out of his chest, a leg protruding from his side and an eye in the middle of his face.

According to Edward C. Ellice in *Place Names of Glengarry and Glenquoich* there was one on the Aldernaig Burn which used to intercept travellers trying to cross the ford above the mill of the same name. As it was the only ford for some distance up and down the burn this was a serious matter. To deal with it a local priest held a midnight mass at the ford for a number of years.

Ellice also tells of 'Big Sandy of the Ghost' in Glengarry who held many midnight meetings with a bochdan which sometimes talked to him and other times fought him.

The first time he met it, the bochdan appeared to him as a deerhound which then changed into a man.

The bochdan warned him about the forthcoming fall of the house of Glengarry and this proved true. It followed Sandy to America when he enlisted and sailed there with the 76th Macdonald Highlanders.

Similar to a bochdan was the *fachan* which had a hand coming out of its chest and a large tuft on top of its head.

The noises heralding the approach of a bochdan were unnerving: shrieks, moans and a clanking of chains. All in all, it was a real spine-chiller.

Bogles

Do children of today know what a tattie-bogle is? It's what we in Perthshire called a scarecrow when I was young and it could be guarding any kind of crop and not just potatoes.

Bogle was also our name for a ghost, although we did not know that at one time a bogle was a particular kind of ghost, one which took delight in scaring the wits out of people.

In parts of England, the name becomes boggle, bogie, boggard, bogie-beast, even, I am assured, bog-a-boo. Like the Scottish ones, they were generally solitary creatures haunting lonely places, where they lay in wait for the night-time traveller.

W. Grant Stewart told of a bogle known as the Ghost of Bogandoran, which lurked in a place called the Bog of Torrans. It used to carry an array of weapons and give the traveller a choice of these for a duel.

One man who encountered it managed to fight it off with a cudgel. Next time he passed that way the bogle tried to push him over a precipice but, after a mighty struggle, the man stabbed the bogle three times. 'The ghost fell down stone-dead at his feet, and was never more seen or heard of.'

In fairness to bogles, the ones in the Border counties had a soft spot for widows, orphans and other needy folk and were known to take their part against their persecutors.

The Boobrie

*I have heard of the boobrie from several people... so he
has a real existence in the popular mind.*
J. F. Campbell, *Popular Tales of the West Highlands*, vol. 4.

Elsewhere in his *Popular Tales*, Campbell describes the boobrie as 'a gigantic water bird' which inhabited the fresh water and sea lochs of

Argyll. He suggests, surprisingly, that it may have been a water horse taking the form of a bird.

They lived on cattle, sheep and other animals and had the hooked bill of a bird of prey, webbed feet and very large claws. The noise they made was a sort of hoarse roar. To get an idea of the boobrie's appearance, one can look up the great northern diver in a bird book. It was said to bear a resemblance to the diver, only much bigger.

Campbell tells of a man who saw one on a moor loch one February day and, despite the cold, waded into the water with his gun. He was up to his shoulders in the freezing water when the bird dived under. After standing there for three quarters of an hour, his gun at the ready, the man returned to the shore. There he waited for five and a half hours watching for the bird resurfacing, but it never did.

Curiously enough, a man driving through Glencoe, in North Argyll, one night in 1998, reported seeing the shape of a huge black bird above his car. It reminded him of pictures he had seen of the long extinct pterodactyl.

As I write there are reports of gigantic birds being sighted in West Virginia, USA, and such claims have been made in the area going back some years.

The Braemar Monster

The village of Braemar, tucked in the hills of Royal Deeside, can claim its very own version of the William Tell story of the boy and the apple. It owes this to a monster kept by Malcolm Canmore (1057-1093), who had a hunting seat here. The ruins of Kindrochit Castle are a feature of the village, but Canmore's seat would have been an earlier and simpler structure.

Just what kind of creature the monster was is not known; the description that has come down is 'like a crocodile'.

He kept it on a small island on the river Dee and, when this part of the country was still Gaelic-speaking, the islet was known as Eilean na Tadd, Isle of the Monster.

Whatever it was, the animal possessed a healthy appetite. To keep it satisfied, Malcolm ordered that everyone in Braemar must, in turn, present him with a cow. This may not have been a great sacrifice for those who owned several cows, but there was a widow named MacLeod who had only one. The prospect for her if she had to give it up was bleak.

She had a son in the village, a skilled archer. He saw his mother's distress and was furious. Seizing his bow he went to the river and fired arrow after arrow at the beast until it was dead.

When King Malcolm heard that MacLeod had killed his pet 'monster' he ordered his instant arrest. A gibbet was built on Craig Choinnich and MacLeod was led there to meet his end.

At the last minute MacLeod's young wife appeared, and, clutching a child to her breast, pleaded with Malcolm for her husband's life.

The King decided to test the strength of her love and her husband's skill as an archer. He told her to stand with the child on the other side of the river. A bannock was placed on the child's head and the father was ordered to shoot an arrow at it from the opposite bank. If he hit it and did not harm the child or its mother, his life would be spared.

It was a terrible moment for father, mother and infant as MacLeod took aim. The arrow sped across the water and struck the bannock in the middle. He was a free man.

Malcolm was so impressed with MacLeod's courage and skill that he invited him to join his personal bodyguard. He became known as Hardy in its old sense of bold and daring, and the McHardies claim him as the founder of their line.

Clearly, fact and legend are interwoven in the story, as they so often are. Was there a monster on the island in the Dee? If so, what kind of animal could it have been? One might be tempted to suspect that the wily Malcolm 'invented' the creature in order to obtain a regular supply of fresh meat for his household and hunting friends.

But if that were true there would have been no beast for MacLeod to shoot at and no reason for him being condemned to death.

It's a puzzling and intriguing local legend.

Bregdi

Shetland fishing crews dreaded meeting one of these at sea for fear it might wrap its fins round the hull and drag the boat under the waves.

There were two ways of fending it off. One was with a knife—like so many creatures it hated cold steel. The other weapon, surprisingly, was an amber bead. Throw one towards it and it would rush off.

Brownies

Of all the Other People, they [brownies] belong most intimately to the countryside. They have their history, their legend and tradition, their code of manners and behaviour which deserve respect.
Marion Lochhead, *Magic and Witchcraft of the Borders*

When the Radio 4 programme *Open Country* came to my hometown in 2000, I was invited to talk for a few minutes about local folklore. The interview was conducted standing beneath the trees on a riverbank, the perfect setting for recalling old rural tales.

One of the stories I told was about two brownies who helped a blacksmith in his smiddy a mile or so downriver. This is a favourite of mine which I love telling. Richard Euridge, the interviewer, seemed to be enjoying it, nodding and smiling as he listened.

When I came to the end of the tale, however, he took the wind right out of my sails when he enquired, 'So what were these brownies—a sort of mini Girl Guides?'

'N—n—o,' I began and explained, falteringly, what they were. It had never occurred to me that he would not know.

'Have you never had a brownie story on the programme before?' I asked.

No, they had not.

Of course Richard is English and most of the programmes in the series are from England where the brownie tradition is localised and not at all common. Nevertheless it is broadcast from Scotland from time to time. Being the kind of programme it is I had taken for granted that the subject of brownies would have cropped up on it.

I did not realise the extent to which brownies have been forgotten, even in Scotland where their presence was once taken for granted.

My local brownies, Redcap and Bluecap, were unusual in that there were two of them. The great majority of brownies were solitaries. The pair were also unusual in that they worked in full view during daylight hours. Most brownies shunned being seen, not coming out of their hiding places till after dark when everybody had gone to bed. Some would come out by day but make themselves invisible. These were usually ones that were intent on mischief.

Many, if not most, brownies were no trouble at all—provided their hosts obeyed the unwritten rules. In fact they could be extremely useful.

A brownie would take up residence in a castle or big house, a farm or a mill, finding himself a cosy hiding place where he could sleep all day undisturbed.

When night came and all was quiet, he would come out and perform the duties he had chosen for himself. In a household these might be cleaning up in the kitchen, scrubbing the floor and general tidying up. On a farm or mill he might do all kinds of useful regular jobs.

No one saw him doing these things, and he would have been furious if anyone had, but if someone had been secretly watching, what they would have seen was a small figure, only about three feet high, in brown, shabby garments, probably a cloak and hood.

Sir Walter Scott describes the brownie as 'meagre, shaggy and wild in appearance'. The shaggyness came from his hair which was thick and reddish-brown. From beneath peeped out a brown, wrinkled face. Some people who claimed to have had a close look said he had no nose, only holes to breathe through. His hands, they said, had no spaces between the fingers. According to the traveller storyteller Betsy Whyte, he had iron teeth.

Not very prepossessing then, and a housewife might not be too keen on the thought of this ugly little creature living in her home and handling her dishes. Yet if she never saw him, what did it matter? And they were such tidy and thorough workers. It must have been very comforting to lie in bed at night and hear the noises from the kitchen as the faithful little brownie scrubbed the pots and pans, swept the floor, and made everything immaculate.

If he was left alone and all the rules were observed, a brownie might stay with a family for generations—they were very long-lived. There is a story of one who lived at Leithenhall, near Moffat, for 300 years, serving one master after another. Every time a new laird took over, the brownie appeared before him for the first and last time.

After the death of one old laird, the house lay empty. The brownie, mourning his late master, wandered the cold corridors, hungry and disconsolate.

At last the new heir arrived from abroad. When the brownie made his ritual appearance, he looked so thin and pathetic his master at once ordered his servants to provide him with food, drink and new warm clothes.

It was the clothes that did it. The brownie was heard to cry:

> 'Ca', cuttee, ca'!
> A' the luck o' Leithenha'
> Gangs wi' me to Bodsbeck Ha'!'

And to Bodsbeck he departed, taking Leithenhall's luck with him—it was to fall into ruin.

The laird had done the unforgivable in presenting Brownie with new clothing. For some reason, he and his kind took instant offence if given a new outfit or garment and would at once up and leave. Any kind of gift or favour had the same effect.

There is a rival tradition that it was at Bodsbeck that the brownie lived and that he was insulted when the family, to show their gratitude for his long service, left him a special reward. According to this version he was heard to shout:

'Ca, Brownie, ca!
A' the luck o' Bodsbeck's
Awa' to Leithenha'!'

It seems that this brownie was accustomed to being given just a little plain bread and milk. Because the family felt they owed some of their prosperity to their brownie they had left him, for a treat, a loaf of bread and a whole jug of cream.

James Hogg's novel *The Brownie of Bodsbeck* deals with the period after the Battle of Bothwell Brig when many Covenanters had gone into hiding. Bodsbeck lies deep in Hogg country and he makes use of local traditions and other strands of local folklore. In his *Journey Through the Highlands of Scotland* he wrote that 'The last brownie that left the south of Scotland haunted Badsbeck (sic) in our vicinity.'

There is a cave at Bodsbeck which is said to have been the brownie's home, though this is unlikely as they were not usually cave-dwellers, preferring cosier quarters.

Sometimes, when a brownie left, he was not just angry but seems to have been genuinely heartbroken, as if he did not want to go but had been forced to do so. There was one on a farm in the Carse of Gowrie whose stay came to an end when the farmer's wife put out for him a smart cloak and hood. All night he sang, outside her window, a sad song beginning:

'Ochone, I maun flit,
I can do nae mair guid,
Since the guid wife has gi'en me
A cloack and a huid.'

It must have seemed natural, when winter was coming on, for the woman of the house to take pity on the poorly clad brownie and leave

Brownie
He scrubbed the pots and pans...

32

him something warm to wear. But it invariably brought the same result. A last cry heard in Glendevon and several other places was:

'Gie Brownie coat,
Gie Brownie sark,
Ye's got nae mair
O' Brownie's wark!'

Half in sorrow then, and half in anger. All they asked of their hosts was that they be left to sleep in peace through the day and that a little cream or small bowl of porridge or bread and milk be left sitting for them in a dark corner of the house at night.

According to William Henderson in *Folk-lore of the Northern Counties*, some people left out little cakes made from fresh meal and spread with honey. When mothers gave one of these to their own children they would say, 'There's a piece wad please a brownie!'

The important thing was that, having started to leave a brownie some modest regular 'reward', the habit be maintained without variation. Be over-generous and you lost him. A lapse into meanness could have the same result.

He enjoyed a warm fire, and some householders always stoked up the kitchen range before retiring so that he could have a heat before starting his duties. There are reports of a brownie's becoming impatient if the kitchen was occupied later than usual. He would make his annoyance known by grumbling audibly in the shadows. Scott tells of a brownie who used to worry in case the fire was allowed to burn too low before it was his turn to enjoy it. He used to snap at the family from his dark corner, 'Gang a' to your beds, sirs, and dinna put out the wee grieshoch [embers]!'

The Carse of Gowrie brownie used to be left sowans after the millworkers had eaten theirs. When they were slow in going for theirs he supped the skin off it, much to their annoyance. He was enraged when he heard them grumbling.

It was never wise to criticise a brownie. You never knew when he might be listening and his revenge could be devastating. Henderson tells of the one at Cranshaws, Berwickshire, who for years had cut the corn and brought it in. A great arrangement. But one year he overheard someone remark that the harvest had been 'no weel mowed'. By morning the whole lot had been dragged to the top of a cliff and flung to the winds. While he did it the brownie was heard exclaiming:

'It's no weel mowed! It's no weel mowed!

> Then it's ne'er be mowed by me again!
> I'll scatter it ower the Raven Stane,
> And they'll hae some wark e'er it's mowed again.'

At Cleiten Mill, Pitlochry, there was a hard-working brownie who was much appreciated by the whole community. A sack of corn could be left overnight and by morning it would be full of meal with some laid aside for the miller and a little kept by the brownie for himself. One day a widow complained loudly that the brownie had kept back too big a share. The brownie heard her and never worked the mill again.

Bad servants could be the cause of a brownie's departure. A brownie at Claypotts, Dundee, had performed valuable duties for many years, his sole reward a nightly bowl of cream. Like most of his kind he was a great stickler for tidiness and he was disgusted when, from his hiding place, he observed a kitchen girl preparing vegetables for the pot. As she did so she was carelessly throwing the kail-runts and unwashed leaves on to the floor creating a mess all around her.

This was too much for him. He sprang out, grabbed several of the stalks and belaboured her with them so that her shoulders ached for weeks.

The brownie left Claypotts with this curious rhyme which includes many local place names:

> 'The Ferry and the Ferry-well,
> The Camp and the Camp-Hill,
> Balmossie and Balmossie Mill,
> Burnside and Barnhill,
> The thin sowens o' Drumgeith,
> The fair maid o' Monifieth;
> There's Gutterston and Wallaceton,
> Claypotts I'll gie my malison;
> Come I late or come I ear',
> Ballunie's board's aye bare.'

Brownies could not abide Christianity, in practice or in symbol. One that lived in Orkney had a good relationship with a young man who did his own brewing and regularly gave the brownie his share. However, the young man always had his nose in the Bible and this annoyed the little creature a great deal.

An old woman warned the young man that he would lose the brownie if he went on reading the Good Book. The young man took no notice and when he did his next brewing it was a failure and he had to throw it away. His next brewing was just as bad. The ale was useless. He tried once more and this time the ale was lovely, but the brownie left and never returned.

A similar story is told of a woman in South Uist who, again, did her own brewing. She refused on religious grounds to give the brownie a share. Twice the brewing went badly wrong but she persisted and the third brew was as good as ever while the brownie left in disgust.

At this point it may be wondered why the Girl Guide authorities decided to give their junior movement the same name as these touchy, cantankerous, anti-Christian little beings. But remember the brownies of folklore possess some admirable qualities. They are independent, hard-working, performing their tasks diligently and faithfully without needing any instruction.

Having taken up residence in a house, barn or mill, they remain there, leaving only if seriously offended. Otherwise their loyalty is unshakeable. There are stories, the best known ones from Dalswinton and Jedburgh, of a brownie going, unasked, to fetch a midwife for a family member in jizzen (childbirth). Alas, both brownies subsequently left, the Jedburgh one because he was 'rewarded' with a smart green coat, and the one at Dalswinton because the local minister tried to baptise him!

The south of Scotland is rich in recorded brownie tales but the area is rivalled by the Highlands and Islands.

In Kintyre, at least two families harboured a brownie, the Mackays and MacDonalds. The latter lived at Largie and when they flitted to the islet of Cara, he went with them. He seems to have been particularly officious, tidying up the whole house every night, airing beds, changing linen, and making sure the dogs were tied up in their kennels. Carelessness on the part of servants was punished with a skelp from his unseen hand. He is said to have shared the family's hatred of all Campbells!

Other Highland homes reputed to have had resident brownies included Castle Lachlan, Loch Fyne; Ardincaple, near Easdale, home of the MacDougalls; Berneray, a MacLeod seat; the Old Castle of Invergarry; Cullachy House; Inchnacardoch, near Fort Augustus, as well as castles, houses and farms scattered through Moray and Strathspey.

Tullochgorum, near Grantown-on-Spey, was unusual in that, like Blairgowrie, it had a pair of brownies. They were male and female, which is also unusual. Records of female brownies are quite rare. This male seems to have been of a playful disposition. He was known as 'Brownie-clod' because of his habit of throwing clods—bits of peat or turf—at people, catching them off their guard.

Again he was unusual in that he had apparently set his heart on acquiring something: a coat and a Kilmarnock cowl. The farm servants who worked alongside Brownie-clod took advantage of the simple creature. They told him that if he thrashed as much corn as two men could do in a whole winter they would find the garments for him.

So while they lolled about on the piles of straw doing nothing, poor Brownie-clod toiled unceasingly, tired when he finished a stint and tired when the time came to start again.

Perhaps his sad face began to trouble their consciences for well before the winter was over the men decided to give him the coat and cowl he wanted. One day when he went into the barn there were the garments waiting for him.

Delighted, he made up his mind he was not going to thrash another sheaf. Being a Highland brownie his parting rhyme was in Gaelic but translated it goes:

'Brownie has got a cowl and coat,
And never more will work a jot.'

The female brownie at Tullochgorum was a sort of housekeeper to the family and, according to W. Grant Stewart, 'for cleanliness and attention she had not the equal in this land'. Her byname was 'Maug Loulach' or 'Hairy Mag', on account of her thick head of hair. Another source places this brownie in the farmhouse of Achnarrow, Glenlivet, and says she was the last of several Glenlivet brownies.

'Laying' or 'hiring away' a brownie, in other words getting rid of it, was never difficult, as we have seen. If you were tired of having one about the place, or if he was making a nuisance of himself, a gift of money would do the trick. Another method was to find out his name and call him by it. Brownies were not the only supernatural creatures to safeguard their name (this is linked with the old belief that with knowledge of the name came power over its bearer).

Angry words could drive a brownie away. The Grants of Rothiemurchus lost theirs when the laird was kept awake one night by noises from the kitchen. It was the brownie at work, but after the laird had shouted to him to 'Stop that din!' the little fellow dropped everything and was never seen again.

The interesting suggestion has been made that in Covenanting times, when fugitives were often given shelter by sympathisers, some households used or even invented a domestic brownie to account for noises in the night. The Covenanter would hide all day in a locked room or attic. After dark, when the servants and any unreliable guests had retired, he would come out for a meal and exercise.

Next morning any questions about strange sounds or missing food would be explained with 'Oh, that would be our brownie.' He could be used to cover up all sorts of nocturnal activities!

In Hogg's *Brownie of Bodsbeck*, already referred to, the supernatural creature is used as a cover-up by fugitive Covenanters.

The brownie's origins, however, go back much further and deeper, at least to Roman times and their household gods, the Lares. A Lar was usually a solitary, devoted to the service of the house and dependent on offerings of simple foods. He was an ancestral spirit, invisible but always present. The folklorist Lewis Spence believed the brownie's anger when given clothing to be similar to the chagrin of a Lar who is not offered the body of a deceased but only his clothes.

There is something in the brownie too of the aborigine. One can see in him a despised survivor of a defeated tribe, skulking in the shadows but creeping nearer the fire at night for warmth and a little sustenance; performing the most menial tasks but with just a touch of his old pride remaining so that one insult too many and he is liable to take the huff and decamp.

Brownies are not solely confined to Scotland. There are accounts of them from the northern counties of England, but in Scotland the tradition is particularly rich with, as we have seen, a great tapestry of tales. It is sad that these rather endearing if prickly little creatures are not better remembered.

I have not heard of any houses or workplaces still claiming a resident brownie but if there are any left I would love to know about them. Surely they can't all have gone?

William Nicholson (1783-1849), the Galloway poet, has immortalised Aiken Drum, 'The Brownie of Blednoch', in his fine poem which combines the sad, the comic and the uncanny. It tells how Aiken Drum makes a frightening though pathetic sight when he goes seeking work.

> 'I seek nae guids, gear, bond nor mark;
> I use nae beddin', shoon nor sark;
> But a cogfu' o' brose 'tween the light and dark
> Is the wage o' Aiken Drum.'

Most of the people are too scared of his terrible appearance but a 'wylie auld wife' recognises a bargain when she sees it. Soon he is making himself useful, not just to her but to everyone, young and old, who needs him.

All goes well until 'a new-made wife' leaves by his brose 'a mouldy pair o' her ain man's breeks.'

'Let the learned decide, when they convene,
What spell was him and the breeks between;
For frae that day forth he was nae mair seen,
And sad missed was Aiken Drum.'

He had disappeared in classic brownie fashion. The whole poem is a masterpiece of Scots writing and it owes its inspiration entirely to folklore.

Cailleach Bheur

She is a monumental figure in our folklore and yet curiously elusive. Dr Katharine Briggs sees her as 'one of the clearest cases of the supernatural creature who was once a primitive goddess, possibly among the ancient Britons before the Celts.'

In appearance she is generally described as lean and blue-faced, a vigorous but time-worn hag. From May Day to Halloween she is a standing stone, aloof and detached. Then she comes alive again, takes up her staff and strides the countryside. Everywhere she goes she withers the leaves and turns green to yellow. She summons the cold winds and brings down the winter snows.

Come the Eve of May she throws her staff under a bush—usually said to be holly or gorse—and turns once more to stone.

A grim figure then, but confusion sets in when you look at the traditions that have her turning, not to stone, but into a beautiful girl. And she has a caring side, for she guards the deer on the hills, herding them, milking them, and protecting them from the hunters.

She has an affinity with other wild animals too—goats, wolves and others that roamed the ancient Highlands. Wells and streams also come under her protection. In one tradition she was responsible for accidentally creating Loch Awe when a spring she was guarding on Ben Cruachan overflowed and filled the glen.

Donald Mackenzie saw the *cailleach bheur* as a primitive form of Artemis, the Greek virgin goddess of the hunt and the moon.

Caoineags

Related to the *bean-nighe*, these melancholy female creatures could be heard wailing in the darkness before a catastrophe such as a disastrous clan battle. They attached themselves to clans and it was said that the MacDonalds' *caoineag* was heard wailing the night before the Massacre of Glencoe. Some people heeded the warning and went into hiding and so survived the slaughter.

Clans and families in Argyll, Skye and elsewhere had their own prophetess of doom, the *caointeach*, whose wails and screams were even more terrible to hear. Some descriptions say she was a little woman in a green dress and white cap. Others say she looked like a small child.

Unlike the *bean-nighe* she was not able to grant three wishes and it was advisable not to try to approach her.

The *caoineag* was well named, for the word is the Gaelic for 'weeper'.

Changelings

In place o' her ain bonny bairn she fand a withered
wolron [wretch], naething but skin and bane, wi' haunds
like a moudiewart [mole] and a face like a paddock [frog],
a mooth frae lug tae lug, and twa great glowerin een.
Nurse Jenny to the young Charles Kirkpatrick Sharpe,
Dumfriesshire, in the 1780s.

It was every parent's nightmare. Leave your baby alone and unprotected for only a few minutes and you might come back and find it gone, replaced by an ugly, ill-tempered creature, a fairy child that would make your life hell.

But was it a child? Many were said to be old fairy men with wrinkled, crabbit faces.

Not all parents realised what had happened and they could not understand why their happy and contented infant had suddenly turned into a cantankerous, wailing monster.

It was often a third party, a friend or acquaintance, who realised the truth of the situation and put forward a solution. It was usually simple and direct: snatch the interloper when it was off its guard and throw it on to a stoked up fire. Instead of burning, it would shoot straight up the chimney and disappear.

Immediately afterwards the missing baby would be back in its cradle, gurgling happily as if it had never been away.

This was almost always the outcome. In nearly every account I have seen or heard, the fairy's expulsion is followed by the instant return of the lost child.

In some cases parents needed convincing that the mewling thing in the cradle had been 'planted' by the fairies. One way of proving it was to put it to the eggshell test. The parents, with some ceremony, would arrange a number of empty eggshells round the hearth, then go into hiding and watch the child's reaction.

The changeling would sit up and stare at the eggshells; sometimes he even climbed out of the cradle and waddled over for a closer look. After gazing at them he would scratch his head (they were invariably male!) and remark that he had lived for so many hundreds of years but had never seen anything like this before.

In some versions of this tale—which is found elsewhere besides Scotland—the parents have made it even more puzzling for the fairy by pretending to be using the eggshells for brewing or holding boiling water.

Many parents were hard to convince. They did not want to believe the child they were nurturing was not theirs. Bewildered though they were by its sudden change of nature, its insatiable appetite and thirst, they could not accept that their child had gone. And the fairy interloper, while giving them a terrible time with its temper and demands, was usually cunning enough not to do anything in their presence which would betray the truth.

As soon as the parents were out of the house, however, the fairy would drop all pretence, even in front of a 'babysitter'. It would talk in an adult way, climb out of the cradle, swagger about the room, drink whisky, dance and even play the bagpipes!

The babysitter would sometimes have to arrange for the mother and father to watch from a hiding place before they would be convinced.

Besides throwing it on the fire, or heating it above the flames, there were equally ruthless ways of getting rid of the cuckoo in the nest. You could drop it in the river, lay it on an exposed hillock or rock and ignore its wails, sit it on a hot girdle, run at it with a sword or red-hot ploughshare, or leave it on the shore for the tide to carry it away.

In the North-east a changeling might be taken to a crossroads and a corpse carried over it. The fairy would disappear and the child would be returned.

In a story told me by Andrew Stewart of the well-known travelling family, it is an itinerant tailor who alerts the parents to their misfortune. His solution to the problem is to heat a girdle over the fire as if to make scones but, instead, to put horse dung on it and, when it is hot, make as if to reach for the changeling. This so terrifies the creature that it flees 'up the lum'.

As it goes, the fairy utters the strange cry: 'I wish I had 'a kent my mither! If I had 'a been longer wi' my mither, I would have kent her better.'

The relevance of which is far from clear.

Occasionally an older human child was taken. From the Isle of Islay comes the story of the smith called MacEachern who had a fine healthy son, in his early teens. Suddenly the boy lost all zest for life, moped about and spent long hours in bed. He ate voraciously but was getting thinner and thinner and his skin turned a ghastly yellow.

It was an old man who told the smith that the boy must be a changeling. He advised him to try the eggshell test to find out for sure. The father did so, filling them with water and carrying them as if they were a great weight.

The boy sat up in bed in amazement: 'I am now 800 years of age and I have never seen the like of that before!'

The father went back to the old man and asked him how he could get his son back. The advice was to build up a huge fire and throw the changeling on to it. The man did this and the fairy disappeared up the chimney.

In this tale the missing son was not instantly returned. To get him back, the smith had to go to a fairy hill on a certain night, armed with a Bible, a dirk, and a crowing cockerel. He was told the mound would be open and he would be invited in, but as he entered he was to stick the dirk in the lintel to make sure he could get out again. The steel of the dirk would ensure his safety.

The smith went to the knoll and, sure enough, it was open. From within came the sound of singing and dancing. Clasping his Bible he walked inside. The fairies gathered round, asking him what he wanted. Seeing his son standing among them he said, 'I want my son and I will not go without him.'

The fairies burst into shrieks of laughter, making such a noise that it startled the cockerel in the smith's arms. It leaped up onto his shoulder, clapped its wings and crowed lustily.

Furious, the fairies pushed the smith, his son and the cockerel out of the mound, throwing the dirk after them. The entrance at once closed behind them.

The smith now had his son back but he found the boy sadly altered. For a year after his return he never lifted a hand and spoke scarcely a word. Then one day when his father was fashioning a sword the boy exclaimed, 'That is not the way to do it!' He took the tools from his father's hands and set to work making the finest sword ever seen on Islay. His skills became famous and he and his father prospered for many years.

According to J. F. Campbell it was well known on the island that the smith and his son lived near the parish kirk of Kilchoman.

The Islay changeling was unusual in that the stolen boy was in his teens. Most children taken by the fairies were unbaptised babies. Until baptism took place there was real dread in the minds of parents and they took careful precautions to protect a new baby.

A minister in the Hebrides told Evans-Wentz that mothers would collect bindweed, burn it at the ends and place it over the cradle. The fairies would then have no power over the child.

F. Marian McNeill, in *The Silver Bough*, writes, 'New-born children were in especial danger, and young mothers would not go out after dark until the christening was over when the fairy power became ineffective. Iron was placed above the bed; mother and child were given milk from a cow that had eaten the *mothan* (trailing pearlwort); and other protective rites were carried out.'

Cold iron was regarded as a certain safeguard against abduction, a belief that stemmed from the time when iron was new, mysterious and had strong powers ascribed to it. Nails might be hammered into the headboard, or a smoothing iron slipped into the bed. Scissors or a knife were believed to be effective.

Longer ago, midwives carried fire—possibly a candle—round the mother and baby, morning and night, or swung it three times round their heads. In some places a Bible and bread and cheese were considered a good defence while in Fife and some other areas it was the custom to place the father's trousers under the mother's head as she lay in bed and to leave them there for the three nights following the birth.

Some parents hung them on the bed, and in the case of a shepherd's wife near Selkirk it was enough to have her husband's waistcoat over her and the newborn child to scare off the fairies who shouted 'Auld Luckie has cheated us o' our bairnie!'

It was a relief to hear a baby give its first sneeze, as it was then believed to be less vulnerable, though not till it was baptised was it completely safe, and not till the moment of baptism would its name be spoken out loud.

Changeling

New-born babies were in especial danger of abduction…

Why would the fairies snatch human children and why replace them? Taking the second question first, there is a tradition that the replacements were either ailing fairy children which might benefit from human love and care (and milk from a human breast), or old men seeking to spend their last days being pampered and cosseted.

As for the first part of the question, mortal children were said to be highly prized by fairies and stolen by them to help renew their stock. There is never any suggestion that stolen children were ill-treated in the fairy world; when returned to earth they were invariably in excellent health and as they grew up they were often peculiarly gifted. The Islay boy is an example of this.

The same belief about using humans to inject new blood into a race is still with us but is now used to explain the abduction of people by aliens. In many parts of the world men claim to have been taken aboard a UFO and 'matched' with an alien female. Women abductees claim aliens have made them pregnant and then later returned and taken away the baby. Aliens on spacecrafts are said to have performed gynaecological examinations on women and are also suspected of removing eggs for fertilisation.

The object of all this seems to be the same: the improvement of the stock by the 'stealing' of human genes. Thus does folklore renew itself.

Since changelings were often thought to be little old men near the end of their days, they did not live long but soon 'dwined' and died. But it has to be wondered how many unfortunate infants died premature deaths at the hands of their parents. Considering how strongly these beliefs were held, and the violent nature of the antidotes, it is not hard to believe that, in corners of rural Scotland, innocent children suffered and died in horrific ways. A child that was sickly, unattractive, and over-demanding could be in danger from its own parents.

It is recorded that, in the parish of Ardersier, Inverness-shire, a man named Munro placed his sickly baby on a so-called fairy knowe, in the belief that it was a changeling. By morning it was dead. In the mid-nineteenth century an old woman in the Slains district of Aberdeenshire was pointed out as the last person to have been placed on a cairn and left there overnight. She was fortunate; she had survived. How many did not?

In the Island of Lewis, E. S. Hartland was told, it was the custom to dig a grave in the fields on Quarter Day and lay the changeling in it until the following morning. By that time, it was believed, the real baby would be returned.

Infant mortality was, of course, high in earlier centuries. Premature child deaths were commonplace. But among the names in those sad lists on some of the old stones in our country graveyards will be a few that hide a terrible secret.

And what, one wonders, were the thoughts of the parents when, the 'changeling' disposed of—by fire, perhaps, or exposure, or physical abuse—their own child was not magically returned to them? Their anguish can only be imagined.

This must be one of the grimmest and most tragic corners of Scottish folk-belief.

Adult Changelings

Sandy Harg had married the prettiest girl in the parish of New Abbey, Kirkcudbrightshire. A few nights after the wedding he was down with his net by the side of the Nith where it opens to the Solway.

There were two old wrecked ships stranded on the rocks offshore. Nobody ever dared go near them for they were known to be the home of a band of fairies who resented human intrusion.

Suddenly, from across the water on the evening air, Sandy heard a voice on one of these wrecks: 'Ho! What are ye doing?' Then came the reply: 'I'm makin a wife to Sandy Harg.'

Sandy threw down his net, leaving it where it fell. He ran home as fast as he could, rushed into the cottage and, to his wife's astonishment, shut every window and locked every door. He then drew her into his arms and held her tight, bidding her be quiet and to listen.

For a long time they heard nothing, until, as midnight struck, there was a soft footfall outside followed by three light taps on the door. The girl struggled to free herself to go and open it. It was as if she felt forced to do so. But Sandy held her fast. 'No,' he breathed. 'No!'

After a silence the footsteps moved away. At the same time the cattle in the byre bellowed and tugged at their tethers. In the stable the horses neighed, snorted and clattered their hooves on the cobbles. The girl was fighting to get free to reach the door and it was all Sandy could do to hold her. All night he held her, and all night the noise continued, the bellowing and the clattering.

Only when dawn broke and the animals fell silent did he slacken his hold. He released her and sat her down while he stepped to the door and went out into the morning light. There, leaning against the garden dyke, he found a piece of oak carved in the likeness of his bride. This was what he would have been left with had the fairies taken his wife.

There are many stories of such a piece of wood being left in place of an abducted person. It was called a stock and some were well carved and others were just a plain length of wood. Some were said to resemble the abductee to begin with but later the resemblance seemed to fade.

A stock was sometimes left in place of a baby, but more often it seems to have been an adult it replaced, often a nursing mother. Those wives were fortunate who, like the one in the story above, were saved by their husband.

In a tale from Shetland, the fairies had planned to abduct a woman who had recently given birth. Her husband overheard them talking near the house. The phrase he picked up was 'Mind da crooked finger!'

This alerted him—his wife had a deformed finger. Like Sandy Harg he succeeded in preventing the abduction, and the stock left behind when the fairies fled was kept in the family for many years, used daily as a chopping board!

The blacksmith at Bonnykelly, in the North-east, was warned when he overheard a fairy telling another, 'Mak it red-cheekit and red-lippit like the smith o' Bonnykelly's wife!'

And from the Carse of Gowrie comes the story of Lord Kinnaird who, riding home alone one night, heard a fairy voice sing:

> 'Mak it neat and mak it sma',
> Like the lady o' the Ha';
> Mak it neat and mak it tidy,
> Just like Lord Kinnaird's lady!'

He spurred his horse home and arrived just as the fairies were dragging his wife from the bed. When he had scattered the Wee Folk he found the stock they had carved lying in the bed.

Another Laird, Balmachie, claimed to have rescued his wife when he came on a troop of fairies hauling her through the night on a litter. He took her home and put her in the care of a friend while he went to her room. They had left, not a stock, but a fairy woman who bore a remarkable likeness to his wife.

Lying in bed she scolded him for having left her alone for so long. He pretended to be contrite and sympathetic and offered to carry her over to the fire where it was warmer.

He flung her into the flames and she shot up the chimney in the usual manner. From her brief appearance in the story it is evident that she would have been as difficult, cantankerous and as ailing as any child changeling.

It was said that fairy women were unable to suckle their own children and that this was why nursing mothers were often targeted. They also considered human milk superior to theirs. R. H. Cromek tells of a nursing mother in Galloway who was visited by a fairy woman carrying a baby. The fairy begged the woman to save the child by putting it to her breast. She did so, the child revived, and the woman was magically rewarded.

One of the most amazing tales is of an English-speaking Lowland woman who was abducted by an army of fairies and, as a result, spent several years in exile in a Gaelic-speaking area.

This happened because a Highlander looked up into the sky one day and saw a crowd of little figures carrying some sort of burden through the air. He took off his cap and flung it into the air, shouting, 'Change this for that!' knowing that the fairies are duty-bound by etiquette to obey such a call. They took the cap and dropped the woman to the ground.

He asked her in Gaelic who she was and where she came from but she just shook her head, for she spoke only in English. As no one in the district had any English they had no way of finding out where her home was. She stayed with her rescuer and his wife, making herself useful. She was grateful to the couple but it was a sad and lonely life, trapped in silence.

One day a group of strangers came into the glen, men from the south engaged in planning General Wade's new roads through the Highlands. When the woman caught sight of two of the men she ran to meet them in amazement and delight. They were her husband and son and they were equally astounded and overjoyed to find her alive and well. She had simply vanished one day and they had no idea where she had gone. She had been carried off by a *sluach*, a crowd of flying fairy abductors, a much feared phenomenon.

When researching this subject of changelings, I wrote to the National Museum of Scotland to ask if they had a stock in their collections or knew where one might be seen. Dr Hugh Cheape, Curator, Scottish Modern Collections, sent me a courteous reply from which I quote: 'I have done a fair amount of research (and have lectured) on the Charms and Amulets collection of the National Museums of Scotland. They are comprehensive but I must say I do not have an example of this [a stock]. I have looked at similar collections in other museums in Scotland and England and have never seen such a thing.

'I suppose, in the general drift of affairs, this would be an unlikely thing to survive. The objects which we have here depend for their survival on the chance intervention of the "educated outsider" perhaps suddenly coming across these things...'

I cannot believe there is not, somewhere, perhaps passed down in family hands, a stock once believed to have been left in place of an abducted child or adult. Maybe the present day generation have forgotten the story behind it and why it was kept. If anyone knows the whereabouts of one I would love to hear about it, and so, I know, would Dr Cheape.

A Changeling Rhyme

Come tae me,
Gin mine ye be;
But gin ye be
A fairy wicht,*
Fast and flee
Till endless nicht.

*in this context, a supernatural being.

The Devil

Wha wad sup kail wi the Deil wants a lang-shafted spune.
Old Proverb.

Some writers have suggested that we Scots have long held the Devil in warm affection almost as one of ourselves. Neil McCallum expressed this view in his book *It's An Old Scottish Custom*. It is our custom, he argues, 'to sup with the Devil'. He describes him coming 'roistering into Scottish company with the persistent impudence of a circus clown.'

Admitting that we are on less intimate terms with him than we used to be, he says, 'To the man in the street, should he ever think of him at all nowadays, the Devil has emerged from the years as a couthie body. Auld Nick, Auld Clootie and a score of familiar bynames show that he has a warm if uncertain place in the heart of the Scots.'

In support of this view McCallum quotes an unlikely source, the Yorkshire-born writer J. B. Priestley, who said of R. L. Stevenson that he was, like a true Scotsman, 'on nodding terms at least with the Devil'.

He is right about the bynames. I have collected over 30. Auld Hornie, the Auld Man, The Black Lad, the Earl o' Hell, the Father of the Lees... the list goes on. How many people know, when they use the expression 'In the name of the Wee Man!' that they are talking of the Devil?

In Gaelic there are, or were, as many names again, including Black Donald, The Big One, The Mean, Mischievous One and, significantly, The One Whom I Will Not Mention.

The belief that we have an affectionate, half-amused attitude to the Devil has, I am sure, been influenced by Burns and particularly his comic masterpiece 'Tam o' Shanter'. Here is how Burns describes the scene that meets Tam's astonished gaze at Alloway Kirk:

> Warlocks and witches in a dance;
> Nae cotillion brent frae France,
> But hornpipes, jigs, strathspeys and reels
> Put life an' mettle in their heels:
> A winnock-bunker in the east,
> There sat Auld Nick, in shape o' beast;
> A tousie-tyke, black, grim, an' large,
> To gie them music was his charge;
> He screw'd the pipes and gart them skirl,
> Till roof and rafters a' did dirl.

By depicting the Devil playing the pipes Burns paints him as a convivial character, the life and soul, if you like, of the party. The choice of instrument—the bagpipes—makes him one of us. He sounds like a good man to have at a ceilidh.

The Devil receives similar treatment in the rollicking song 'The Deil's Awa Wi' the Exciseman':

> The Deil's awa, the Deil's awa,
> The Deil's awa wi' the exciseman;
> He's danced awa, he's danced awa,
> He's danced awa wi' the Exciseman!

So now the old rascal is dancing, and he is clearly on our side since he is ridding us of the hated Excise officer.

It's all great fun, Burns at his humorous best, but, in truth, it in no way reflects the cold dread in which Satan was once held in Scotland. The couthie-sounding bynames were only very faintly affectionate. More seriously, they were, I would submit, a defence mechanism. Just as people protected themselves by calling the fairies by other names, so they did not dare be heard talking of the evil one directly.

And little wonder. Was he not, in one guise or another, constantly stalking the land in search of souls for his dark kingdom? He might, on the slightest invitation, make an appearance, perhaps as a dog or other creature or, as he often did, as a handsome, civil, apparently harmless stranger.

The traveller John Stewart told me a typical tale in the 1950s. 'The Girl and the Devil' illustrates not just his guile but how dangerous he was.

The story tells of Mary, a quiet girl who lived with her mother and father in a house a little way outside a village. Her parents were concerned because she would not go out. She was very happy helping them in the house, but they felt she should go down to the village now and then and meet others of around her own age.

At last one day they persuaded her to attend a dance in the village hall although, as she reminded them, there was little point as she could not dance.

She was sitting watching the dancers when a young man came over and invited her on to the floor. 'I can't dance,' she told him, but he assured her that anyone could dance. 'Just try it. You can dance all right.'

And to her surprise she found she could. She danced with him all evening. Afterwards he walked her home. At the gate he asked her, 'What about next Saturday? Will you be down at the dance?'

She went down and the same thing happened. They danced all evening. As he walked her home he asked her if she had a boyfriend and when she said no he said, 'What about me? We could get married.' He asked her to think about it and give him an answer the following Saturday night.

After the dance the next Saturday they stood at the gate and he asked, 'Well, are you going to marry me?'

She had made up her mind. 'Yes, I will,' she said.

He told her he was going away for a year, but at the end of it he would return and they would be wed. Here is how John Stewart described what happened next:

'When he was turning away and she was shutting the gate, she lookit down at his feet and she saw the cloven hoof. It was the Devil! She didn't know what to do. She went away into the house and next day she couldn't do nothing at all. She couldn't work, she couldn't do anything. She'd promised herself to the Devil.'

Her father knew there was something wrong. 'What's the matter with you? Have you had a row with your boyfriend?'

She told him what she had seen.

'My God,' he said, 'You'd better go down to the priest.'

This she did. 'That's terrible,' said the priest. 'You must tell me when the time comes for him to collect you. Be sure to do that now.'

So when the year was nearly up she went and told the priest, 'He's coming for me at six o'clock tonight.'

'Very well. Let's go down to the chapel.'

John Stewart again: 'So they went down to the chapel and the priest stood right in the middle of the floor and he put holy water round the two of them, and they're standing in the centre of this circle of holy water. And he's reading the Bible.'

At six o'clock there was a knock at the door. The priest called, 'Who's there?'

The young man's voice said, 'I've come for my wife.'

The priest went on reading the Bible.

The young man banged on the door and shouted, 'I've come for my wife!'

A third time he banged on the door and roared till the chapel shook.

The priest called quietly, 'If you have come for your wife, come in and put your hand in mine and I'll give you your wife.'

The young man roared again and the chapel shook and shook.

'Come in,' said the priest, 'If you're a man at all, come in.'

'No!' roared the voice. 'Send my wife out!'

But when he saw that she would not come out of the chapel he made to enter but couldn't. 'He just took the half of the chapel away and he turned into a ball of fire. And the lassie never seen him after that.'

Because of the Catholic flavour to this story, it has been suggested at the School of Celtic and Scottish Studies that Mr Stewart may have picked it up on his travels in Ireland. If he did he brought it over to Scotland and spread it here. Songs and stories have been crossing and re-crossing the Irish Sea, both ways, for a very long time, whole shiploads of them.

The glimpse of the cloven hoof is a dramatic image that occurs again and again in Devil stories. When it does there is not so much as a hint of affection or goodwill towards the sinister stranger. He is the sworn enemy who must be warded off, defeated. The hoof has its parallel in water horse stories in which a girl finds traces of sand and waterweed in a young man's hair.

In the Highlands the hoof may be a pig's foot. The pig was long held to be unclean in parts of the Gaeltacht. There is a tale of boys playing a game of cards in a room when they hear a noise at the fireplace and see a pig's foot coming down the chimney. When it withdraws, it does so in a cloud of smoke. Other versions of this tale have it as a hare's foot. The Devil, as we have seen, takes many shapes.

A game of cards is always attractive to the Devil—cards are his books. It is fatal to start a game with him for it will never finish. In a secret room in Glamis Castle he sits playing with Earl Beardie who was foolish enough to say, when no one in the company would play with him, that he would play the Devil himself till Doomsday.

The Devil appeared, polite and suave as usual, and they sat down at the table. When the game showed no sign of ending and Beardie was making too much noise—he was a rumbustious character—the room was walled up and they were left to get on with it.

Of course there were always some people willing to make a compact with the Devil, or too weak to resist him. He ran classes for his disciples at which he taught them the Black Airts (Arts). At these classes, witches, warlocks and wizards learned their spells and were trained in evil.

They learned how to fly through the air, change into an animal, bird or insect, and how to do the maximum harm to those they regarded as enemies. They could spoil their crops, steal from them by hidden means, inflict diseases on them and bring about their death.

A common method of killing someone was to make a little clay or wax figure of the person and stick pins in it. For a slow death, the figure would be placed between stones in a burn where it would gradually be washed away. As the last fragments crumbled, the victim died.

Sometimes the perpetrator was suspected. If a person was suffering a long illness and it was thought a certain woman was responsible—it was very often a woman—she would be invited to the house. While there, a piece of her dress would be secretly snipped out. After she had gone, it would be flung on the fire. The sick person would at once start to recover.

Another way of harming someone, of exerting the Devil's power over them, was to carry out a mock baptism.

It was, as I have said, never wise to speak the Devil's name. To do so could trigger a personal appearance. There is an example of this from Glen Lethnot, Angus. A miller called Black quarrelled with a farmer two miles down the glen. Later, as night was falling, he determined to go and see him to continue the argument.

His wife was aghast. It would soon be pitch dark. She tried everything to dissuade him, at last appealing, in tears, 'Wha will keep me company while you're awa?'

Recklessly he replied, 'The Devil if he likes!'

The Devil

*A game of cards is always attractive to the Devil—cards
are his books…*

He stamped out of the house, slamming the door. Mrs Black sat down by the fire to await his return. She was not alone, for her son, a small boy, was also in the house.

An hour had gone by when she smelled sulphur ('brimstone reek' she called it). It grew stronger and stronger. She knew only too well what it meant and she told her son to run to the Manse as fast as he could and fetch the minister.

When he heard what was happening, the minister threw on his gown and, clutching his Bible in front of him, hurried to the mill house and flung open the door. The Devil was behind it but, on the minister's entrance with the Bible, he gave a terrible yell and vanished, leaving a gaping hole in the floor.

This minister, whose name was Dow, was evidently a fearless character but his bravado was to prove his undoing. In 1745 one of his parishioners committed suicide. He should, as a suicide, have been buried in unconsecrated ground but Dow insisted that he was to give him a resting place in the kirkyard.

His flock were horrified and warned him that no good would come of it. He scoffed at their fears and, to prove there was no danger, jumped over the open grave three times.

That night he was sitting in the firelight in his study when he saw a pair of eyes gleaming in the darkness, staring at him.

Dow strode to the door and opened it and called to his servant lass to bring a candle and a pitchfork. She brought them as fast as she could and when he raised the candle he saw, on the landing outside the study door, a huge black cat. He lunged at it with the fork, lost his balance, and crashed through the banister, breaking his neck as he struck the floor below.

Dow was laid to rest in a grave within the church. Years later, when the church was rebuilt, his coffin was dug up, but instead of being re-interred, it was left propped up against the wall outside. It would seem the congregation were not happy to have this unconventional minister back under their roof, even as a corpse.

Curiously I have heard of a similar series of events leading to the death of a minister, again in Angus, but involving a farmer and a minister named Thomson.

It is not so many years since, on some farms, there was preserved a 'Guidman's Croft'. For 'Guidman' read 'Devil'. This was a small piece of ground which was left untouched and never broken by the plough. The hope was that, by leaving this small plot for the Devil, the farmer would be left in peace.

There were also so-called 'fairy rings', but whether these were indeed left for the wee folk or were 'Guidman's Crofts' romantically disguised I cannot say.

There are strong and ancient links between the fairies and the Devil. Dr Katharine Briggs believed, with other folklorists, that the Devil's characteristics, his cloven foot, the (sometimes) horns and shaggy hide, have no roots in Christian theology but were derived from early heathen gods and nature spirits. If this theory is correct, the Devil we see in our mind's eye has been around for a very long time and predates Christianity.

Doonies

One day a boy started to climb the steep rocky face above Crichope Linn, near Thornhill, Dumfriesshire. He had spotted young rock-doves up on a ledge and wanted to catch them and take them home.

He had climbed to quite a height when he realised, to his horror, that he was stuck. He could move neither up nor down. He grabbed hold of the branch of a hazel bush but knew that, at any moment, it must break and he would fall to the rocks or waters of the Linn below.

At that moment he saw, some way below him, the figure of an old woman. She held out her apron inviting him to jump into it.

Somehow he trusted her. He released his grip and let himself fall. The apron did not hold him but it broke his fall and when he landed it was not on the rocks but in the water.

He felt a hand pulling him out and found himself looking into the face of the strange old woman. She beckoned him to follow and led him by a path through bushes and undergrowth to safety.

She then told him to go straight home and never to go near the doves again, warning him that if he did, 'The doonie will maybe no be here tae help ye.'

She disappeared before he had time to thank her for saving his life. He never did go near the doves again and though he searched often for the path she had taken out of the Linn, he never found it.

There are other stories of doonies rescuing people in difficulties and guiding them to safety. Some of the doonies were old women, others old men. They could also take the form of a pony, but in all cases it was their role to be friendly and helpful to people in trouble.

Fairies

One thing is certain, that the notion that there exist supernatural men, women and animals who inhabit subterranean and submarine regions, and yet can indulge in intercourse with the human race, is of very great antiquity and widely spread.
James Napier, *Folk Lore of Superstitious Beliefs in the West of Scotland Within This Century* (1879).

The word fairies has been so trivialised and romanticised in modern times that it is tempting not to use it at all. There are plenty of other names which, thankfully, have not suffered the degradation into which 'fairies' has sunk. But let's stick with it and look behind the stereotyped storybook image it conjures up.

We must first dismiss all those quaint illustrations of dainty, pure-skinned creatures flying and dancing in the air and peeping from behind leaves. Generations of little girls have loved such images and adored the sweet coyness of the Flower Fairies of Cicely Mary Barker's series of books. There is nothing wrong with any of that except that these 'fairies' are a Victorian invention which has been so successful it has swept the fairies of our folklore, the 'real' fairies if you like, off the earth and out of the sky.

Our forebears would not have recognised these pretty storybook confections as the fairies they knew. The ones they believed to be 'out there' were neither cute nor adorable, but dangerous, vindictive, cruel and not to be trusted for an instant.

It is true that in height some could be as small as the figures shown in the storybooks, but they could also be the same height as ourselves, or any size in between. They often, but not always, wore green. Importantly, they did not have wings. The gauze wings of the illustrations are sheer invention. Fairies that flew through the air did so without the aid of wings.

I speak about them in the past tense though there are people still claiming to have seen one or more. Imagination? Wishful thinking? It is not for me to say.

There are not many travelling people on the road now, but when they were still moving from one campsite to another, living close to nature, they saw and experienced many strange things. Here are just three examples I have been told about by different individuals:

A little man spotted running into the rocks by a burn in the Sma' Glen; a tiny woman wandering in a forlorn manner in a wood at night; a small coffin found on a wall which, when opened, contained the body of a dead fairy, perfect in every detail.

Non-travellers have reported strange sightings as well. Mary Tredgold, a children's writer, was crossing the Isle of Mull in a bus on a day of driving snow when the bus pulled into a lay-by. Through the window she was astonished to see a little figure, about 18 inches high, digging on the moor with a spade. He was not dressed for the weather but wore a white shirt, sleeves rolled up, and what looked like blue dungarees.

The quotation at the top of this section confirms how deep and widely spread belief in fairies used to be even as late as the end of the nineteenth century. With the belief went fear. In her book, *Troublesome Things*, Diane Purkiss puts it well: 'In journeys into the fairy past we are going back from safety into terror. Into the dark.' And again: 'We need to recover the fear of fairies in order to understand their importance to pre-industrial people.'

Many of our 'pre-industrial' ancestors lived in constant fear of offending the fairies. They were afraid even to speak about them by name. If the fairies overheard them there could be terrible repercussions. The fairies' anger, as said earlier, had its roots in the belief that a mortal who knew their name gained power over them (hence the story of Whuppity Stoorie, the Scots Rumpelstiltskin, who was defeated when her name was discovered).

People disguised the fact they were talking about the fairies just as parents of very young children still do when discussing something that is not for their youngsters' ears. It was hoped the fairies would not realise they were the topic of conversation and there was also the thought that, if they did, they might not mind being referred to as the Guid Neibours, Guid or Honest Folk, People of Peace (because they moved silently), Still (or Restless) People, Klippe, Green Goons, the Seelie Court, or a number of other names used in different parts of the country.

In Gaelic areas they were the *Sidhe*, though again there were other names. The *sluagh* or fairy host was the term to describe them when they moved through the air in a crowd borne on eddies of wind.

All the names appear to have been non-critical and placatory though one suspects there surely must have been others, less complimentary, muttered under the breath but not recorded by folklorists!

In parts of the Highlands, if the fairies were being talked about, the person speaking might add an aside such as 'A blessing attend their departing and travelling' as a protection against reprisal.

One of the greatest fears was of abduction. The section on Changelings deals with the stealing of human babies by fairies. Adults, too, were taken, and there are many tales of husbands having to rescue their wives who had been dragged from their beds by a horde of determined little creatures. Sometimes they left a doppelganger in her place who betrayed herself with her peevish ill nature. She could be got rid of and the wife restored by flinging the impostor on the fire.

Nursing mothers were always in danger of abduction to help suckle a fairy baby, and midwives could find themselves delivering a difficult birth for a fairy woman.

There are stories of women being carried away by fairies on a sleigh-like contraption but frequently the *sluagh* swooped down from the air and swept the person off their feet. Hebridean folklore is filled with tales of men and women being lifted up and carried to another part of their island or across the sea to another. Sometimes the fairies brought them back while others had to find their own way.

There often seems no reason for these abductions other than mischief-making or mild wickedness. Occasionally, though, the fairies needed a mortal's help, for instance to throw an arrow at some person or animal. The arrows, tiny sharpened objects, were not fired with a bow but flung, or flicked with a thumbnail, and it was said that the fairies were not able to do this themselves.

According to J. G. Campbell, a person or beast struck by an arrow became paralysed and seemed as if dead, but was actually taken away by the fairies and belonged to them thereafter.

Many people claimed to have come upon these fairy arrows, or 'elf-shot', and there may still be families who cherish one or more. What they will have are probably flint arrowheads or scrapers used by prehistoric man.

The most famous fairy relic in Scotland is the so-called fairy flag at Dunvegan Castle, Skye. The popular story about it is that it was first wrapped around a MacLeod infant heir by a fairy woman and it has long been believed to have magical properties.

There is a theory that it is a banner brought back to Skye by a MacLeod who had been on a Crusade to the Holy Land. Perhaps the time has come for the flag to be scientifically examined to establish its age and origin.

A Mackay clan member is said to have been given a flag by a fairy sweetheart; the Macrimmons treasured a fairy silver chanter; and a

Macpherson piper was presented with 'the black chanter of Clan Chattan' by a fairy woman who loved him.

What purported to be a detailed study of fairies, their speech, dress, customs and much else, was written by the Rev. Robert Kirk, who was minister of Aberfoyle, Perthshire, in the late seventeenth century. His book *The Secret Commonwealth* was completed in 1691 and was described on the title page by its author as 'A Treatise Displaying The Chief Curiosities Among The People of Scotland As They Are In Use To This Day'.

Kirk's first charge was Balquhidder where he stayed for 20 years before moving to the manse at Aberfoyle in 1685. An Episcopalian, until he was forced to turn Presbyterian, he was a Gaelic enthusiast and spent much time translating the Bible and the metrical psalms into Gaelic for use by Highland worshippers. Some of this work he did during a lengthy stay in London, so it is a mistake to think of him as a simple and ingenuous country preacher.

The best account of Kirk and the most reliable version of the *Commonwealth* was edited by a former director of the School of Scottish Studies, Dr Stewart Sanderson, and published by the Folklore Society in 1976. Sanderson shows Kirk to have been an assiduous scholar who 'engaged in a variety of literary labours'. He corresponded with academics and during his time in London he met some of its leading clergymen and attended services in a variety of different churches. He was clearly a man of enquiring mind.

His book is based on his researches among his parishioners, first in Balquhidder and then Aberfoyle, though I would give a word of caution. There is no way of knowing now how much of it was taken from the lips of the people, how much is his own theorising, how much even the work of other hands. Sanderson describes the history of the book's composition and publication as 'an involved tale of confusion, error, hypothesis and speculation.'

Having said that, he rather surprisingly goes on to say that Kirk's treatise is 'an important contribution to social history since it presents an authentic portrait of the nature and state of fairy belief in the Scottish Highlands and Islands during its heyday.'

How Kirk could speak for the Islands I don't know. At the most he could be reflecting beliefs in two small corners of Perthshire. But Sanderson's faith in Kirk's integrity allows for few if any doubts.

Two contemporary folklorists have also placed their trust in the *Commonwealth*. Lizanne Henderson and Edward J. Cowan are co-authors of the best and most serious book on the subject of fairies in recent years, *Scottish Fairy Belief.* They quote extensively from Kirk and claim that his work provides 'an unrivalled corpus of information and a rare insight into various aspects of belief in the latter half of the seventeenth century.'

Readers interested in exploring the subject further should obtain copies of both books. The seventeenth-century language of the *Commonwealth* does not make for easy reading but it repays close study and opens up a bewildering 'other world' filled with creatures invisible to mortals except the small select number possessing visionary powers.

There is evidence that the expression 'second sight' was applied originally to people who could see supernatural beings and that it was only later narrowed to mean the ability to foretell the future. Kirk believed that it was possible for some individuals to see the unseen and it is surely not insignificant that he was that rare thing, a seventh son. I have no doubt that it was this which encouraged him to search out the supernatural, a subject that would hardly have been encouraged on his divinity course.

There is an old Aberfoyle tradition that, since his 'death' in 1692 Robert Kirk has been 'living' in the fairy kingdom that so fascinated him. His coffin in the kirkyard is said to contain, not his body, but a heap of stones, and he himself is literally 'away with the fairies'.

Differing versions of this tradition have been collected in the Aberfoyle district over the years but all seem to agree that Kirk was abducted by the creatures in whom he took so much interest. In a play on the subject, 'The Shepherd Beguiled', Netta Reid gives a dramatic and moving account of Robert Kirk's extraordinary life and strange fate.

The most numerous stories about fairies are those which deal with the adventures of the many individuals who are said to have spent a night in one of their underground homes or palaces and have emerged to discover that they have, in fact, been absent for a very long time, it may be a year and a day, or 100 years or more. Many of these unfortunates crumble to dust or a bundle of bones upon learning the terrible truth.

Because the fairies are so fond of fiddle music many of the tales are about fiddlers. Loving to listen to and join in good dance music, they are easily coaxed into joining the revelries. In parts of the Highlands and Islands bagpipes replace the fiddle in the fairies' affection.

The fairy home or country is invariably below a green mound or hillock which opens up to admit the mortal and closes again when he leaves. There is no long journey to a strange and beautiful land; for that you almost always have to go to what I am tempted to call the 'top end' of fairy lore as in the ballad of True Thomas of Ercildoune, who was discovered sitting under a tree by a beautiful lady who may or may not have been the Queen of the Fairies.

She transported him to a land within the Eildon Hills and he was fortunate, since he was there for only seven (blissfully happy) years and returned to earth with the gifts of poetry, prophecy and a tongue that would never lie.

But that is the glamorous, literary side of fairy lore. For ordinary folk in their cottages and blackhouses, fairies, and encounters with them, were nothing like that. They lived from day to day hoping not to attract their attention and certainly not to arouse their animosity.

One of the worst things you could do was interfere with their homes. Anyone who tried to dig the ground above them was very quickly stopped, and many a new building was abandoned when the previous day's work was, again and again, scattered during the night.

Glamis Castle is the most famous example we have of a building that had been intended to stand on another site. Melgund Castle, near Brechin, is another. It could happen with churches as well. Fordoun, Kincardineshire, had to be moved from its original site and so did the kirk at Old Deer, Aberdeenshire, although here the supernatural intervention is sometimes said to have been by 'The Spirit of the River'.

Many farmers and shepherds made sure their animals kept off the 'roof' of a fairy dwelling and might even tend it, keeping it clean and tidy. This old folk rhyme has come down to us from these times:

> He wha tills the fairies' green
> Nae luck again shall hae,
> And he wha spills the fairies' ring
> Betide him want and wae,
> For weirdless days and weary nights
> Are his till his deein day.
> But he wha gaes by the fairy ring,
> Nae dule nor pine shall see,
> And he wha cleans the fairy ring
> An easy death shall dee.

The fairies' 'ring' or 'green' here was the spot where they were believed to meet and dance, and it was usually of a different colour of green to the surrounding area.

Fairies did not live in idleness. The men had trades similar to those of their mortal neighbours and the women spun and weaved, baked and cooked. They were, by all accounts, industrious and hard-working.

They strongly disapproved of slovenliness when they encountered it in homes or crofts.

Today most of us probably regret that we cannot hope ever to see a fairy and that, despite claimed sightings that appear in the press from time to time, no one can produce hard evidence of their existence in the past or present.

Our rural ancestors, on the other hand, would have given much to live in a fairy-free world. They had enough to contend with in the harsh conditions of day to day life without having to worry about the Guid Neibours who were often, in modern parlance, Neighbours from Hell.

However, it was not like that for everybody. Some families, it was said, managed to establish a working relationship with their local fairy colony. Perhaps they felt they had to if the colony was under a mound close to their door. In some cases fairies seem to have lived under the very doorstep, so friction of any kind had to be avoided and it would pay both sides to respect one another.

There are also reports from various parts of the country of men meeting fairy women and having affairs with them, often in secret places in the hills or on the moors. A Vatersay woman, Nan MacKinnon, said the island shepherds used to go courting them. The fairies did not need to entice them—the men went chasing after them.

Today we read with a certain sadness the accounts of how the last fairies left Scotland; for most people in the past it would have been great news. Like hearing that the dreadful family at Number 29 have loaded their goods into a furniture van and departed.

Hugh Miller tells in *The Old Red Sandstone* how, one Sabbath morning, a little herd-boy and his sister watched the fairies leave the Black Isle. The children lived in a clachan called Burn of Eathie on the south side of the steep-sided glen down which the burn tumbles in a series of falls. At the bottom it reaches the lovely bay where Miller found many of the fossils which won him fame as a geologist. Eathie is about a half-hour's tramp from his one-time cottage in Cromarty, now an NTS property.

That Sunday morning everybody from the huddle of cottages had gone to church, leaving the two children on their own. They were outside enjoying the mid-day sunshine when up from the glen trooped a long cavalcade of little riders on horseback.

Miller describes the scene thus:

> The horses were shaggy, diminutive things, speckled dun
> and grey; the riders, stunted, misgrown, ugly creatures,

attired in antique jerkins of plaid, long grey cloaks, and
little red caps, from under which their wild, uncombed
locks shot out over their cheeks and foreheads.

The boy and his sister stood gazing in utter dismay
and astonishment as rider after rider, each one more uncouth and dwarfish than the one that had preceded it,
passed the cottage and disappeared away among the brush-
wood which at that period covered the hill, until at length
the entire rout, except the last rider, who lingered a few
yards behind the others, had gone by.

'What are ye, little mannie? And where are ye going?'
enquired the boy, his curiosity getting the better of his
fears and his prudence.

'Not of the race of Adam,' said the creature, turning
for a moment in his saddle. 'The People of Peace shall
never more be seen in Scotland.'

Miller would almost certainly have heard the details of this story
from a native or natives of the district. Note his description of the
fairies: 'stunted, misgrown, ugly' and 'uncouth and dwarfish'. Their
garb is drab and colourless except for their red caps.

It is all a very far cry from the trim, brightly clad sprites of the picture
books and paintings. Even the horses are dull, 'shaggy...speckled dun and
grey.' Not handsome, and there is no glittering silver or gold harness.

These are, of course, the last remnant of their race. As such they
bear a defeated air, though their reasons for leaving Scotland and what
happened to all the others is not explained.

Nan MacKinnon of Vatersay explained the absence of the fairies by
saying that 'They are here for a century and away for another century.
This is their century away.' When they were on the island, she said,
'They weren't near the houses.'

Her view that they would be back seems a fairly isolated one. The
general opinion is that they have gone for good. Allan Cunningham
collected a tradition, similar to Miller's account, in Nithsdale in the
South-west. This time it was a fine summer's evening and farm workers were on their way home when they saw, on Burron Hill, a procession
of small figures like little boys.

One, taller than the rest, ran ahead and entered the hill, then appeared on the summit. After this had happened three times they all
disappeared. Said Cunningham, 'The people who beheld it called it
"The Fareweel of the Fairies to the Burron Hill."'

These leave-takings can be seen as symbolic, illustrating the decline in belief in fairies, for which education has been largely responsible. The Reformation was the turning point. Folklore in all its many forms could survive, even flourish, alongside Catholicism but the new Presbyterian rule would not countenance it. It set about rooting it all out and heaping it on the bonfire. Had Episcopalianism gained the ascendancy and become the national church, the old beliefs would almost certainly have lingered longer. In general it took a more benign view (Kirk was a reluctant conscript to the Presbyterian tenets and never gave up his fascination with folklore).

It is easy to explain the 'disappearance' of fairies; not so simple to account for them in the first place. Theories about the origins of fairy belief abound. A Gaelic rhyme is a clue to one theory. Curiously the first line echoes the words of the little man in Miller's story:

> We are not of the seed of Adam,
> And Abraham is not our progenitor;
> But we are the offspring of the Haughty Father
> Who out of Paradise was driven.

This places them in the role of fallen angels, cast out of Heaven with Satan, and condemned to live below the ground.

Another theory has them as spirits of the dead. Easy to understand why when you remember their homes were often in tumuli, ancient burial mounds. People said to have spent time with the fairies often swore that they had recognised friends or relatives among them whom they knew to be dead.

When W. Y. Evans-Wentz interviewed folk for his book *The Fairy Faith of Celtic Countries* (1900), several of them told him they believed the fairies were spirits which could appear and disappear at will.

A third and very interesting suggestion is that they are a folk memory of an early small-sized race, a conquered people reduced to living in holes in the ground. The Picts are obvious candidates but there is no evidence to suggest that they were appreciably smaller than ourselves, nor that they were the sort of people to lurk below ground. Modern archaeology tells us they did nothing of the kind. Their houses were above ground and their underground passages, the souterrains, were used, it is believed, for storing grain and foodstuffs, and possibly for keeping one or two animals in winter.

Since there is no evidence for another, smaller race ever having lived in Scotland, the folk memory theory seems no more convincing than the other two.

We are maybe getting closer to the truth with the suggestion that our fairies may be a degraded version of the gods and goddesses of our ancestors. This, in fact, may well apply to very many of the creatures described in this book.

History tells us a lot about early deities and ancient forms of worship, but there is much we do not know. Clearly there were pre-Christian deities of many kinds and, just as clearly, these evolved, faded, became distorted in the minds of succeeding generations.

In my own lifetime I believe I have seen another stage in this never-ending evolution. Instead of seeing fairies, people now report strange craft in the sky and what are called 'aliens' landing on earth. Instead of little people in green, they are grey.

The whole UFO phenomenon can be viewed as simply an extension of the body of belief that embraced fairies, mermaids, gruagachs, kelpies, brownies and all the others discussed in these pages.

To say that is not to dismiss all the many reports of UFOs and their 'crews'. Like most of the contents of this book they cannot simply be brushed aside as impossible. But the continuity from fairies to aliens has been remarkably smooth and seamless.

The fairies abducted people: so, we are told, do the aliens; their abductees did not realise the passage of time: neither do people taken aboard spacecraft; fairies sometimes abducted people in order to renew their stock: aliens are said to do the same. People who have been abducted by space men are often subtly changed by the experience just as others were after a spell in 'fairyland'.

The major difference between fairies and aliens would seem to be that the former lived below our feet and the aliens are above our heads in the sky. There are, however, theories that they enter the earth through huge holes in the mountains or fly their UFOs into the sea or a deep lake.

As far as Scotland is concerned, there is an aerial photograph in existence of what looks like a strange large craft lying on the bed of Loch Nevis and there have been reports of flying objects apparently disappearing into the sea off our coasts.

Ben MacDhui, home of the Big Grey Man, is said by some students of space to contain a huge domed auditorium in which members of a group known as the Great White Brotherhood monitor equipment far in advance of human knowledge.

All of this echoes older beliefs. In his *Minstrelsy* 200 years ago Sir Walter Scott wrote that 'Wells or pits, on the top of high hills, were...supposed to lead to the subterranean habitations of the fairies.'

It was believed, he said, that persons abducted by the Devil could be reclaimed from mountain top lochs.

In the past, if small objects went missing in a house or were mysteriously moved from one place to another, people blamed the fairies. Now, when such things happen, often a poltergeist is held responsible. Many of the things poltergeists are said to get up to—opening and slamming doors, breaking dishes, scattering items on the floor—are the same things the fairies were likely to do when in mischievous or vindictive mood.

Scientists, so far as I know, are no nearer 'explaining' the activities of today's poltergeists than they are of understanding yesterday's fairy folk. The mystery—and the magic—are with us still.

Fairy Boys

The port of Leith is celebrated for many things nowadays, from the Royal Yacht *Britannia* to its swish Ocean Terminal, and its trend-setting bars and restaurants. All a far cry from the stir caused, in the seventeenth century, by the so-called fairy boy.

The name by which he has ever since been known, the Fairy Boy of Leith, is misleading for, although we don't know his name, he appears to have been no fairy but a local child.

He was aged about ten when he came to the attention of a visitor to Leith, Captain George Burton. Burton was on a business trip which entailed staying several nights in Leith. Fifteen years later he sent an account of what had taken place to a writer called Richard Bovet. This was published in 1684, in Bovet's book *Pandaemonium, or the Devil's Cloyster Opened*.

Burton told how, when he was in Leith, he used to meet with others at a howff for a glass of wine. It was the woman who kept the howff who told him about the boy. What she said intrigued him so much that he asked if he might see the child.

He was in luck, for not long after, she pointed him out in the street where he was playing with other boys. Burton went out and 'by smooth words, and a piece of money, got him to come into the house with me.'

Burton had evidently been told that the boy possessed superior knowledge, because he proceeded to ply him with what he called 'astrological questions'. These the boy answered 'with great subtilty' and 'cunning much above his years.'

While they were talking, Burton noticed the boy drumming with his fingers on the table. 'Can you beat a drum?' Burton asked, to which the boy replied that he could 'as well as any man in Scotland'.

He then told Burton that every Thursday night he played the drum for people who met 'under yonder hill', pointing towards the Calton Hill, which Burton describes as lying between Leith and Edinburgh.

The people for whom he played were, said the boy, men and women, and they were entertained by other music besides drumming. There was always a big selection of foods and wines and often he was transported with the revellers to France or Holland for the night.

Burton wanted to know how the boy got into the hill and was told it was through a pair of great gates invisible to others. 'Within there were brave large rooms, as well accommodated as most in Scotland.'

The boy then proceeded to tell Burton's fortune, saying he would have two wives; he could see them sitting on Burton's shoulders and they were both very handsome.

An amusing incident then took place when a woman who had come into the room demanded the boy tell her future as well. Burton wrote, 'He told her that she had two bastards before she was married, which put her in such a rage that she desired not to hear the rest.'

Further conversation followed during which Burton learned from the woman of the howff that nothing would stop the boy going to Calton Hill on Thursday nights. Burton promised him more money if he would meet him at the howff the following Thursday afternoon.

Burton's idea was not, as one might expect, to accompany the boy to the hill, but to prevent him going there. To this end, on the Thursday afternoon, he brought along some friends. When the boy arrived they asked him question after question, determined to keep him there. However, at about 11pm, Burton suddenly realised that the boy had slipped away.

Burton sprang after him and caught him at the door. He recalled that he 'took hold of him, and so returned him into the same room. We all watched him and, of a sudden, he was again got out of doors. I followed him close, and he made a noise in the street as if he had been set upon; but from that time I could never see him.'

And not surprising after the way the boy had been treated by Burton and his friends who had all, no doubt, consumed more than a few drinks. One can imagine the scene in the crowded room as the child was bombarded with questions and hauled back when he tried to escape. It is no wonder he avoided Burton from then on.

But what about that 'noise in the street'? Was the boy set upon?

Burton did not trouble to go and find out. Perhaps he was too much of a coward. It is possible that some of his cronies had followed the boy and attacked him.

There is another possibility. The boy could have realised he had been delayed too long and was going to be too late for his appointment inside Calton Hill. The noise he made may have been a cry of disappointment and distress.

Whatever you think of it all, Burton's account has a ring of truth. There is nothing in it that sounds false. And it is interesting that the boy was so open about his involvement with the people in the hill. He is never quoted as calling them fairies, though the folk of Leith evidently believed that was what they were, since they called him the Fairy Boy.

From the way the boy talked it is almost as if he did not realise there was anything untoward about his 'friends' or the things they did, including the night-time flights abroad.

What is one to make of it all? The obvious explanation is that this was a slightly simple boy who invented these Thursday night adventures to impress everyone. That may have been so, but a fool he was not. Remember the 'great subtilty' with which he answered Burton's questions. The inference is that he had gained knowledge and psychic powers from the fairies. Remember too his clever put-down of the pushy woman who demanded that he tell her fortune.

One is left wishing that Captain Burton had handled the situation with greater tact and certainly some compassion. Instead of cruelly trying to stop the boy from going to Calton Hill, he could have asked to be taken along. What a story he then might have had to tell!

Another child who claimed to consort with the fairies lived at Borgue in rural Kirkcudbrightshire. His name was Johnny Williamson, and his father, an itinerant packman, having been drowned at sea, he was brought up by his mother and grandfather.

The boy used to disappear for several days at a time and it was firmly believed that he was then with the fairies.

There was an incident when local folk were cutting peats for the Laird of Balmagachan. Johnny had not been seen for ten days, and as they were sitting on the moor having their dinner, the peat-cutters were discussing where he might be.

Suddenly, there he was, sitting amongst them.

'Johnny!' said someone, amazed. 'Where did ye come from?'

'I came with our folks,' he said.

'Your folks? Who are they?'

The boy pointed to a hole in the peat bog and told them he had come from there.

An old man advised Johnny's grandfather to send him to a priest who could give him something to scare away the fairies. When Johnny came back he was wearing a cross hanging round his neck on a black ribbon.

The grandfather, and the man who had advised him, were both members of the local kirk but were banned from it for approaching the priest and accepting the cross. But it evidently worked, for there is no record of Johnny going off with his fairy friends again.

In Kinloch Rannoch there is a tradition that a little herdboy formed a rapport with the hill fairies and that, as a result, the cattle in his care always gave the best and sweetest milk.

Fairy Dogs

The existence in Highland supernatural bestiary of this creature indicates the belief that animals as well as humans populated the spirit world of the Celts.
Francis Thompson, *The Supernatural Highlands.*

These were much feared in the Highlands and Islands. Their size alone made them formidable beasts. One man who had seen the paw-prints of a fairy dog described them as being as broad as his outspread palm.

They were hideous to look at, with dark green coats, and ears of an even deeper green. The colouring was lighter on the lower parts of their legs towards their paws. The tail varied in shape. Some had a flat, plaited tail, while in others it was long, coiled over its back.

They usually ran in a straight line, silently and rhythmically, and people dreaded their bark. They would bark three times, an interval between each one, and a lone traveller at night, hearing a single bark, would dread a second and even more a third, for after that he might at any moment be attacked and torn to pieces. There was no escape from the *cu sith.*

During the day their unseen and unknown owners usually kept them tethered as watchdogs, but at times they were allowed to run free and they would make a lair for themselves on a rocky hillside. After lying in hiding through the day they would set out on the hunt for prey when darkness fell. Sometimes they hunted in packs, at other times singly. Although it is usually said that they ran silently, there are also reports of them making a noise like a galloping horse.

They were much feared on the island of Tiree. The folklorist John Gregorson Campbell is not the only one to provide evidence of this. He tells of a young girl who was playing out of doors after nightfall when she heard the first bark of a fairy dog from the beach on the north shore. It was, says Campbell, 'like the baying of a dog, only much louder.'

Her father recognised the sound, grabbed her hand and rushed her indoors.

There is also a report of two Tiree women gathering driftwood on the beach when they heard the ominous bark. They at once hurried home to safety.

Campbell speaks of a recess in the rocks by the island shore which was known as the Bed of the Fairy Dog.

Two boys spending the night in a summer shieling at the foot of Tiree's Hynish Hill did not hear a bark but they did hear 'loud howlings' and large-pawed creatures treading the turf roof over their heads. In the morning, when they ventured out, they saw the fairy dogs' pawmarks.

A slightly different version of this story is also told, but whatever the true facts the boys had a terrifying experience.

More in the realm of fantasy is the old tale from Benbecula of two men who were sitting by the peat-fire in a longhouse when a pair of fairy dogs rushed in. They were fastened together by a glittering leash studded with precious stones.

As the men sprang to their feet they heard a voice from outside calling the dogs by name. The beasts turned and dashed out and when the men went outside they saw them high in the air heading west with a fairy host or crowd. The fairies were evidently going hunting for they had hawks on their wrists. The night air was filled with music like the tinkling of innumerable bells mingled with the voices of the fairy spirits calling to their hounds. The dogs' unlikely names were Slender-fay, Mountain Traveller, Black Fairy, Lucky Treasure, Greyhound and Seek Beyond.

More credible is a report from Lorn, Argyll, of a shepherd who claimed to have looked over rocks and seen, curled in a lair, two pups with green backs and sides. Although they were young they were already larger and longer than his sheepdogs.

He—and his dogs—were terrified and quickly left the scene.

Another shepherd, an old man, is said to have spent a night with a fairy dog. It had scratched at his door and, when he opened it, it trotted in and lay by the fire. It looked tired and hungry so, despite his fear, he put food and water in front of it. It drank the water but left the food untouched.

In the morning the shepherd opened the door to let it out. As the dog passed it gave his hand a warm, soft lick.

The following winter there was a terrible storm and, with his sheep-dog injured, the old shepherd was struggling on his own to gather his flock. It was a hopeless task and he was tired out and nearly giving in when the green dog appeared out of the snow. It again licked his hand, and whenever it did so he felt his strength surge back. Next moment a pack of green dogs was scouring the hill collecting his sheep.

When the sheep were all safely gathered the dog accompanied the shepherd back to his cottage and then, with one last lick, disappeared into the night.

The collector Affleck Gray recorded this story, which is so untypical as to make it extremely suspect. The lore on fairy dogs makes it clear they were objects of terror with no tender side to their nature.

However, despite the dread these animals inspired, it was considered great good fortune to find a fairy dog's tooth. They held special powers. If a cow was sick the crofter would place the tooth in its drinking water and this acted as a cure. It would also restore to milk the goodness stolen from it by a witch.

Alasdair Alpin MacGregor knew a family who had the tooth of a fairy dog which one of them had found in a potato in his barn. At the time MacGregor wrote of this in the 1930s the tooth was in the possession of a widow in Canada.

The last fairy dog is said to have been seen near the old castle of Ruthven, Kingussie, just under 200 years ago.

Fatlips

Sir Walter Scott knew of this creature who was said to lurk in a dark vault in the ruins of Dryburgh Abbey. A deranged woman shared the vault with him. She had been jilted and had made a vow that, until her lover returned, she would never again look upon the sun. Her lover never came back but she still kept her promise, year after year, never venturing outside until night had fallen.

Two local gentlemen took a kindly interest in her, Haliburton of

Newmains and Erskine of Shielfield. When she came out she made her way to the home of one or the other. Fatlips, she told them, looked after the vault while she was gone—she seems to have had no fear of him.

What was he like? Locals said he was a little man with heavy iron shoes on his feet. The clay floor was damp and he used to try to trample the moisture into the ground with his heavy footwear.

Whichever house the woman was visiting, she always bade her host goodnight when midnight struck. Lifting a candle she would then make her way back to her underground home and strange companion.

The Fearsome Man

A tall grey figure with a face shaped like an egg, wild and gleaming eyes, and a thick black mane...that is the description that has been given of the apparition called *An Duine Eagalach*, the Fearsome Man.

His territory is on Rannoch Moor and the best known encounter was experienced by a man who was walking from Kingshouse to Rannoch. A mist had come down and he was glad to hear footsteps coming from behind. Company on the way would be welcome. He was not prepared for the hideous sight that bore down on him and strode past without a word or a glance.

It was a very shaken traveller who arrived at the inn at Rannoch Station and gulped down a large dram. Had the proprietor seen anything of a strange tall man? He had not. Apart from two guests at the inn, no one had called or passed that day.

Darkness was falling when he set out to complete his journey. As he approached the old stone bridge at the head of Loch Rannoch, the moon came out and he saw someone sitting on the parapet. It occurred to the traveller that he might be a gamekeeper or shepherd who could explain what he had seen.

He stopped and started to ask him. The figure slowly raised its head—the head like an egg which he had seen earlier that day. The face broke into a most ghastly smile...

This story has similarities to one from another part of Perthshire, the tale of the Headless Man of the Beech Hedge, Meikleour. According to the story, he was seen one dark night by a young tinker lad hurrying to fetch a doctor for his wife who was about to give birth.

Like the man on Rannoch Moor the lad heard footsteps behind him as he passed the hedge (the world's tallest). He was horrified to see it was a man with no head.

On his return to the campsite, he paused by a drinking trough at the hedge only to find the headless figure kneeling beside him. To add to the mystery, he later found that the trough did not exist.

Fideal

One of these strange water demons haunted a loch in the Gairloch district. It looked nothing more than a tangle of grasses and water weeds but, like something in a horror film, it dragged men down to their death.

The last man to die in its clutches was named Ewen. He had set out to kill it and succeeded but lost his own life in the struggle.

Finn Folk

This is an extract from *Description of the Isles of Orkney*, written by the Rev. James Wallace of Kirkwall, and published in 1693:

> Sometimes about this country are seen these men they call Finn Men. In the year 1682 one was seen in his little boat at the south end of the Isle of Eda. Most of the people of the isle flocked to see him, and when they adventured to put out a boat with men to see if they could apprehend him, he presently fled away most swiftly. And in the year 1684 another was seen from Westra.
>
> I must acknowledge it seems a little unaccountable, how these Finn Men should come on this coast, but they must probably be driven by storms from home, and cannot tell, when they are any way at sea, how to make their way home again...

These reports of strange men in small boats seen off Eday and Westray are typical of sightings of which records exist. Most are from Orkney and Shetland but they occur on the Scottish mainland coast as well. All describe a small fur-clad man paddling what sounds like a kayak covered with sealskins.

One of the men is said to have been swept into the mouth of the Don at Aberdeen. He spoke a language no one knew and died three days later. A report of this incident, which took place in the early eighteenth century, describes the man as an 'Indian', while a later description says he 'was all over hairy'.

Ernest Marwick, the Orkney scholar, believed that the Finns (or Fins) were an aboriginal race who lived in Norway at least until historical times. In a chapter in *An Orkney Anthology* (1991) he says the Norwegians use the word Finn as the equivalent of Lapp. They believe the Finns to have been endowed with magical powers.

Marwick found evidence of an old Orkney belief that parts of their islands once belonged to the Finn Folk, the last stronghold being Eynhallow. This is not impossible for, if the Finns existed, the Norse invaders may have brought some of them, possibly as servants or because of their skills in healing, prophecy and magic.

The island of Fetlar, Shetland, contains traces of a construction known as the Finnigard, the Finn Wall. The Finns may have built this for their Norse masters or it could have marked the boundary of land in their own possession.

If the Finns were never in Orkney or Shetland it would be difficult to account for the islands' folklore concerning them, although, of course, the Norse brought their lore with them. Like the Norwegians, the islanders believed that the Finns possessed magical powers. They were said to be able to turn themselves into seals or otters, and to converse with ravens.

It was believed they had a land of their own under the sea which was called Finfolkaheem, also a paradise island with green valleys and clear streams, which appeared to human gaze only now and again and was known as Hildaland.

Orcadians tell the story of Annie Norn, a young girl who went down to the beach one evening and never came home. Years later, a cousin of hers was on a boat which had been battered by a storm. The crew was helpless but suddenly a young woman in a kayak came alongside and told them to follow her.

It was Annie, and she took them to her beautiful home in Hildaland and introduced them to her Finn husband. After they were rested and refreshed she set them on their way and in a magically short time they were back in Orkney. Journeys made by the Finns were believed always to be lightning quick: only a few strokes of the paddle took them from Orkney or Shetland to Norway.

Stories from the Isles invariably illustrate the Finns' ability to perform magical deeds. If the Norwegians believed them to be gifted in this way, so did the natives of the northern islands.

Some Shetlanders used to claim to be descended from the Finns. Jessie M. E. Saxby, in *Shetland Traditional Lore*, writes:

> I remember seeing a woman who went by the name of Finne. She was very short, less than five feet in height, and very broad in the body. She had black hair and black eyes, and it was said that she 'could do things we canna name', but her doings were always of a kindly nature, 'just the way o' a' the Finns'.

Marwick mentions another woman, who lived on Sanday, Orkney, and was reputed to have Finn ancestors. She was known as 'Baabie Finn'.

The evidence for Finns having at one time lived in the islands is strong, but were some individuals still visiting our shores by kayak as late as the seventeenth century? Were some of them still living in remote corners of Norway at that time? The question then has to be asked, would it have been possible for them to paddle one of their tiny craft from Norway and back?

These are questions I cannot answer, nor this one: if these small hairy strangers were not Finns, who, or what, were they?

Fride

Although they rarely if ever saw them, many Hebrideans believed there were tiny elves, the *fride*, living under the ground. The entrances to their homes were hidden in rocky places and the elves used to come out at nights and go into houses in search of crumbs on the floor.

A crofter was once having very bad luck with his cattle. He was losing them one by one. Then he discovered that the woman working in his kitchen was picking up every crumb that fell from the table.

He told her to leave the crumbs for the *fride* and from that day his cattle thrived.

Some islanders used to scatter crumbs and pour a little milk amongst the rocks where they believed the *fride* lived. If this was done every day, the elves would not harm them or their stock.

Ghillie Dhu

Everyone in the Gairloch district knew that the Ghillie Dhu lived in the birch woods. Few people had seen him and nobody had ever spoken to him, until little Jessie Macrae got lost in the woods.

She had wandered off on her own and could not find her way back. She walked and walked, and circled and circled, and then, as darkness closed in, she sat down and cried.

It was then that the Ghillie Dhu appeared before her.

'Why are you crying?' he asked.

Jessie blinked at the little figure clad in moss and leaves.

'I'm lost,' she told him.

The Ghillie Dhu smiled and told her to follow him and she got to her feet and did so. It was a long way through the strange dark wood but somehow she was no longer frightened. She trusted the Ghillie Dhu.

As the sun rose they came to the edge of the woods. He pointed the way, smiled, and slipped back into the greenery of the trees.

You might think, after that, that local people would feel kindly towards the Ghillie Dhu. And so the ordinary folk did. However, some years later, the Laird, Sir Hector Mackenzie, decided he wanted to hunt down and kill the little creature. Jessie, by now, was grown up and married to a Mackenzie and she and her husband did their best to have the hunt called off.

It went ahead, led by Sir Hector and four other lairds. For a whole night they searched through the birch woods, beating the bushes and looking in every nook and corner. To Jessie's great relief they never caught as much as a glimpse of him. The Ghillie Dhu had proved as elusive as ever.

The name of this attractive creature means 'Black Servant' and he is clearly one of the many tutelary fairies or guardian spirits.

Giants

It is a matter of some difficulty to distinguish the fairy-
tale giant from the giant of legend.
Dr Katharine M. Briggs, *A Dictionary of British Folk-Tales.*

The most famous giant and, sadly, the only one many people have heard of is the one that lived at the top of Jack's beanstalk. The story of 'Jack and the Beanstalk' or 'Jack the Giant Killer' makes wonderful bedtime reading and great pantomime:

> 'Fee, fi, fo, fum,
> I smell the blood of an Englishman!'

Who, as a child, has not thrilled to that roar, whether in the bed-room or the theatre?

It is a pity though that the tales of our own Scottish giants are so little remembered. The largest and rowdiest of our supernatural beings have become an elusive race. They were never that on earth.

The Red Yetin certainly deserves to be remembered. He was a particularly hideous giant for he had three large heads. His story goes back a long way: Sir David Lyndsay entertained the young James V with tales of the Yetin. The creature was, by the way, no relation to the hairy Yeti of the Himalayas. The word Etin is from a Scandinavian term for giant.

Tradition says the Red Yetin came here from Ireland. Arriving in Scotland he forced the King's daughter to marry him then kept her locked up, taking her out for frequent beatings.

At this time there were two widows dwelling side by side and living off little bits of land. The first had two sons and the other had one. The widow with two sons decided it was time her older boy went out to seek his fortune. She called him to her and told him to take a pail to the well and bring water so that she could bake a cake for the journey. The size of the cake depended on how much water he brought. 'And mind, the cake is a' I can gie ye,' she said.

The boy went to the well and filled the pail. But he was careless and failed to notice, as he carried it to his mother, that there were holes in the bottom of it. By the time he handed it to his mother most of the water had trickled away, and it was a very small cake she baked for him. When it was ready she told her son, 'Ye can tak half o' it wi' my blessing or the hale cake wi' my malison [curse].'

The boy thought of the long, uncertain journey ahead, looked at the small cake and said he would take the whole thing, malison and all.

Before he left he went to his brother and handed him a knife. 'Look at this every day,' he told him. 'If it's still clean, ye'll ken I'm a'richt. If it turns rusty, ye'll ken I'm in danger.'

The boy was three days on the road when he came on an old shepherd with a flock of sheep.

'Wha's are these?' asked the lad.

The shepherd replied:

> 'The Red Etin of Ireland
> Aince lived in Bellygan,
> He stole King Malcolm's daughter,
> The king of fair Scotland.
> He beats her, he binds her,
> He lays her on a band;
> And every day he dings her
> With a bright silver wand.
> Like Julian the Roman
> He's one that fears no man.
> It's said there's ane predestinate
> To be his mortal foe;
> But that man is still unborn,
> And lang may it be so.'

The young man went on his way and met an old man herding pigs. 'Wha's are these?' he asked and received the same reply.

Next he met a man with a flock of goats. They, too, he was told, belonged to the Red Yetin. But this old man said more. He warned the boy about a herd of beasts he would meet along the road. They would, he said, be very different to anything he had seen so far.

Sure enough, as the boy walked on he sighted a herd of big, fierce animals unlike anything he had ever seen. They all had two heads and four horns sprouting from each one. As they moved towards him he took to his heels and, seeing a hilltop castle, he ran up to it and in at the open door.

In the kitchen he found an old woman sitting by the fire. Frightened of going out again to face the animals he begged her to let him stay the night. She warned him it would not be safe. He was in the home of the terrible Red Yetin. He still implored her to let him stay.

'Let me hide,' he said. 'The Red Yetin will never ken I'm here.'

She gave in and showed him a hiding place where the boy crouched down out of sight. Almost at once he heard the Red Yetin enter the kitchen and roar:

> 'Snouk [sniff] but and snouk ben,
> I find the smell of an earthly man;
> Be he living, or be he dead,
> His heart this night shall kitchen [flavour] my bread!'

The Yetin went straight to where the lad was hiding and dragged him out. The boy looked up at the towering monster with its three great heads and pleaded for mercy.

The Yetin glared at him. 'Very well,' he boomed. 'I will spare your life if you can answer me three questions.'

The lad nodded and gulped.

'The first question is, Which was inhabited first—Ireland or Scotland?'

The boy did not know.

'The second question is, Was man made for woman or woman made for man?'

The boy did not know.

'The third question is, Which were made first—men or beasts?'

The poor lad stood silent. The giant gave a mighty roar, seized a mallet and banged him on the head. The boy turned to stone.

Now, every morning the lad's brother back home had been taking out the knife and having a look at it. Up till then it had remained bright and shining. But the morning after the lad was turned to stone his brother looked at the knife and found it brown and rusty.

He went at once to his mother and told her it was time he went after his brother.

'Very well,' said his mother. 'Fill a pail o' water and I'll bake you a cake for the journey.'

Off he went to the well and he did the same as his brother; he lost most of the water through the holes in the bottom of the pail and ended up with a very small cake and his mother's malison.

On the road he met the old man with the sheep, the old man with the pigs, and the old man with the goats, and was given the very same answers to his questions. He was chased by the two-headed beasts, hid in the castle, and was discovered by the giant who asked him the same questions. When he could not answer them, the Red Yetin hit him on the head with the mallet and turned him into stone.

As time passed and no word came back from the two brothers the other widow's son made up his mind to go and find them. His mother told him to fetch water from the well to make a cake and he went and filled it. As he walked back with it a raven flew over and cried out that the pail was leaking. He looked down, saw the water dripping out and at once patched up the holes and refilled the pail.

Thus the cake his mother made was a large one. 'Now,' she said, 'will ye tak half o' it wi my blessing or the hale cake wi my malison?'

He said he would take half with her blessing. And somehow the half was bigger than the brothers' two cakes put together.

The boy had walked a good way along the road when he met a woman who asked him if he would give her something to eat. He at once broke off a big piece from the half cake and handed it to her.

She thanked him and in return gave him a magic wand, for the truth was that she was a fairy woman. 'That will help ye wi' what lies ahead,' she said, and she told him some of the things he could expect and what he must do. Then she vanished.

He walked on and came to the old man with the sheep.

'Wha's are these?' he asked.

The shepherd looked at him and said:

> 'The Red Etin of Ireland
> Aince lived in Bellygan,
> He stole King Malcolm's daughter,
> The king of fair Scotland.
> He beats her, he binds her,
> He lays her on a band;
> And every day he dings her
> With a bright silver wand.
> Like Julian the Roman
> He's one that fears no man.'

Then he added:

> 'But now I fear his end is near,
> And destiny at hand;
> And you're to be, I plainly see,
> The heir of all his land.'

The lad walked on till he came to the man with the pigs.

'Wha's are these?' he asked, and received the same reply. The same thing happened when he met the old man with the goats.

Walking on he saw, ahead of him, all over the road, the herd of two-headed beasts. Instead of running away, he walked right in amongst them. One came up to him, bellowing and pawing the ground. It was going to attack him but he remembered the wand the fairy woman had given him. He touched the beast with it and it fell dead at his feet. The other animals stood back and watched him pass through.

He climbed the hill to the castle. The door was shut so he knocked boldly and walked in. The old woman who had hidden his two brothers now did the same for him.

In crashed the Red Yetin and stood glaring about him with his three great heads. He roared:

'Snouk but and snouk ben,
I find the smell of an earthly man;
Be he living, or be he dead,
His heart this night shall kitchen my bread!'

The lad stepped from hiding and stood before him. The giant put the same three questions to him as he had put to the brothers. The boy had been given the right answers by the fairy woman on the road. He spoke them now in a loud clear voice. With each answer the giant seemed to shrink in size. His power was slipping away.

When the giant was quite small the lad lifted an axe and cut off the three heads one by one. Then, laying down the axe, he ordered the old woman to show him where the giant had imprisoned the King's daughter whom he had heard about from the old men. She led him upstairs and unlocked a door, then another and another. There were many doors and behind each one stood a beautiful girl. The most beautiful of them all was the King's daughter.

Once they were freed, the lad asked to be taken to the two brothers. The woman led him to a low room and pointed to where the two stone statues were standing side by side. He touched them with the wand and they came back to life. There were many other statues there, for the giant had quite a collection. A touch of the wand was enough to restore them to life.

Next day the whole company set out for the King's palace, the lad and the princess, the two brothers, and all the others who had been turned to stone.

The King was overjoyed to see his daughter again and he threw open his doors to all of them. The lad and the princess had fallen in love and in time the two brothers fell in love with the daughters of two rich nobles. So the three couples were married and lived in happiness for the rest of their days.

It will be seen that the story of the Red Yetin has features in common with 'Jack and the Beanstalk', particularly when it comes to the giant sniffing out the intruder in his castle. It is not clear why the hero of the tale is given unfair advantage over the two brothers through receiving the raven's warning and the advice and wand from the fairy woman. Presumably it is because he *is* the hero, and therefore deserves to be helped. To make it a level playing field, as we would say today, the brothers would have to be given the warning by the raven but ignore it, and refuse the fairy a piece of cake and so not receive her 'reward'. These things do not happen in the versions I have seen, though one feels they should.

Despite these reservations, the story is at least as striking as 'Jack and the Beanstalk' and might well have retained its popularity in Scotland had it not been eclipsed by the English tale. Pantomime has a lot to answer for.

Shetlanders have their own version of the story complete with the giant's scenting out of the presence of an 'earthling'. The hero in this one is a little boy who herds cows for his mother. One day when he comes home tired and hungry she tells him she has nothing for him to eat as there is no meal left. He asks her to shake out all the bags and collect what is there. She does so and finds just enough to bake him a small 'bruni'.

She puts it by the peat fire and tells him to watch it. He does so, turning it to get it brown all over. But when he lifts it he lets it slip through his fingers on to the floor. It falls on its edge and runs out through the open door with the boy after it.

Just as he bends to pick it up it rolls into a hole in a hillock in front of the cottage and vanishes from sight. The boy is amazed to see smoke coming out of the hole. He starts to dig and soon the hole is big enough for him to crawl through. He squeezes in and finds himself in a passage, makes his way along and comes to a big room.

Seated in it is a giantess who is sifting meal from a huge pile. She has a large sieve which she is shaking from side to side. As he watches her the boy realises she is blind and has no idea he is there. His eyes shine as he gazes at the pile of beautiful meal. Next moment he has slipped off his breeks (trousers) and fastened the legs together. Then, using them as a bag, he fills them with the lovely meal. He then turns and crawls back along the passage and out through the hole, dragging his breeks behind him.

He hurries home to his mother who is delighted to see the pile of meal and starts baking with it right away. From then on, every time she needs more meal, the boy takes a sack, goes back into the hole and helps himself from the pile under the nose of the blind giantess.

The pile is beginning to go down, though, and one day, when he is in there filling his sack, the giantess mutters, 'If only I kent wha's stealin' my meal.'

The next time he goes and is busy helping himself the giantess's great hand suddenly gropes across the meal and catches him by the wee finger.

'Ah,' she shouts. 'Here's the thief that's been stealin' my meal!'

As the boy wriggles to get free there comes the sound of heavy footsteps and in comes the husband of the giantess. He roars:

'Fi fum fi fen,
I fin da eir
O' an earti man.
An' bi hi whik
Ir bi hi did,
A'll he his hid
Wi' may supir brid,'

(Fi fum fi fen,
I find the smell
Of an earthly man.
And be he live
Or be he dead,
I'll have his hide
With my supper bread.)

He is about to grab the boy when his wife stops him. What he is smelling, she tells him, might be a crow that came down the chimney into the fire. To the boy she puts a question: what would he have done if he had caught *her* stealing meal from *him*?

He thinks a moment and then he answers, 'I would have tied you up and fed you till you were so fat you went deaf and blind. Then I would have boiled you and eaten you.'

'Well,' she said, 'That's what I will dae wi' you!'

She ties him up and feeds him so much food he thinks he must surely go deaf and blind. Every day she gives him more and more. When she thinks he must be fat enough for eating she lights a big fire and hangs a cauldron over it, full of water.

After a time she asks the boy to go over to the fire and listen if the water is boiling yet. He goes over and listens but goes back to the giantess and says the cauldron is so deep he can't hear if it is boiling or not. 'You had better listen yourself,' he says.

She goes over and bends an ear to the cauldron. As she does so he creeps up behind her and gives her a great push so that she tumbles head first into the boiling water. Then he bangs the lid on top.

When she is cooked he takes her out, cuts her up, and puts the best bits on a great plate for the giant's supper. He comes in, picks up his knife and fork and eats her with relish. He says it is the best thing he has eaten for a long time. It is so good he gobbles it up too quickly and chokes on a bone. He falls off his chair, dead.

The boy helps himself to all the meal in the kitchen. He also finds a hoard of silver plates and other treasures which the two giants had stolen from people they had killed over the years. He takes all this home with him.

His mother is overjoyed to see him again safe and sound and she claps her hands when she sees all the meal. She claps them even louder when she sees the silver plates. From that day she and her son never want for anything again.

If the reader thinks that this was a rather cruel and nasty end for the two giants, it is not unusual. Most stories have the giant or giants dying a violent death at human hands. No sympathy for them is expected. In any case it would be difficult to sympathise with some of the monsters described. Take the one who captured Oscar, the son of Ossian.

Oscar was a fine strapping fellow, the tallest and strongest of his age-group. But even he had no defence when a giant came ashore in a rowing boat and took him and his friends prisoner, stringing them along a branch like a row of fish.

The giant was hideous, his whole body covered in green scales. He put the branch in his boat and rowed for hours till he reached his island home. There he carried the branch up to his castle and called for his housekeeper.

'I'm going to rest now,' he told her. 'When I wake I want the biggest lad among these cooked for my supper.'

The biggest was Oscar. When the giant had gone, the woman went to the branch to fetch him. He begged her to spare him this time.

'Very well,' she said, and she cooked the next biggest instead.

When the giant awoke and came for his supper he looked at the portion on his plate and bawled, 'There was a bigger one than that! I'm going to sleep again. If you don't have him cooked when I come back I will eat you instead!'

He stamped off.

'I will have to take you now,' the woman said to Oscar.

'I have a better idea,' said Oscar. 'You would like to be free, wouldn't you?'

'Oh yes!' said the woman. She told him she had been the giant's prisoner for seven years. Every day she feared he would kill and eat her.

'Then if you help me,' said Oscar, 'I will help you.'

When the giant returned, they were ready for him. Oscar was armed with a red hot poker and the woman with the giant's sword. Oscar stepped up to the giant and drove the poker through the scales on his head so that he fell to the ground. The woman then sliced off his head with the sword.

As soon as this was done, they untied all the other young men from the branch and while they were rubbing their aching limbs the house-keeper showed Oscar where the giant had a cache of gold and silver hidden in the castle. They all took as much of it as they could carry, piled it into the giant's boat and, taking the woman with them, rowed home.

In *Popular Tales of the West Highlands* J. F. Campbell gives several version of a traditional giant story which is known as 'The Battle of the Birds'. The title is misleading, a misnomer, for although the most frequently told version opens with a King's son going to watch such a battle it is over by the time he arrives and all he sees is a fight between a raven and a snake.

The Prince saves the raven from defeat by cutting off the snake's head and he is rewarded by the bird which is, in fact, a young man who has been placed under a spell.

The tale is filled with magical happenings, the second part dealing with the adventures of the Prince's son who marries a giant's daughter after accomplishing three impossible tasks with her aid. The two lovers take flight pursued by the giant who intends to kill his son-in-law but he himself drowns in a loch.

That is not the end of the young lovers' travails but, through perseverance and magic, the giant's daughter and the Prince overcome all the obstacles put in their way. How they overcome the obvious one of the difference in their sizes is not explained!

The version I have outlined was collected in 1859 from a fisherman called John Mackenzie who lived near Inveraray and was, at the time, building dykes on the Ardkinglas estate. A second version was related to Campbell by a stable boy 'then employed at the ferry at St Katharine's, who repeated it in Gaelic while rowing the boat to Inveraray.' (What times for story collectors!)

Like some other versions it opens with an apparently minor inci-dent, a quarrel between a mouse and a wren. This develops into a staged battle watched by mice, rats and all the birds of the air. A young Prince comes to watch, befriends a raven, and they agree to travel together.

The Prince meets and falls in love with a giant's daughter who helps him with the impossible tasks set by her father. The giant is killed when, on the girl's advice, the young man places an apple under a horse's hoof: the giant's heart was inside the apple. Even the progeny of giants felt no sympathy for them and destroyed them without compunction!

A giant story with a ripple of humour running through it was told to Hamish Henderson and myself by a 14-year-old traveller boy, Jimmy McPhee, in the 1950s. He said he had been told it by his grandmother. The giant in the story has even more heads than usual—seven in all.

It's the story of a young boy called Jack whose brother had disappeared and no one knew where he was. One morning Jack went out to catch rabbits. He met a wee bird which said to him, 'Don't go into that wood or you'll meet the Giant with the Seven Heads.'

'I'm only looking for rabbits,' said Jack. 'I don't want a giant with seven heads.'

He went on and met a snake which said, 'Don't go into that wood or you'll meet the Giant with seven Heads.'

Jack said, 'I'm only looking for rabbits. I don't want a giant with seven heads.'

On he went and met an owl. The owl asked him, 'Will you do something for me?'

'What is it?' asked Jack.

'Take this sword and go and kill the Giant with the Seven Heads.'

'I'm only looking for rabbits,' said Jack. 'I don't want a giant with seven heads.'

However, he took the sword and walked on and presently he saw, coming towards him, the Giant with the Seven Heads, riding on the back of a huge, tall horse.

As the boy stood wondering what to do he heard a voice call 'Jack! Jack!' It was the wee bird he had met earlier and now it told him to take hold of one of its wings. Jack did so and the bird said, 'Now draw your sword.'

He did, and at once he turned into a bird. He flew up and cut off one of the giant's heads. As the giant tried to catch him he fluttered back then swooped in again and cut off a second head. And so it went on until all seven heads were off. The giant's body and all the fallen heads then vanished and there stood Jack's long-lost brother.

His brother thanked Jack for breaking the spell he had been under and Jack said, 'Go and tell them at home because I've still got to catch my rabbits!'

One could imagine what a really good storyteller would do with that narrative and the gales of laughter it would raise. I would love to have heard Jimmy McPhee's granny in full flight. On the other hand it could be told in all seriousness with emphasis on the dangers facing Jack as he approaches the huge and terrible creature.

Most giants were regarded as a natural enemy to be destroyed at all costs and without mercy. The exceptions were their daughters, some of whom, as we have seen, could become the wives of ordinary men. The fear and hatred of giants would seem to have been well justified: they cooked and ate people, were cruel, ill-tempered and destructive.

Destroying them could be a formidable undertaking, for their soul might be hidden somewhere, and until it was found and destroyed you could not kill or even injure its owner. Aware of this, giants could be very cunning in concealing their soul: it might be in an egg, a stone, an animal or fish, a tree or bush. Sometimes it was buried under the ground or even below a house.

Hugh Miller, in *Scenes and Legends*, reminds us of the tradition that at one time the whole country was populated by giants. Belief in them used to be widespread and thankfully they are not completely forgotten: fragments of folklore associate them with places and natural features up and down Scotland.

Miller recounts the legend that our giants were all descended from the 33 daughters of Diocletian, King of Syria. He had put them in a boat and set them adrift as punishment for their unpleasant custom of killing their husbands on their wedding night.

They landed on our shores and found the country uninhabited. For a time they lived on roots and berries until they were discovered by a race of demons who took them as their wives. The progeny resulting from these unions were of huge size and ferocity—the giants of our myths.

In his hometown of Cromarty, on the Black Isle, Miller knew all about giants from his earliest childhood. Every time a boat left the harbour to go seaward, she would pass between the two great promontories that guard the entrance to the Cromarty Firth. One of them rises from just outside the town, the other looks across at it from the Nigg side of the water.

These are known as the North and South Sutors, this being the old Scots term for a shoemaker. The headlands, Cromarty folk said, were the work-stools of two giants who sat opposite each other as they toiled at their lasts, throwing tools to and fro across the basin.

Miller goes on to say that, according to tradition, a woman giant created nearly all the hills of Ross-shire when the bottom fell out of the pannier she was carrying. It was filled with earth and stones and they scattered over a wide area.

Just a few miles from Cromarty two giants waged daily war against one another from the headlands guarding Munlochy Bay. They were husband and wife and they threw missiles at each other until one day the husband flung a battle axe and injured his wife with it. Next day she flung it back and it stuck fast in his forehead. She shouted in glee, 'That will keep you quiet for one day at any rate!'

More usually it was boulders that giants threw at one another. Two of them tossed stones across Loch Ness, and in many parts of Scotland there are, or were, large stones, sometimes single, often in groups, said to have been flung by giant hands. In Orkney rows of large stones going out to sea were believed to have been the start of bridges giants had begun to build and then abandoned.

Look at a map of the Outer Hebrides and you see the outline of a nine-headed giant killed by an intrepid Skye man and a kelpie from the Cuillins. The giant had abducted the young man's sweetheart and other female prisoners with the intention of eating them at his leisure at his home on the Stack Rock.

The avenging pair followed him to his lair, sliced off eight of his heads and then finished him off with a stab through the heart. The great trunk, limbs and heads were impossible to bury so they were left to float in the sea where, in time, they became the Isles of today.

Another enterprising young man was responsible for dispatching two giants who lived on Rannoch Moor. Local folk were desperate to be rid of the pair who rampaged through the district at nights destroying everything in their path. They killed anyone who tried to stand up to them.

Such was their ill temper that the couple were constantly quarrelling and trying to get the better of one another and it was this that was to be their undoing.

The young man persuaded them to compete against each other to see which could hurl stones the farthest. They tried harder and harder, growing more and more angry as each sought to outdo the other and all the time the young man was urging them to throw ever heavier boulders.

At last one of them, exhausted, fell to the ground. The other turned and dropped a great rock on top of him, crushing him to death. He then staggered and fell, breathing his last. The rocks they threw in the contest can be seen strewn across the Rannoch landscape.

Still in Perthshire there was another pair of quarrelsome giants, Colly Camb and Smoutachanty. They were husband and wife but could not bear to live together. Colly lived in a cave on Mount Blair while his wife had a cave of her own a little distance away at Auchintaple.

No one who ventured into one of their caves ever came out alive and Colly had a terrible habit of throwing rocks from the top of Mount Blair, often inflicting great damage on houses and farms.

Giants

*The young man persuaded them to compete against each
other to see which could hurl stones the farthest…*

After he raided a mill and stole all the oatmeal, the local people decided they had had enough. They marched up to Colly's cave and challenged him to come out. When he did they set about him and, through sheer force of numbers, beat him to death.

It is maybe a pity Colly Camb was not still there when, a few years ago, a mobile phone mast was erected on the summit of Mount Blair, despoiling this most beautiful of hills. Colly, I am sure, would have made short work of it!

Some of the other places with strong giant traditions are: Norman's Law, Fife; Invergowrie, near Dundee; Kinveachie, Inverness-shire; Knockfarrel, Strathpeffer; the hills of Torvean, Dunain and Craig Phadrick, all Inverness; the Isle of Mull; Ben Ledi, Perthshire; Edderton, on the Dornoch Firth; Hoy, Rousay and Wyre, all Orkney; Portree, Skye; Weisdale, Unst and Fetlar, Shetland. Even Arthur's Seat, Edinburgh, has its giant associations.

Great heroes, such as King Arthur and William Wallace, are sometimes elevated to giant status in our folklore. In such cases a 'modern' name has almost certainly superseded an old one.

The Highlands are particularly rich in giant lore. In Gaelic they were known as *Famhaireans* (or Fomarians), and their strongholds were scattered widely through countless hills, caves and islands.

According to the Highland folklorist Alasdair Alpin MacGregor, the last of the giants lived in a cave on the Hills of Fearn, Ross-shire. His daughter had married an ordinary man who had little time for the old giant, despite the fact that he no longer presented any danger. His riproaring days were long over and he was now blind and growing feeble.

One day as he dined with his son-in-law on a large cut of roast ox the young man asked him, 'Did you giants ever eat beef from as big an ox as this?'

The giant replied: 'The legs of the birds we ate were heavier than the hindquarters of your biggest oxen.'

The young man laughed scornfully, thinking it was a foolish boast and no more was said, but the giant's pride was hurt and later that day he called his manservant.

'Bring me my bow and three arrows,' he said, 'and lead me by the hand to yon corrie in the Balnagown Forest.'

When they reached the corrie he told the servant to take him to a step in the face of the cliff.

'Now tell me what comes,' he said.

'I see birds,' said the servant.

'Are they larger than usual?'

'No. No larger than in Fearn.'

'What do you see now?' asked the giant.

'More and more birds.'

'Are *they* larger than usual?'

'Three times bigger than eagles!' exclaimed the servant.

'And what do you see now?'

'The sky is black with birds. The biggest of them is three times bigger than the biggest one!'

'Give me my bow and guide my hand,' said the giant.

The servant did so and the giant fired an arrow which brought down the largest of the birds. It was enormous.

Said the giant: 'Cut off a hindquarter.'

It took the pair of them to carry it home.

When his son-in-law saw the size of it he could hardly believe his eyes. From that day he treated his father-in-law with proper respect and never contradicted him again.

So the last of the once great race of Scottish giants lived out the rest of his life in peace and contentment.

The Ghost Elk

Only two people are known to have seen this phantom animal. One is the present Laird of Ardblair, Perthshire, Laurence Blair Oliphant. This is what he told me:

> 'When I was a small boy I was playing at the side of the castle by what used to be the kitchen garden. It was nearly lunchtime and I was expecting my mother at any minute to call me in.
>
> 'Suddenly, in a plantation on the west side of the building I saw this large, red, antlered animal, running through the trees. The trees were planted pretty close together and it would have been impossible for such a huge beast to run between them so swiftly and without making a lot of noise. But there was no sound of breaking branches or pounding hooves. It just ran quickly and easily through the wood and disappeared.'

Many years later Laurence's wife Jenny came to him and said, 'I have just seen the most extraordinary thing.' She had glimpsed the animal running through the same piece of woodland.

Over the years, when Laurence recalled his sighting he thought of the creature as being like the American moose. However, when he told me about this in 2002 he had recently watched a programme on television about the giant Irish elk and realised how similar it was to what he and Jenny had seen.

Elk roamed Scotland for a very long time, probably not becoming extinct until around AD 1300. They were a forest animal, as red deer were originally, and as man cleared the forests they lost their natural habitat and became easier to hunt down.

Glaistigs

The names glaistig and gruagach seem sometimes to be interchangeable. Take J. G. Campbell's definition: 'The glaistig was a tutelary being in the shape of a thin grey little woman, with long yellow hair reaching to her heels, dressed in green, haunting certain sites or farms, and watching in some cases over the house, in others over the cattle.'

That sounds like a description of a typical gruagach. It does not help when he goes on to say: 'In the south Highlands, the glaistig was represented as a little wan woman, stout and not tall, but very strong. In Skye, where most of her duties were assigned to a male deity, the gruagach, she was said to be very tall, "a lath of a body", like a white reflection or shade.'

Alexander Carmichael, on the other hand, in *Carmina Gadelica*, describes a glaistig as 'a water-imp...a vicious creature, half woman, half goat, frequenting lonely lakes and rivers.'

Katharine Briggs tries to make sense of it all in *A Dictionary of Fairies*. The glaistig was, she says, 'a composite character'. She explains: 'She sometimes has the attributes and habits of the *cailleach bheur*, sometimes assumes animal form, often that of a goat, but more often she is described as half woman, half goat. She is a water spirit, but when she is regarded as a *fuath* she is murderous and dangerous. As the green glaistig, however, she is more like a banshee, mourning the death or illness of her favourites.'

The truth would seem to be that whether you called a certain creature a glaistig or a gruagach depended on where in the Highlands you lived.

There is dispute too about the derivation of the name. Campbell says it is from *glas*, grey, wan or pale green, and *stig*, a sneaking or crouching object. Carmichael, on the other hand, states: 'from *glas*, water, *stic*, imp.'

Some sources suggest that the glaistig was not a full member of the fairy race but occupied a mid-position between ourselves and supernatural beings. It is also suggested that she was a mortal who had gone over to the fairies.

She usually lived close to a large house, making her home in a little glen or ravine. Some lived at the back of a waterfall or in a ford. In Mull she lived in a yew tree.

Although she seldom if ever entered the house to which she bore an attachment, she felt fiercely protective towards it and the site it occupied. Should the house be destroyed by fire or demolished, the glaistig would be heard wailing in distress.

Her protectiveness did not extend to the people living in the house though she shared their joys and sorrow in her own way, making exultant noises when there was something to celebrate and wailing at times of sorrow.

Like the gruagach she often watched over sheep and cattle and, according to Donald Mackenzie, she cared for horses, goats and dogs, and could herself take the form of any one of them.

MacDonald Robertson picked up a tale of a man in Lorne who claimed to have encountered a woman in green at a spot called Doire nan Each. His dog ran at her and she fled, leaving him convinced he had seen the glaistig who lived in a ravine by a mansion in the district. It was believed she was a former mistress of the house.

There is a popular Lochaber story of how a man known as Big Kennedy of Lianachan was riding home late one night when he came on a glaistig on the bank of a stream.

He grabbed hold of her and swung her up in front of him, using the belt of his sword to hold her fast. When he got her home, he threatened not to release her until she had built him a large new barn. She set to and toiled all night so that the barn was finished by morning.

One version of this tale has it that, in the morning, when the barn was built, Kennedy heated the coulter of his plough in the fire until it was red hot and then ordered the glaistig to swear on it that she would never again interfere with anybody in Lochaber.

She placed a hand on the coulter and burned it to the bone. Shrieking in agony she rushed from the house screaming, first a blessing, and then a curse, on the house of Kennedy. They would, she said, grow like rushes but wither like ferns.

This is said to have been fulfilled, for future members of the family grew tall and straight before inexplicably declining and wasting away.

I have seen a version of this which has it that, as the glaistig left after building the barn, she leaned in at the window to shake Kennedy's hand. Instead of his hand he held out the hot coulter. In either case the glaistig's curse seems not undeserved.

Sometimes it was glaistigs who were on the offensive. They would jump up behind a rider and pin his arms to his sides. This seems to have been done more in mischief than malevolence, but it rebounded on one glaistig who seized hold of a chief of the MacMillans. As soon as she released him he turned and stabbed her to death with his dirk.

It is said that a glaistig would sometimes be found sitting by a stream or river waiting to be given a lift across, though why, if she was a water sprite, she would require a lift, I do not know.

Great-hand

Parts of Edinburgh's Old Town are a maze of underground cellars and passages. The crowds of tourists who wander up and down the High Street are blissfully unaware of the horror that may be lurking below their feet.

Great-hand, according to the tradition, lives in a passage that runs the length of the Royal Mile from the castle to the Palace of Holyrood. It was said to have been used by soldiers in the distant past. They could file down the passage, emerge at the other end and attack their enemies from the rear, taking them by surprise.

They stopped using the passage when Great-hand took up residence in it. From then on no one who went into the passage came out alive.

The description given of Great-hand was sketchy. All that had been glimpsed of him was a gigantic grisly hand and fingernails like an eagle's claws.

For a long time the tunnel was unused. Then a local piper said it held no fears for him. He was going to explore it and he would take his dog with him. He told folk he would play his pipes all the way down so if they listened from the street they would be able to follow his progress.

A big crowd gathered to watch him and his dog go into the tunnel from a cave under the Castle. He was playing bravely and they followed the sound down the hill. Suddenly at just about the spot now known as the Heart of Midlothian, the music stopped abruptly as if the pipes had been wrenched from the piper's hands. There was complete silence.

After a time the crowd returned to the entrance in the cave. There they saw the piper's dog run out, terrified, without a hair left on its body.

Later, when all hope of the piper was gone, the entrance was blocked up, as was done at the other end as well. Great-hand was to receive no more victims.

The story of a piper entering a cave or tunnel and not being seen again may be familiar to readers who have heard it told in another part of the country. There seem to have been a lot of brave, if foolhardy pipers!

Invariably it is claimed that the sound of ghostly pipes has been heard long afterwards.

Similarly there are many local legends of dogs going into caves or holes and emerging, often miles away, without a hair on their body.

All of which reflects man's fear of the underground, its total darkness and hidden, unseen horrors.

Green Ladies

True Thomas lay on Huntlie bank;
A ferlie spied he wi' his e'e;
And there he saw a ladye bricht
Come riding doun by the Eildon Tree.
Her skirt was o' the grass-green silk,
Her mantle o' the velvet fine;
At ilk tett o' her horse's mane
Hung fifty siller bells and nine.

The mysterious and beautiful seductress who carried off Thomas of Ercildoune to fairyland (or Elfland) for seven years is in a class of her own. The ballad which tells how 'she led him in at Eildon Hill' is a striking and imaginative piece of literature. It tells how, when she brought him back to earth (in more than one sense) she endowed Thomas with the gift of prophecy, a gift he used liberally for the rest of his life. Very many predictions attributed to him are still being quoted in towns and villages across Scotland.

Whatever the identity of the green-clad 'ladye', Thomas was a real life thirteenth century figure who lived at Ercildoune, the old name for Earlston, Berwickshire. The ruins of the family seat are still there.

A later addition to the story told in the ballad, tacked on, it seems, by Sir Walter Scott, claims that he afterwards returned to Elfland and is still there, but will one day come back to earth as he did before. The prophecies he made on his first return were gloomy enough; what will they be like next time?

The temptress in the ballad is the queen among our green ladies. Most of the others, and there are many of them, tend to fall into distinct categories. One of the categories consists of fairy women. Highland folklore contains many accounts of lone fairy women appearing to someone at a cottage door or in the fields, usually seeking a favour such as a bite to eat. Their request granted, they go away as quietly as they came.

A second category is that of ghosts. Green ladies are generally solitary and sad. They are usually believed to have died a tragic death and to be lingering between this world and the next.

The one at the Castle of Mey is typical. Tradition says she is a member of the Sinclair family who owned the castle when it bore its old name of Barrogil. She had fallen in love with a handsome ploughman who worked on the castle farm. Her father, the Earl, forbade them to meet and locked her in a room in the tower. What he had forgotten was that one of the windows overlooked the fields where the young man worked. She was able to watch him from her eyrie and exchange waves and throw kisses.

When the Earl found out, he flew into a rage and ordered the window to be blocked up. Some time later, in despair, the lovesick girl threw herself from the remaining window.

A little along the coast at Bighouse, Melvich, there is another green wraith, the ghost of a woman who hanged herself in her bedroom.

Blairgowrie, Perthshire, has two fine old castles and two different green lady legends. The Macphersons of The Newton have it that their apparition, Lady Jean, was tricked into surrendering herself to the fairies in an attempt to win back the affections of her lover, Ronald. She won him back but, clad in fairy green, she died on her wedding night. She is buried on the hill behind the castle but returns every Halloween and re-enters her old home in search of Ronald.

Ardblair, just outside the town, has an equally sad story handed down in the Blair Oliphant family. The present laird, Laurence Blair Oliphant, told me it thus: 'She was Jean Drummond and I assume of The Newton [The Drummonds were at Newton Castle in the seventeenth century].

She was betrothed to, or at least, courting one of the Ardblair family, a Blair. This chap left on a military mission and was away for some time, during which Jean would visit Ardblair and walk about the house.

'Then news reached her that he was dead. In a fit of grief she drowned herself in the river Ericht. Since then she has been seen wandering forlornly around Ardblair or, dripping and rather sinister, in the grounds of Newton.

'We often hear footsteps in the upstairs rooms and occasionally doors will open on their own, but whether this is caused by the green lady or not I don't know.'

Although Mr Blair Oliphant says that no present occupant of Ardblair has ever seen Jean, his mother, later Lady Duncan of Jordanstone, once told me of an encounter. 'I was going up the staircase to the gallery, carrying a coal scuttle. We had a guest staying, a lady, and when I caught sight of a figure standing there I thought "That's funny, I didn't think she was here." Then the figure just vanished. I have always believed it was Jean I saw that day."

Mr Blair Oliphant says that, from what his parents used to say, the green lady made frequent appearances in the time of his grandparents and earlier. 'They spoke of guests seeing her at parties and I got the impression that nobody then thought very much about it!'

The Jeans of the two legends would seem to be the same person, making this an interesting example of how different versions of a story are cherished within long-established families, even when they live in such close proximity as the Macphersons and the Blair Oliphants, with just a few fields separating the two homes.

In Banffshire there is a tale of a laird's wife who colluded in concealing the murder of a pedlar and the theft of his wares and gold. She was forced to remain in limbo as a green lady until she had arranged for his body to be disinterred from its hiding place and given proper burial. His gold was then sent to the dead man's window.

An old house in the heart of Stonehaven was known by local people to be the home of a green lady but after the building was cleared away in the 1940s she was seen no more.

Green ladies are invariably harmless, arousing pity rather than fear. Those fortunate enough to have encountered one are not greatly alarmed as they might be if they met, say, a ghost dog or a man from an earlier century.

The Countess of Munster described in her book *My Memories and Miscellanies* (1904) how the Christmas celebrations were enlivened one year by two sightings of 'Green Jean' at the family home, Wemyss

Castle, in Fife. She was first seen by a young member of the household and a friend and later by Lady Millicent Wemyss who had the strange experience of walking alongside the figure until it disappeared.

The green lady of Huntingtower, Perth, used to be kindly thought of by local people because of the warnings she would give them of approaching dangers. She was also said to have saved the life of a sick boy in a cottage near the castle by placing her hand on his brow.

In this respect she is like the Banffshire green lady who showed concern for the well-being of her husband's servants and saved children from drowning by warning an old nurse of the danger threatening them.

The above are only a handful of examples of 'lady' ghosts attired in traditional fairy green, green signifying enchantment. Less well known are the white ladies and grey ladies associated with certain places. So called white ladies have been seen at intervals at Ardoe House, Aberdeen, Balvenie Castle, Dufftown, Castle Huntly, near Dundee, and Kilbryde Castle, Dunblane.

Some, like the White Lady of Kilmany, Fife, haunt a place or locality rather than a building. Most of them, like green ladies, are inoffensive, though the one at Edzell Castle, Angus, is accompanied by an obnoxious smell.

The most famous grey lady must be the little figure who has been seen kneeling in prayer in the chapel of Glamis Castle. Grey ladies have also been reported from Dalhousie Castle, Lasswade, the Traquair Arms Hotel, Innerleithen, and the House of Monymusk, Banchory.

Some of these may well be clad in grey. Others may be so called because their insubstantial figures, glimpsed for maybe only a few seconds, convey the impression of greyness.

Sightings of green, grey and white ladies are still being reported today while many of the other phenomena in this book seem to have become extinct. Our imagination, in the twenty-first century, can still, apparently, accept female ghosts though they have rejected the brownie, the giant, and the merman. Or is it because the 'ladies' are still with us and the others are not?

Folklorists see them as descendants of ancient tutelary gods or guardian spirits. The stories of suicides and tragedies have been grafted on to them in modern times to 'explain', for the benefit of our puzzled minds, who and what they were and why they linger on.

The truth, as so often in folklore, lies deeper and further away.

Gruagachs

At one time it was an everyday sight in the Highlands. When the evening meal was finished, the woman and daughter of the house would rise from the table, pick up the left-over milk and take it outside. There she would walk over to a hollowed-out stone and carefully pour the milk into it. Having done this she would return to the house.

The stone was a *Clach na Gruagaich*, a Gruagach Stone, and the milk was the daily offering to the creature the family might never see but on whom they depended. On some crofts the milk was poured onto the stone immediately after the milking.

Most of the gruagachs were female, though males were not unknown. All had a good head of beautiful hair. According to J. F. Campbell, the root of the word is *gruag*, the hair of the head.

Some crofters kept the stone in the byre and this was appropriate as the gruagach took it upon herself to look after the cattle. She would be in amongst them when they were at pasture and would drive them away from danger.

The daily milk offering was essential because, if she was not given it, she could cause trouble, leading the cows astray or setting them loose from the byre at night. She could make them go dry, or stop the cream from rising to the surface.

Although many of the gruagachs were long-haired girls, J. G. Campbell tells of some in Skye who were tall young men, also long-haired and surprisingly smartly dressed for the job. Folk who had glimpsed one amongst their cattle said he wore a beaver hat and carried a stylish little cane or switch for dealing with the animals.

The female carried a strong reed for this purpose and if someone annoyed her she had been known to give him or her a brisk flick with it.

Some people claimed to have heard the gruagach singing and said they had very sweet voices, but there is also a report of one swearing savagely when her will was crossed.

As with the brownie, families who wanted to retain the services of their gruagach took pains not to offend it and so drive it away. One that lived at Skipness Castle seems to have been particularly valued. According to J. F. Campbell, she did not confine her duties to the care of the cattle but helped the servants with odd jobs about the house. Campbell also mentions one at Kerrisdale, Gairloch.

Some gruagachs were great swimmers. One such is said to have lived in a cave at East Bennan on Arran. She used to sing of her frequent sea travels:

> 'A night in Arran,
> A night in Islay,
> And in green Kintyre of the birches.'

Her services as a herd were highly valued by the islanders and they were dismayed when, after some slight, she took offence and left Arran. It seems she did not get far, for tradition says that she placed her left foot on Ben Bhuide on Arran and her right foot on Ailsa Craig as a stepping stone to the mainland.

While she was moving her left foot, a three-masted ship passed below and struck her such a blow on the thigh that she toppled into the sea. 'The people of Bennan mourned…long and loud.'

One wonders why she used the 'stepping stones' when she normally swam everywhere. This folk memory of a gruagach would seem to have become confused with another Arran creature, one of giant proportions.

The original Gruagach was a sun-god. In the Isle of Skye some Standing Stones were known as gruagach stones and were believed to represent the god.

The Gunna

A little man with flowing yellow hair, wearing a fox-skin, the gunna (pronounced 'goona') was always welcome on a Highland croft. He slept during the day but came out at night and watched over the cattle, keeping them clear of dangerous places and preventing them from trampling the crops. If a cow strayed, he would take it by the horns and steer it to safety.

Like the brownie, the gunna could not accept gifts of clothing and the only food the crofter could give him was a handful of scraps. Give the gunna more and you lost him. There was one on Tiree which acted as herdsman from sunset to sunrise until one of the crofters offered him breeks and shoes, when he immediately left.

Only people with the gift of second sight could see a gunna and those who did said he was a pitiful sight, thin and wasted. The fox-skin was all he had to cover him and he suffered in cold weather.

According to Donald Mackenzie, no matter how cold the gunna was, he could not enter a house for warmth, forbidden to do so, just one of the punishments inflicted on him when gunnas were evicted from the land of the fairies for some unknown misdemeanour.

Gyre Carlin

It used to be considered essential, in Fife, for a woman to finish off the garment she was knitting before Hogmanay. If she left it unfinished the gyre carlin (or gy-carlin) would take it away.

Even earlier, spinners and weavers had the same belief and they went to great trouble to complete their work.

A carlin is a witch or crone and there is little doubt that the gyre carlin was a witch figure. I have seen her described as the Queen of the Fairies but this is very improbable.

Originally she was perhaps a patroness of spinners and weavers.

Habetrot

This old fairy woman, an expert spinner, lived in Selkirkshire and the story is that she and her many helpers did a young girl's spinning to save her from punishment by her mother.

When the girl married a local laird, he expected her to spin the finest yarn. She took him to see Habetrot and her assistants and when Habetrot pointed out that they all had thin long lips with pulling out the thread, he told his pretty bride that she must never sit at a spinning wheel again. They sent all the spinning to Habetrot instead and she was delighted, so everyone was happy.

Habetrot was one of the fairy creatures who guarded her name, not wanting any mortal to know what it was. Whuppity Stoorie was another, and in Rousay, Orkney, there was a peerie (small) boy called Peeriefool.

If a mortal found out the secret name, he or she had power over the fairy, who was invariably very angry but unable to take revenge. It was usually the fairy's own fault that the name was discovered as they had a habit of singing about it. Whuppity Stoorie, for instance, sang:

'Little kens oor guid dame at hame
That Whuppity Stoorie is my name.'

101

Habetrot was less of a poet. She sang:

> 'Little kens the wee lassie on the braehead
> That my name is Habetrot.'

The Roman goddess of wisdom, Minerva, was also the protector of spinners and weavers. When the Romans left Scotland they left altars to her. Old Habetrot, supervising the work of her helpers, may be Minerva in Scottish clothing.

Hogboons

In the old days in Orkney, it was a common thing for a crofter's wife, at the end of a meal, to leave the house, go over to a small green mound, and pour the left-over milk on top of it. Later she might do the same with the ale.

This was for the hogboon who lived in the mound. Offerings of food were often left for him as well.

A family considered themselves lucky to have a hogboon on the croft and they wanted to keep him there. If they moved to another croft, they always hoped he would follow them and take up residence in the nearest green mound.

At nights, when they were in bed, the hogboon would sometimes come into the house for a few scraps. Some wives would leave a residue in the bottom of the pot so that he would not be disappointed.

Tom Muir, in *The Mermaid Bride and Other Orkney Folk Tales*, tells of a laird's daughter who was going to be married. It was the custom for the bride-to-be to have her feet washed beforehand. She decided hers were to be washed in wine.

After this had been done the servants took away the wine and drank it, much to the dismay of the housekeeper. 'I meant,' she wailed, 'to pour the wine on the house-knowe whar the hogboon bides for good luck to the wedding!'

Muir also gives an example of why it was wise to keep a hogboon happy. A crofter at Hellihowe, on Sanday, had brought home a new wife who cared nothing for the hogboon. She never poured anything on his mound nor left him any food.

The hogboon started to make their lives a misery, hiding kitchen utensils, turning things upside down, and generally creating mayhem. It got so bad the poor crofter appealed to the laird to let him move to a house at the other end of the island. To the couple's relief the laird agreed.

They set out one day with a string of ponies carrying all their belongings. The further they got away from Hellihowe the happier they felt.

Then, as they neared their new home, the lid of the kirn flew off and the hogboon's head popped up: 'We're getting a fine day to flit on, Goodman!'

Similar stories are told of certain household brownies, with whom the hogboon has a lot in common.

The name hogboon is a link with Orkney's Nordic past, being from the Old Norse, 'Haug Bui', a mound dweller.

It

This is surely a subject for a film of the horror genre. No two Shetlanders, looking for It, saw the same thing, such was its power of glamourie.

Jessie Saxby, in *Shetland Traditional Lore*, writes, 'One said It looked like a large lump of "slub" (jellyfish). Next It would seem like a bag of white wool. Another time It appeared like a beast wanting legs.' And so the descriptions go on, all entirely different.

She tells of an attempt once made to kill It with an axe. Although they were not certain if It was alive or dead some men piled earth over It. Later, one of them cleared away the soil. 'Something rose out of the hole and rolled into the sea.'

A creature of nightmares.

Killmoulis

This ugly little man lived in mills, mainly in the south of Scotland. He was never so common or so widespread as the brownie, many of which also took up abode in mills.

He had a huge nose and no visible mouth and the folklorist William Henderson suggested that he may have eaten his food through his nose. He says that the killmoulis was inclined to play practical jokes but could be thoroughly relied upon to help with the hard work.

When he was needed the miller could summon him with these words:

'Auld Killmoulis wanting the mow [mouth],
come to me now, come to me now!'

There are reports of him running for the midwife in the same way
as the brownie, and weeping and wailing before a family disaster or
bereavement.

King Otters

These magnificent beasts led packs of seven otters. A king otter's skin
was highly prized. Even just a piece of it, kept in a household, protected the family from ill luck. Soldiers thought themselves fortunate if
they could carry a bit, believing it gave them immunity in battle.
Sometimes a scrap of skin would be sewn into their banner. Another
way of using it was to place a tiny scrap over the eye.

Obtaining the skin in the first place, however, was very difficult.
The animal had a small white spot, the only place on its body a bullet
could enter. Some said the spot was below the chin, others that it was
hidden under a front leg. If a hunter fired and failed to hit the spot,
says J. G. Campbell, 'he fell a prey to the animal's dreadful jaws.' And
always, after a king otter was killed, a man, woman or dog would die.

In some parts of the Highlands it was believed there was a jewel in
the animal's head. A similar belief was widespread about the toad.

Another name for the king otter was water dog and he was said by
those who had seen him to be brown, while the seven he led were
black.

Alexander Carmichael was told that if you touched the liver of a
king otter with your tongue, the tongue would have the power to heal
burning for the rest of your life. The burn would not blister but would
heal instantly. Carmichael's informant said he had not only seen this
done but had done it himself, always successfully.

The Lame Goat

A lone wanderer, this was a not unwelcome visitor since it could give
limitless quantities of milk, enough for a whole army. It was a compli-
ment if it lay down on your land as it was said always to choose the best

in the district. Known to Gaelic-speakers as the *gobar bachach*, it was long said to be a wanderer in the Isle of Skye.

Loch Monsters

Something rose from the water like a monster of prehistoric times, measuring a full 30 feet from tip to tail. It had a long sinuous neck and a flat reptilian head. Its skin was greyish black, tough looking, and just behind, where the neck joined the body, was a giant hump...
A 1934 witness of the Loch Ness Monster. From *Loch Ness Monster*, Tim Dinsdale.

Is the Loch Ness Monster, as described above, one of the last of the 'supernaturals' to haunt man's imagination? Does it, perhaps, fulfil a need, a desire in us to believe that we have not yet discovered and dissected *everything*, that there still remains one creature we can neither name nor explain?

There is possibly an element of this. Many people cling to a belief in 'Nessie' and love to shudder a little at the thought of this strange, wild, unknown beast, still at large, still a mystery.

I like the thought of Nessie myself; I like to know that no entrepreneur has been able to lay a finger on her and no scientist has yet put as much as a tissue from her skin into one of his cold, cruel jars.

It will be a sad day when both of these things happen—as surely they will. For I am convinced that there are, not just one, but several examples of an unknown species alive and thriving in Loch Ness and, that being the case, it must be only a matter of time before somebody proves it.

Pity poor Nessie then! If she is subject to too much intrusion now, what will it be like when everybody *knows* she is there? Commercial pressures to film her, display her, examine her, pick her apart, will be intolerable.

Up to the time of writing this in the spring of 2002, the hundreds of people who have tried so desperately to obtain *That* photograph, *That* piece of film, have failed. They have been dogged with such incredible ill luck that many of them have come to wonder if there is a jinx on their efforts.

One of the most consistently enthusiastic of them, Tim Dinsdale, wrote of one fruitless season:

'It was maddening. On two occasions, cameras had been in one place one day and another the next, only to find the move had robbed us of photography. It was difficult not to fall into a state of despondency—or not begin to believe some of the older people who would shake their heads and mutter seriously, "Ye'll never film the Beast."'

'The Beast'... The local name is so much better than the Monster label stuck on it by the Press back in 1953 when it first hit the headlines. Perhaps if it had been called a 'beast' from the start, more folk would have believed in it.

But 'Loch Ness Monster' it is, 'Nessie' for short, and she and her clan hoodwink us all still. Long may they continue to do so.

Some of my readers may now be asking why, if the monster in Loch Ness is no myth but living flesh and hide, it is included in this book. I deal with it here because there are numerous tales of unknown and sometimes frightening creatures skulking in Scottish lochs, and we have to differentiate between the real ones and the fabulous.

Donald Mackenzie, writing in the 1930s, said, 'Most of the Scottish lochs have their monsters.' If this was so, they are now largely forgotten. Loch Ness obviously contains the most famous of our living monsters. Nessie is known across the globe. 'Morag' is not so celebrated and, mindful of the circus on Loch Ness-side, maybe we should be glad of that. They are certainly glad of it on the shores of Loch Morar where the creature lives.

Although lying only a short distance from the bustle of Mallaig and Arisaig, this highly scenic stretch of water is little visited by tourists. Any who do turn off the A830 to take a look soon find that the road along the north side does not take them very far. Most of Morar's 11 mile length is roadless on both sides.

The most dramatic encounters with 'Black Morag' have involved local people out on the water in their boats. Some of the incidents have been quite frightening. In 1969 two men were convinced the monster deliberately thumped into their motorboat. One of the men fired a shot to scare it off. The thing they saw had at least three humps, was dirty brown in colour and had a snake-like head. The other man struck it with an oar, which broke in two (a man who saw the broken oar told me he examined it for pieces of skin or hairs but unfortunately he found nothing).

In August 1990 two men and two boys, out fishing on the loch, became aware that a creature with three humps was 'shadowing' their boat. The animal has also been spotted lying on the shore, on one occasion by a party of schoolchildren in a motor launch.

Witnesses are generally awed by its size. It has been described as 'like a full-grown Indian elephant' and 'a huge, shapeless, dark mass rising out of the water like a small island.'

Adam Malcolm, a retired schoolmaster, and his wife Mollie, told me of their sightings. For several years they leased a house overlooking the loch and spent many holidays there. One fine day he was sitting reading in the front room with his back to the window. 'Something made me turn round,' he said, 'and I saw a hump in the water off the far shore. Next moment Mollie came into the room and joined me.'

Mollie took up the story. 'I'd had a sudden feeling, "I have to go and look at the loch." We stood staring at it and then a neighbour came to the door and called, "What's that across the loch?"'

Adam and Mollie rushed to the door and all three stood watching. Adam hurried back in for his camera—he was a very keen photographer—but by the time he returned, the ladies had seen the hump sink below the surface.

'It must have been 20 feet long,' said Adam, 'dark in colour and shaped like half of a huge rugby ball.'

A few years later, Mollie had gone up to the telephone kiosk. 'There was no phone in the house so we went to the box to make any calls. The view from it was tremendous—a great, long stretch of water.

'I had dialled and was waiting for an answer when I glanced through the glass and saw a large shape in the water where I knew there shouldn't be one. As I was staring at it my call was answered and I was distracted. It was only for a few seconds but when I looked out again the thing had vanished.'

The Malcolms believe there will have been many more sightings by local people than have ever been made public. Adam knew a man living on the lochside who told him he regularly watched a creature in one of the bays. Morag's a sensitive subject locally for a very good reason: the tradition that an appearance presages a death in a certain family. Because of this, a sighting is not something to boast about or spread abroad.

Besides being seen above the water, there is at least one reliable account of a monster animal being sighted lying on the bed of the loch.

So whatever is swimming in Loch Morar, it is made of solid stuff and is no myth. The creatures in Morar and Loch Ness probably belong to the same race, a species not yet named by science. It seems most unlikely that they are a couple of one-offs. Which leads me to speculate that there may be specimens in other Scottish lochs, as Mackenzie suggested.

They are shy in their habits and therefore elusive. They live underwater, surface rarely, and avoid observation by man. They dive noiselessly and can swim off at great speed. It is surely not inconceivable that there are a number of them in our waters.

Loch Oich has yielded reports of a strange beast, not surprising in view of its closeness to Loch Ness. And if Oich, why not Lochy, the third in the chain?

In Scottish folklore, lochs have long been regarded as the home of strange and dangerous creatures. I deal elsewhere in this book with water horses and water bulls. Other even more terrible things were once believed to lie in wait for the unwary. It is possible some of the creatures were exaggerated descriptions of the animals still found in Ness and Morar. They may well, in earlier times, have been more widely scattered, but being shy, were glimpsed only briefly, just long enough to lodge in the folk mind.

The Big Beast of Loch Awe, for instance, was said to be a powerful creature with twelve legs. Some said it was like a huge horse, but so many years have passed since it was last sighted that descriptions are now sketchy. I have seen it described as like an enormous eel.

Whatever its shape it used its twelve legs to good effect in wintertime when it could be heard smashing the ice on the loch. Now it seems to be largely forgotten on Loch Aweside. A longtime resident at Ford, questioned in 2001, had hardly heard of it and could tell me nothing.

The Beast of Barrisdale was equally formidable. It lived in the vicinity of Loch Hourn, and while Loch Awe's denizen boasted a dozen legs, this one had only three. However, it was capable of flight, and around the end of the nineteenth century, a Barrisdale crofter was claiming that he had not only sighted it high over the hills of Knoydart but had been pursued by it, just reaching the safety of his cottage in time.

Its roars sometimes echoed across the water and its three-legged tracks could be traced in the sands of Barrisdale Bay.

In the lochs of Skye lived the *Biasd na Srogaig*, the Beast of the Lowering Horn. Descriptions are sketchy except for the single large horn sprouting from its forehead. This Skye version of the unicorn had none of that animal's grace and beauty for it seems to have been tall, gangling, and awkward in its movements.

Loch Garten, in Strathspey, had its monster, a beast that was like a cross between a bull and a horse. It preyed on young children and lambs and often frequented the south end of the loch where a burn joins it to the smaller Loch Mallachie. There is a tradition that a crofter, sick of its depredations, succeeded in drowning the beast, using a lamb as bait, a large hook and a rock which dragged it to its death.

The monster that lived in Loch Chon, near Aberfoyle, was like a huge dog. It was a creature of the deep and could swallow a child whole.

Clearly, one had to gang warily on or close to lochs. Belief in this evil and motley throng instilled in our ancestors a deep respect for all lochs, large and small. That respect carried more than a hint of earlier beliefs, for behind and beyond the monsters can be sensed the presence of goddesses and sacrifices made at the water's edge, a lamb, perhaps, or a calf, but it could be a virgin or a child.

The rituals may have been forgotten, but the old fears lingered on and one could argue that we are still seeing some traces of them today among the watchers by Loch Ness. F. W. Holiday, in *The Great Orm of Loch Ness*, speaks of the horror and repulsion felt by people who have seen one of the beasts at close quarters.

Loireags

'A small mite of womanhood that does not belong to this world, but to the world thither.' The words of a Benbecula woman describing a loireag to the collector Alexander Carmichael in the latter half of the nineteenth century.

A 'small mite' she may have been, but she was a formidable if usually invisible presence. Women waulking cloth in the Islands would never see her but would always know she was there. Loireags took it upon themselves to 'supervise' the entire waulking process. If the loireag was not satisfied the work was being done in the proper traditional manner she was quite likely to interfere with what had been done so that they had to start all over again.

She was also a stickler for a high standard of singing by the women at the waulking. One of the women singing out of tune or too loud would arouse her ire and she might seize the warp and remove it from the web. Even too much repetition of the same song would throw her into a rage. The women would know they had incurred her wrath when something went badly wrong.

To appease the loireag, or repay her for overseeing the waulking, the women used to leave out some milk. If they failed to do this she would suck the milk from their goats, sheep or cows.

It was believed that one way of getting rid of a troublesome loireag was to swear at her! It did not always work. The daughter of a South

Uist crofter came upon one sucking at the udder of their cow at the foot of Ben More. This seems to have been one of the rare occasions when a loireag was visible to the eye.

The girl's father gave it a swearing but the loireag calmly went on sucking the precious milk. Furious, he lifted a stone and flung it at her, hurting his cow more than the thief.

Only when he grabbed one of the cow's horns and spoke the name of St Columba did the loireag release the udder and run up into a corrie screaming over her shoulder at him and his cow.

This loireag plagued the lives of crofters in the vicinity of Ben More for many years.

The Benbecula woman who described the loireag as a 'small mite' also said it was 'a plaintive little thing'. Perhaps she did not want to risk its anger by criticising it too harshly, though she did add that it was 'stubborn and cunning'.

Luideag

The name means 'The Rag' and it was used to describe a vicious female demon which haunted the vicinity of a lochan in the eastern half of the Isle of Skye. She was said to be drab and hideous in appearance and anyone venturing near the lochan was destined to meet a violent death.

According to the Skye authority, Frank Thompson, she was last seen about 150 years ago wandering near the road between Broadford and Sleat. He said she finally disappeared after a man was found lying dead near her favourite haunting-place.

Marool

Jessie Saxby described this Shetland monster as a 'sea-devil'. It was like a large fish, with 'a crest of flickering flame, and eyes all over his head.' She said it delighted in gales at sea and could be heard singing exultantly when a ship went down and its crew were drowning.

Mermaids

O passion's deadler than the grave,
A' human things undoing!
The Maiden of the Mountain Wave
Has lured me to my ruin!

Many of the creatures in this book are so fantastic it is impossible for us to believe they existed. Others the reader may find not at all hard to accept. And mermaids? Perhaps they should be put into the 'don't know' category.

The distinguished folklorist Calum I. Maclean met an old fisherman on the Isle of Muck who swore that in 1947 he plainly saw a mermaid sitting amongst his lobster-pots. She was combing her hair, but when she realised she was being watched she slipped into the sea.

In 1892 lobstermen at their creels at Deerness, Orkney, claimed they saw a mermaid. She was, they said, small with long slender arms and black hair. There had been a report of a sighting locally two years earlier, and then, in June, 1893, several Deerness people said they saw one swimming offshore. Around the same time, at Birsay, a farmer and his wife reported watching one in a rock pool. When they approached she made off quickly out to sea.

Then there is the famous case of the little Benbecula boy who apparently killed a mermaid. A group of islanders was gathering kelp on the shore on a day around 1830, when one of the women heard splashing. She looked up and there, not far out, was a small figure turning somersaults in the water. The whole party stood watching the creature until one of the boys picked up some stones and flung them as hard as he could. One of them struck the creature and she immediately sank.

A few days later, two miles along the coast, a small figure was found washed up. It was said to be about the size of a three or four year old child, but with very large breasts. The lower part of the body was like a salmon, though without scales. The hair was long, dark and glossy and the skin 'white, soft, and tender'.

A coffin and shroud were made for the little creature and many islanders attended the burial in Nunton graveyard.

A Miss Mackay published an account of what she and a friend believed to be a mermaid which they saw in Caithness in 1809. It was a cold wintry day and they were walking on the shore when they were amazed to see a figure swimming in the icy waters. Every now and again it raised a hand to sweep its long hair.

When the report was published it was read by the schoolmaster at Reay, James Munro. He wrote to a London paper telling how he had watched a mermaid at another Caithness spot, Sandside Bay.

He had seen her in the classic mermaid pose, sitting on a rock and combing her hair 'which flowed about its shoulders, and was of a light brown colour.' He finished his letter: 'I can only say of a truth that it was only by seeing the phenomenon that I was perfectly convinced of its existence.'

Also convinced was Colin Campbell, a Barra crofter, who told Alexander Carmichael that he saw what he took to be an otter on a reef holding and eating a fish. He had raised his gun to fire when he suddenly realised it was a woman holding a child. Putting down his gun he lifted his telescope and looked through, getting a clear view of a mermaid, head, hair, neck, shoulders and breasts.

As he shifted the glass it gave a click and the mermaid and child slipped under the sea with a splash. Carmichael concludes this account by saying that Campbell was 'an honest, intelligent, middle-aged man.'

One of the most detailed descriptions of a mermaid was given in the early nineteenth century by members of the crew of a fishing boat out from Cullivoe in the Shetland Isles.

They had been startled to find what they believed to be one in their catch and had studied her carefully before removing the hook from her neck and putting her back in the sea. This is how James R. Nicolson repeats their description in his book *Shetland Folklore*:

> About three feet long, with breasts like those of a woman and short arms with fingers like those of a human being. On each shoulder was a fin which, when extended, covered both breasts and arms.
>
> The head was not so round as a human being's and had no ears, although it had two small blue eyes. In place of a nose there were two small openings immediately above the mouth, which was wide enough to admit a man's fist. From the waist down the body tapered off to a tail which resembled that of a halibut.

If this was not a mermaid, what was it?

In the 1930s local people used to see what they took to be a mermaid in Loch Inchard, Sutherland. They would see her swimming or lying on the rocks. Also in Sutherland there was a celebrated sighting by a respected smallholder, Sandy Gunn of Balchrick, who died as recently as 1944.

He came on her reclining on a ledge of rock near Sandwood Bay. She was only a few steps away and he got the impression she was marooned, unable to reach the sea until the tide would come in. She stared at him, he thought half in anger, half in fear, until he turned and ran, following his dog which had already fled, howling in terror.

To his dying day Sandy Gunn swore he had seen the real thing.

These, then, are a few claimed encounters from comparatively modern times. They all portray the mermaid in a sympathetic light: shy, delicate and harmless.

They were not always thought of in these terms. In fact there are two widespread misconceptions about mermaids: one, that they were all timid and harmless, and the other, that they lived only in and by the sea.

On the first point, there is no lack of evidence that many looked on mermaids as vicious and dangerous creatures to be avoided at all costs. Like the German Lorelei, they were believed to lure men to their death. Often they did this with their seductive singing, but at least one had a more novel method. The story was told by Chambers in *Popular Rhymes of Scotland* and has been retold often since. It is worth repeating here.

The young Laird of Lorntie, in Angus, was riding home one evening with a servant when he heard a woman's voice crying for help from a loch. Thinking it was someone drowning he rushed into the water where a figure was struggling and splashing.

Her long hair, like hanks of gold, was streaming on the surface and he was about to seize hold of it when his servant shouted, 'Bide, Lorntie, bide! It's the mermaid!'

The warning came just in time to save him from being pulled to the bottom of the loch. As he turned away the creature half-rose above the surface and called, in mocking anger:

> 'Lorntie, Lorntie,
> Were it not for your man,
> I had got your heart's bluid
> Skirl in my pan!'

This is very different to the almost sugary-sweet image of the mermaid that has become so commonplace. Notice, too, that this one's 'home' was an inland loch. Mermaids lived in freshwater lochs, rivers and streams as well as in and by the salt sea.

Since Robert Chambers published the story in 1826 it has been copied by many writers and collectors of folktales. None that I have seen has questioned the location of 'Lorntie' which Chambers placed in Forfarshire. I have searched but have not been able to find a Lorntie in what is now Angus, but in East Perthshire there is a Lornty Burn which runs from Loch Benachally to join the river Ericht north of Blairgowrie.

There is a story of a particularly vindictive mermaid which haunted the Stinchar, near Ballantrae, Ayrshire. Every night she used to come out of the river and sit on a black rock to comb her hair. As she sat she used to sing and her voice carried to the nearby house of Knockdolian.

The Lady of Knockdolian had a young baby and she got it into her head that the singing was disturbing the child. To put a stop to it she ordered her servants to break up the rock. The servants smashed it to pieces and the Lady thought, 'That will put an end to it.'

The mermaid came that night and was heard singing for the last time, but instead of her usual beautiful melody, this is what she sang:

> 'Ye may think on your cradle,
> I'll think on my stane;
> And there'll never be an heir
> To Knockdolian again!'

Soon afterwards a mysterious thing happened. The cradle was found overturned with the baby dead underneath it. No other child was born and the family line died out.

Fishermen at sea did not like to see a mermaid following their boat. They would try to distract her by throwing empty barrels overboard and then, while she examined them, they would speed out of reach.

According to Tom Muir, if a mermaid gripped the bow of a boat and asked the state of the tides, a fisherman would give the wrong answer. If he gave the right answer she would have the power to pull the boat below the waves.

Peter Buchan, the North-east writer, wrote:

> Some old men remember a mermaid pitching upon the
> bowsprit of a small vessel belonging to Peterhead, which
> was driven among the rocks near Slains Castle, and all
> hands perished save one man who bore the tidings to land.

Here the mermaid was clearly blamed for the tragedy.

Despite this, there are countless tales of men deliberately setting out to capture a mermaid and force her to become his wife. When a mermaid comes ashore she often slips off the skin that covers the lower part of her body and tail. Without that she cannot return to the water. The stories tell how a man creeps up and seizes the skin, then takes the helpless mermaid home with him to be his bride.

Invariably she has several children by him and makes a model wife and mother, though she often gazes sadly and wistfully out to sea. Her husband has hidden the mermaid skin somewhere in the house or in a barn. One day she or one of the family finds it. She runs down to the water, slips it on and escapes. When the skin is off she has human-like legs and feet.

Some of the absconding wives are never seen again but, according to folklorist Donald Mackenzie, many of the mermaids did not entirely desert their husband. If he was a fisherman she watched over him at sea, guiding him to the best fishing grounds and out of storms.

The sons of these mermaid wives were said to possess unusual skills as fishermen, and their descendants were among the finest of navigation pilots.

Not surprisingly, mermaid wives possessed knowledge that was a mystery to their mortal husbands. A Skye man kept a mermaid for a year and 'she gave him much curious information.' She must have hinted at the strange properties of the water in which eggs have been boiled, for when he let her go he asked her, before she went, to tell him the secret.

'Ah,' she answered enigmatically, 'If I told you that, you would have a tale to tell!'

They were her last words to him.

Although most of the men who captured a mermaid did so by stealing her tail-skin so that she could not swim, there were other ways of doing it. A man called Paterson picked off some of the scales from a mermaid on the shore near North Kessock. Her tail immediately vanished and she stood before him a perfect and beautiful woman.

He kept her as his wife against her will until the day one of the children found the scales hidden in an outhouse and gave them, in all innocence, to his mother.

When Paterson came home the mermaid had gone but, like so many others, she bore her husband no ill will and was said still to be watching over his descendants many years later. Mermaids were known to be long-lived.

A Sutherland fisherman stole a mermaid's 'pouch and belt' without which she could not swim. He concealed it in a corn stack and when the stack was being taken down she spotted it and escaped.

Johnie Croy of Sanday, Orkney, gained power over a mermaid by seizing her golden comb and taking it home. His mother pleaded with him to throw it back into the sea but he refused. Finally, the mermaid made a bargain with him: she would live with him for seven years and then the whole family must go to visit her people.

Johnie agreed, and when the seven years were up the two of them and six of their children sailed away never to be seen again. The youngest child had been left at home thanks to a subterfuge of his grandmother's. He grew up to be a soldier of great distinction.

Mermaids could grant wishes and there are many tales of them doing so in exchange for their freedom. What would happen was that a man would stalk a mermaid on the shore and trap her in his arms. When she pleaded with him in vain she would offer him three wishes if he would let her go free.

In this way a Skye man was given the ability to foretell the future, a gift for music, and the secret of how to cure scrofula. A seaman at Tain asked for, and was given, health, wealth and happiness.

Hugh Miller told of a Cromarty shipmaster, John Reid, who was deeply in love with a local beauty, Helen Stewart. She did not return his affections, so when he heard a mermaid singing outside the Dropping Cave near the village, he decided on a desperate plan. He crept up on her, overpowered the creature and demanded three wishes: one, that neither he nor any of his friends should die at sea; two, that he should succeed in all his enterprises; and three, that Helen should return his love.

'Quit, and have,' said the mermaid succinctly.

Miller tells us that all three wishes were realised. The couple were wed and enjoyed a happy, prosperous marriage. It turned out to be a real love match. By the time Miller was recording their story, Helen had been buried for 70 years in the ruins of the local St Regulus Chapel (Miller would know the whereabouts of the grave for he was, in his earlier years, a monumental sculptor in the district). The last of John Reid's family, his grandson, died in London leaving property and a large legacy to a Cromarty relative.

Unlike Reid, some men made a modest single request. One of them was a boat builder at Port Henderson, Gairloch. He asked only that no one should ever be drowned when sailing in a boat of his construction. J. H. Dixon, who recorded this fact in a book published in 1886, said that he himself was proud to possess a boat the man had built.

Another who asked for only a single wish was McComie Mor, an intrepid character, some of whose adventures are still remembered in

Mermaids

Mermaids could not help hurting mortals, no matter how much they loved them...

Glenshee and Glenisla. Most recently several of the tales associated with him have been recounted by Antony Mackenzie Smith in his book *Glenshee:Glen of the Fairies*.

McComie Mor was a great swordsman, a heroic fighter who feared nothing and no one. It is quite in character that when he encountered a mermaid in a burn deep in the hills he determined to take her home with him.

He was living in Crandart, Glenisla, at the time and he believed that if he took her across running water she would escape him. To prevent this he made a long and arduous journey involving several hilltops, never slackening his hold on her for a minute.

At Crandart she pleaded with him to let her go and at last he relented. He said he would release her if she would tell him how he was going to die. She led him to the window and pointed to a large stone on the hillside.

'You will die,' she said, 'with that stone under your head.'

McComie freed the mermaid and next day ordered his servants to bring the stone down to the house and build it into the wall under the head of his bed. Years later he died peacefully in the bed with the stone still under it.

I should mention that Mackenzie Smith, in his book, describes the captive creature as the 'wife' of a kelpie that lived in the river Shee. I prefer to believe she was one of the strange race of inland mermaids.

Another of them lived in a loch just over the hills from McComie Mor's original home, Finegand, Glenshee. The name of the loch, Loch Mharaich, means the Loch of the Mermaid, so there is no doubting this one's identity. She had a typically destructive nature and used to leave the loch to wreak havoc in Strathardle. Local tradition has it that she was hunted down and killed by Bran, the famous hunting dog of the Fingalians.

In Gaelic a mermaid is a 'Maid of the Waves' or 'Maid of the Sea'. Some speakers refer to it simply as a *ceasg*.

Far from the Highlands, in Galloway, there is a tale told of a mermaid who fell deeply in love with a young married seaman whom she watched secretly from the Solway. Her favourite haunt was a cleft in the rockface known as the Needle's Eye. From there and sandbanks offshore she watched his comings and goings.

After she had saved his life in a storm, he returned her love and for a whole summer they met at a secret rendevous. She bore him a child and after he had drowned in a second storm, he joined her and their son in the water. For many years afterwards they were known to warn seamen of danger on dark nights in rough weather.

A final example of the power wielded by mermaids comes from South Uist and the renowned storyteller, Angus MacLellan. He told of a Lochboisdale man, Donald MacLeod, who was a member of the crew of a fishing vessel. They were in East Coast waters when they spotted a mermaid following the boat.

Anxious to get rid of her the skipper threw out a herring, hoping she would stop to consume it. She passed it by and still followed. He told one of the crew to throw her another herring. The mermaid still came on. One by one the crew flung out herrings. The mermaid still followed.

It came to Donald's turn, and as soon as his herring hit the water the mermaid seized it and dived out of sight. She did not reappear.

The skipper said nothing, but when they came into port he paid Donald off and told him to return home and not to go to sea again for it was certain sure that one day he would die by drowning.

Donald was ashore for a year and then a man called Mackerchern from Loch Skipport bought a boat and asked Donald to help take it home with him. The two set out from Lochboisdale on a lovely calm day. Loch Skipport is at the other, north, end of the island and the boat was seen by two lighthouse keepers at Uishernish as she neared her destination. Ten minutes later, when they looked again, the boat had vanished. Neither body was ever found and it was assumed the weather must have made a rapid change for the worse and upset the boat.

These latter details were supplied by Major Finlay Mackenzie of Lochboisdale Hotel whose father sold the boat to Mackerchern.

On the neighbouring island of Barra, fishermen believed that if a mermaid was seen there would be a storm and the danger of drowning. John Macpherson of Barra, who passed on so much island lore, told of a crew who only just managed to survive a gale after two of them saw one swimming near the boat. What worried them most was that she was between them and the shore, a bad omen.

Macpherson, who was known to all by his byname, The Coddy, said he knew a man from Eriskay who had once found a dead mermaid washed up on a beach. Apart from the fish's tail she looked very human and had beautiful hair.

Mermaids were generally solitary creatures so it is a surprise to come on a tradition involving a group of 24. Perhaps they gained courage from their numbers, for an old rhyme tells how they swam to Inchkeith in the Forth to torment, with their wiles, the holy man living there:

> Four and twenty mermaids left the port of Leith
> To tempt the fine auld hermit who dwelt upon Inchkeith;
> No boat, no waft, nor crayer,
> Nor craft had they, nor sails;
> Their lily hands were oars enough,
> Their tillers were their tails.

Poor man, I fear he didn't stand a chance.

It was fishermen who felt most at risk from mermaids. The deep dread of drowning as a result of seeing one may well have its roots in the fear of some long forgotten sea goddess who demanded human sacrifice. Who knows what rituals may have been enacted to propitiate her? Victims may well have been deliberately drowned, their bodies offered up to the goddess.

As we have seen, however, mermaids, captured and domesticated, made good and loving wives and mothers until the opportunity came to return to the sea and this they could never resist. However, their love for their mortal husband and children was sincere and they suffered pangs of regret in leaving them when the time came. They would often continue to watch over them from a distance and they would help them prosper with good catches—two roles probably originally filled by the goddess.

There is a sense here that mermaids could not help hurting mortals, no matter how much they loved them. This is the message of Hogg's poem 'The Mermaid', a verse of which opens this chapter.

In the poem a young man falls in love with a mermaid who warns him:

> 'O laith, laith wad a wanderer be
> To do your youth sic wrang;
> Were you to reave a kiss from me
> Your life would not be lang.

> 'Go, hie you from this lonely trake,
> Nor dare your walk renew;
> For I'm the Maid of the Mountain Lake,
> An' I come wi' the falling dew.'

The warning is not heeded, and the young man takes to his death-bed saying (unfairly) that 'the Maiden of the Mountain Wave has lured me to my ruin!' In fact, she had done her best to put him off!

The poem finishes with the mermaid, over a century later, sitting by his grave 'braiding her locks' and lamenting his death still.

So mermaids were capable of sincere feelings towards us. One is credited with saving the life of a young lady dying of consumption. As the young lady's lover wrings his hands, the mermaid rises from the water and sings:

'Wad ye let the bonnie die i' your hand,
And the mugwort flowering i' the land?'

Mugwort or muggan are old names for the shrub southernwood. The young man gathered the flowers from it, pressed them and gave them to his loved one who recovered.

Mermaids must have been strong believers in the curative powers of mugwort, for one in Renfrewshire rose from the water as the funeral of a young girl passed by. Mournfully she sang:

'If they wad drink nettles in March
And eat muggans in May,
Sae mony braw maidens
Wadna gang to the clay.'

Some folk credited mermaids with prophetic powers, which may offer one explanation for Thomas the Rhymer's amazing ability to foretell the future. There is a tradition that the Borders seer was born of a liaison between a mortal and a mermaid.

Some members of Clan McLaren may have inherited a gift for prophecy—there is said to have been a mermaid in their lineage.

Introducing a poem about a MacPhail of Colonsay and the Mermaid of Corrievreckan, the collector John Leyden made the comment that 'the mermaid of the northern nations resembles the siren of the ancients.' He adds the intriguing suggestion that the comb and mirror may be a Celtic adornment to the prototype.

An ancient link perhaps with the comb and mirror symbols found on so many of our Pictish carved stones?

Mermen

Do ye think, man, that there's naething in a' yon saut wilder-
ness o' a world oot wast there, wi' the sea-grasses growin', an'
the sea-beasts fechtin', an' the sun glintin' down into it, day by
day? Na; the sea's like the land, but fearsomer.
Robert Louis Stevenson, *The Merry Men.*

Considering the huge number of stories about mermaids, and the many reported sightings over the centuries, the male of the species is a very elusive creature indeed; so elusive one is apt to forget him in the scheme of things. Did they never draw themselves up on a rock and comb their hair with a golden comb? Did no girl ever fall in love with one and take him for a husband?

Mermaids sometimes spoke of their mermen husbands whom they said they loved as dearly as their mortal ones, but little more information seems to have been given and there are few stories of incidents involving mermen.

Dr Katharine M. Briggs, in *A Dictionary of Fairies*, sums them up thus: 'Though generally wilder and uglier than mermaids, mermen have less interest in mankind. They do not, like the selkies, come ashore to court mortal women and father their children.'

She goes on: 'They seem to personify the stormy sea, and it is they who raise storms and wreck ships if a mermaid is wounded.'

Mermaids themselves, of course, were blamed for doing both these things too.

The most famous reported encounter with a merman happened off the Banffshire coast on 15 August 1814. On that day two Port Gordon fishermen sailed into their home harbour full of what they had seen. So convinced were they that their eyes had not deceived them that they described their experience in detail to George McKenzie, the schoolmaster at Rathven.

Impressed with their story, Mr McKenzie wrote a letter to the *Aberdeen Chronicle* which printed it on 20 August. He wrote that the men had been on their way back at 'about three or four o'clock yesterday afternoon, when, about a quarter of a mile from the shore, the sea being perfectly calm, they observed, at a small distance from their boat, with its back towards them, half its body above the water, a creature of a tawny colour, appearing like a man sitting, with his body half-bent.

'Surprised at this, they approached towards him till they came within a few yards, when the noise made by the boat occasioned the creature to turn about, which gave the men a better opportunity of observing him.

'His countenance was swarthy, his hair short and curled, of a colour between a green and a grey; he had small eyes, a flat nose, his mouth was large, and his arms of an extraordinary length.

'Above the waist, he was shaped like a man, but as the water was clear, my informants could perceive that, from the waist downwards, his body tapered considerably or, as they expressed it, like a large fish without scales, but could not see the extremity.'

In Orkney and Shetland, mermen are often confused with Finn Men who are dealt with in a separate chapter.

A rare instance when mermaids and mermen were apparently seen together forms the opening of a tale from the island of Unst. A man there came on a mixed company dancing on the beach. Their tailskins lay in a pile but when they saw the man watching they hurriedly slipped them on and disappeared into the sea.

One skin lay near where he was standing so he seized it, carried it up from the beach and hid it behind some rocks. He then went back to the beach where a beautiful girl was wandering in distress. He took her home and she had no choice but to stay with him, becoming in time a loving wife and mother.

He had gone back and retrieved the skin which he hid in an out-house. As in countless other cases one of the children found the skin a long time after and showed it to her mother. The lure of the sea was stronger than her love of husband and children and she departed.

In the previous chapter we heard about the Cromarty Firth mermaid who used to sit on a rock outside the Dropping Cave. On one occasion, a local man who had been catching crabs farther along the shore was returning to Cromarty by way of the rocky beach as darkness fell.

As he passed the cave he glanced towards it and saw, sitting in the entrance, an old grey-haired man with a beard to his waist.

Was he a merman? The crab-fisher did not linger to investigate.

Mothman

This seems to be a new addition to the canon of Scotland's supernatural creatures. Generally spoken of in the singular, the mothman is mostly confined to certain states of America where he is described as looking like a winged man. Despite his name, the wings are feathered, like a bird's, and there seems to be little resemblance to a moth.

There is at least one sighting claimed for this country. A strange creature apparently answering his description was seen one night in 1992 by an Edinburgh lady. She looked from her window and saw it crouched on the branch of a tree in her garden. She studied it for some time and was convinced it was half-man, half-bird.

Muireartach

It was fatal to admit this sea spirit if she came to the door begging for a warm seat by the fire. She would, as many witches did, grow larger and larger, until she dominated the room.

Her chief role was one of raising storms and destructive winds. According to some, she had a blue-black face, a mane of white hair, and only one eye. Her roar was terrible to hear.

Njuggle

This Shetland water horse (see p.149) would be sighted grazing quietly by a stream or loch. Many a Shetlander, thinking he had come on a stray horse, climbed on its back. Instantly the njuggle would race for its watery home carrying its helpless victim.

It differed from an ordinary horse—or, indeed, a kelpie—in that it had a rounded tail, but this it kept hidden between its hind legs until it had the innocent person on its back, when it would bolt towards the water.

It seemed to like being near mills, perhaps enjoying the rushing water and the deepness of the sluice. Millers sometimes glimpsed the creature as it plunged and wallowed.

Shetland parents used the threat of the njuggle to warn their children from going too near the sea, swift burns or deep lochs, although they would also tell them that, if they stood at a safe distance, they might listen to the njuggle's singing.

Some Shetland lochs are named after these creatures, the best known being Njuggles Water, north of Scalloway.

Nuckelavee

It is an extraordinary name for an extraordinary creature, surely the most hideous and nightmarish of all Scotland's monsters. It would be difficult, in the folklore of any country, to find a creature as ugly and as terrifying as the nuckelavee.

Did it exist? According to Tammas it did. He claimed he not only saw it but was pursued by it and years later his terrible experience was described by the Orkney writer W. Traill Dennison.

Tammas lived on Sanday in the North Isles, and he said he was returning home late one night, walking along a narrow strip between the sea and a freshwater loch, of which there are several on Sanday.

Suddenly he became aware of something huge lumbering towards him. He was hemmed between the sea and the loch so could go forward or back but not out of the thing's path. He had been taught that the worst action to take if you encounter a supernatural creature is to turn your back on it so, despite mounting fear, he went slowly forward, peering toward the big ungainly monster which was gradually taking shape.

'The lower part,' reported Dennison, 'was like a great horse with flappers like fins about his legs, with a mouth as wide as a whale's, from whence came breath like steam from a brewing kettle.'

This horse-like creature had only one eye, glaring like a red-hot coal.

On the monster's back was what looked to him like a huge man, though to Tammas he seemed as if he might be part of the 'horse', for he appeared to have no legs. He did though have long arms stretching nearly to the ground. His head lolled about on his shoulders as if at any moment it might topple to the ground.

Dennison goes on, 'But what to Tammas appeared most horrible of all was that the monster was skinless; this utter want of skin adding much to the terrific appearance of the creature's naked body, the whole surface of it showing only red raw flesh, in which Tammas saw blood as black as tar, thick as horse tethers, twisting, stretching, and contracting as the monster moved.'

No wonder Tammas was terrified, but even in his terror he remembered that the nuckelavee is a sea monster and cannot stand fresh water. He moved as close as he could to the side of the loch, still keeping his eyes on the beast before him.

'The awful moment came when the lower part of the head of the monster got abreast of Tammas. The mouth...yawned like a bottomless pit. Tammas found its hot breath like fire on his face; the long arms stretched out...'

As they reached out to seize him, one of Tammas's feet went into the loch, splashing water on the animal's foreleg. It shied away with a thunderous snort. This was Tammas's chance. He turned and ran. Behind him he heard galloping hooves. The monster was in pursuit, bellowing now in rage.

'In front of Tammas lay a rivulet, through which the surplus water of the loch found its way to the sea, and Tammas knew, if he could only cross the running water, he was safe; so he strained every nerve.

'As he reached the near bank another clutch was made at him by the long arms. Tammas made a desperate spring and reached the other side, leaving his bonnet in the monster's clutches. Nuckelavee gave a wild unearthly yell of disappointed rage.'

You can make what you like of that account, which seems to have been accepted by Dennison in good faith and reported by him in the same spirit.

It is the only recorded sighting I have seen, though the nuckelavee was held in awe by old Orcadians who believed it used to come ashore and roam overland, devouring sheep and cattle and destroying crops with its evil breath.

Thankfully it seems not to have been seen or heard now for many years.

The Old Man of the Barn

According to J. G. Campbell every farm in Highland Perthshire used to have its *bodachan sabhaill*, who helped gather the grain into sheaves and thresh the corn. They had the appearance of little old men and, like brownies, toiled by night, as this old verse records:

> Whan thair wes corne to thrashe or dichte,
> Or barne or byre to clene,
> He had ane bizzy houre at nichte,
> Atween the twall and ane.

In his *Scottish Folklore and Folk Life*, Donald Mackenzie quotes these lines:

> When the peat will turn grey and shadows fall deep,
> And weary old Callum is snoring asleep...
> The Little Old Man of the Barn
> Will thresh with no light in the mouth of the night,
> The Little Old Man of the Barn.

Puddlefoot

This was the charming name of a happy little fellow, a brownie, that used to splash about in a burn between Dunkeld and Pitlochry. There was a farmhouse nearby and he used to go up to it, leaving wet footprints and pools of water all over the floors.

A mischievous soul, he would go around the rooms tidying where it was untidy and untidying where it was tidy.

He left the district abruptly after a man passing the burn one night heard splashing and called out, 'Weel, and is that you, Puddlefoot?'

Puddlefoot retorted angrily, 'Oh, so I hae gotten a name then! It's Puddlefoot they call me!'

Some folk who tell this tale say that he left because he hated the name he had been given. It is more likely to be another example of a supernatural creature's fury at its name being discovered and used by a mortal.

Redcaps

According to Scott in his *Minstrelsy*, every ruined tower in the south of Scotland was believed to harbour an inhabitant of this species. They were particularly drawn to castles and peel towers which had been the scene of evil deeds.

'Malignant' is the word that seems best to describe redcaps. They lurked in dark corners of their chosen ruin ready to creep out and pounce on any benighted wayfarer who sought shelter for the night.

Some reports say that they poured the blood of their victim into their cap, others that they kept the colour of the cap bright by dying it in the fresh blood of their latest kill.

In appearance, a redcap was a thick-set old man with fierce red eyes, long tangled hair, protruding teeth and fingers like talons. He wore iron boots and carried a pikestaff.

Physical strength was of no avail against a redcap's attack. Confronted by him the only ways to save your life were to make the sign of the cross, quote holy scripture or utter the Lord's name. He would back off and slink away, wailing, leaving behind on the ground one of his long teeth.

> Noo Reidcap he was there,
> And he was there indeed;
> And grimly he girned and glowered,
> Wi' his reid cap on his heid.
> Then Reidcap gied a yell,
> It was a yell indeed,
> That the flesh neath ma oxter grew cauld,
> It grew as cauld as leid.

Besides this old rhyme, a redcap features in one of the Border ballads, 'Lord Soulis'. Soulis, of Hermitage Castle, was a thoroughly unpleasant individual suspected by his neighbours of dabbling in sorcery. Perhaps they were right, for he treated the castle redcap as his familiar and took advice from him.

The first verse finds this evil pair together:

> Lord Soulis he sat in Hermitage Castle,
> And beside him Old Redcap sly;
> 'Now, tell me, thou sprite, who art meikle of might,
> The death that I must die?'

Redcap promises him protection against 'lance and arrow, sword and knife'. All he has to fear is 'threefold ropes of sifted sand' twined around his body.

A number of attempts are made to kill Soulis but none of them succeeds. Even the ropes of sand fail, thanks to Redcap's magical intervention. In the end Soulis dies a horrific death, wrapped in a sheet of lead and plunged into a boiling cauldron.

> And still beside the Nine-stane Burn,
> Ribb'd like the sand at mark of sea,
> The ropes that would not twist nor turn,
> Shaped of the sifted sand you see.

The ballad does not tell us what became of Redcap after the death of his master, whether he moved to new quarters or remained at Hermitage to lurk in the shadows and prey on the unwary.

The rhyme quoted earlier gives us a last glimpse of one of these malignant creatures:

> Last Reidcap gied a leugh,
> It was a leugh indeed;
> Twas mair like a hoarse, hoarse scraugh,
> —Syne a tooth fell oot o' his heid.

The Red Dummy

One of the most impressive archaeological sites in Easter Ross is the Grey Cairn, a huge pile of stones heaped up by men long since crumbled to dust. Their names, their ways, are forgotten, but the stones remain.

According to more recent inhabitants of this lovely corner, the stones of the cairn were home to a little man with a red coat and cap. Somewhere in their midst he had a cosy den though no one had ever seen it.

The little man was deaf and dumb but a more cheerful character you could not meet. He used to look in at the door of the nearby mill and give the miller a wave and a smile which put the miller in good humour for the rest of the day.

In return, the miller put a cog of porridge and cream on his windowsill every night and the wee man thoroughly appreciated it.

He used to have great fun whirling round on the mill wheel, revelling in the glittering, splashing water and the speed of the wheel. Most of all, though, he used to watch from a seat on the cairn for a horse and cart coming along the road. As it went by he would run out and jump on the axle of one of the wheels and cling on as it went round, bumping along the rutted track. The men on the carts were always pleased to see the happy face of the wee man they called the Little Red Dummy.

After the cart had gone a short distance the little fellow would jump off and run back to his home in the Grey Cairn.

When the miller grew old and frail the Red Dummy used to go into the mill and help him with the heavier jobs that were now too much for him.

It was said that he was an exile from the land of the fairies and that his dumbness and deafness were a punishment, though what crime this jolly little fellow could have committed to deserve that, it is hard to imagine.

Redhand

It was best to avoid this nasty piece of work which used to stalk Glenmore. In Gaelic he was *Lamhdearg* (Ly-erg) and he appeared in soldier's garb, stepping in front of an innocent traveller on the road and challenging him to fight.

According to an old manuscript, in 1669 three brothers, one after another, were challenged by Redhand and all died from their injuries.

Sea Serpents

Seven herring to fill a salmon,
Seven salmon to fill a seal,
Seven seals to fill a whale,
And seven whales to fill the Cirean Croin.
Gaelic rhyme.

The *Cirean Croin*, or sea serpent, was believed to be the biggest creature in the world. One of its Gaelic names means the Great Whirlpool of the Ocean. Seafaring men from around our coasts would tell wide-eyed family and friends of their encounters with these fearful monsters, hideous to look at and dangerous because they could capsize a fishing boat.

In the Northern Isles they told of the mester stoorworm (mester, superior; stoor, large, powerful). It was, they said, thousands of miles long, with scorching breath and a forked tongue that could sweep a whole village into the sea. It could swallow ships at one gulp.

One year the people of Orkney were terrified when it started coming into their waters. To placate it they gave it seven maidens for breakfast every Saturday morning. This would have gone on long enough, had it not been for a brave lad called Assipattle. The curious name comes from his habit of lying amongst the ashes at home (assi, ashes; pattle, to grovel).

He was despised and bullied by his brothers, but it was he who rid the world of the mester stoorworm. He simply steered his little boat down the creature's huge throat, made his way through his stomach and planted a glowing peat in its livers. He escaped, but the animal was destroyed by fire.

The first lot of teeth it spat out in its fury and agony became the islands of Orkney, the second lot became Shetland, and the third ones became the Faroes. As it died, it curled itself into a great lump, now Iceland.

Assipattle was hailed a hero, married the king's beautiful daughter, Princess Gemdelovely, and inherited the kingdom.

More modestly sized and, thankfully, less ferocious, sea serpents have frequently been reported in the waters round our coasts by thoroughly reliable observers. There is nothing supernatural, for instance, about the animal seen one warm day in July 1931 on the west shore of Arran.

Dr John Paton, of Langside, Glasgow, was cycling with his 14-year-old daughter on the coast road between Imachar and Dougarie when he saw what looked like an upturned boat on a rock a few yards from the beach. He dismounted and went to investigate, but as he approached was amazed to see a head turn towards him. He wrote:

> I waved my daughter's attention to the creature and made an effort to get as close as possible. The legs or flippers could not be observed, and I wanted to be sure of just what kind of extremities it had. I was disappointed, as the movement evidently frightened it, and it wobbled off the rocks into the sea. It made off at a good pace and left a considerable wake behind it.
>
> The head was parrot-shaped—that is to say, it had a kind of beak. It was a rather light grey colour. The body was longer than that of a large elephant—of a similar colour, and just as shapeless.

Dr Paton said he was familiar with seals, sharks and other sea life but this was something entirely new to him.

I could list many other reports of—for the want of a better name—sea serpents, all testifying to the existence of an animal in our seas not yet identified by scientists. In appearance and habits it seems very similar to the creatures in Loch Ness and other lochs and may well be of the same species or at least the same family.

Similar creatures have, of course, been reported from many other parts of the world. In recent years, for instance, people claim to have watched them at various points along the Australian coast.

In his ground-breaking book of 1968, F. W. Holiday insisted on calling the inhabitants of Loch Ness 'orms'. His book *The Great Orm of Loch Ness* proved deservedly popular, but the term 'orm' has not caught on. You can't picture an 'orm' as you can a 'monster' or 'serpent'.

However, Holiday's contention that the freshwater loch creatures and sea serpents are all orms or giant worms may well be correct. Belief in both is deeply rooted in Scotland.

Alasdair Alpin MacGregor was shown 'serpent mounds' in the Highlands. They were shaped like serpents and were though by local folk to have been used for burials. Intriguingly an old man told him he believed serpents had once been worshipped in the district. Part of that

131

worship may well have involved casting offerings into the tide to satisfy a serpent's appetite and ward off its destructive powers. But what lies buried in those mysterious mounds?

Seefers

These creatures are found in Shetland waters. There is argument as to what seefers looked like, some saying that they were like a pig and others that they were the shape of a coffin!

They had the habit of leaping out of the water, and when fishermen at sea saw one doing this they watched to see how it fell back. If it landed on its side they would cheer for it meant 'death tae fish', but if it fell face down there was gloom as it meant 'death tae man'.

Tom Henderson, the Shetland historian, was told by an old fisherman that he had been on a boat when they saw a seefer make three great leaps, landing the right way each time.

'Boy,' said the fisherman, 'What a simmer o' fish we had!'

Selkies

The selkies are Orkney folks' cousins, so the selkies are
sib tae me.
Orkney saying.

If all the stories are to be believed, the selkies, or seal people, are sib (related to) quite a number of folk in the islands and round our coasts. Anyone, for instance, bearing the name MacCodrum has a selkie ancestor. They were a North Uist family, but the name seems to be extinct there now and I have not traced MacCodrums anywhere else in Scotland. There are said to be some on Cape Breton Island and there could be others in communities overseas where there are descendants of Uist emigrants.

If ever you meet a MacCodrum, ask to see his or her hand. If the tales are true, it will be unusually rough and horny. The Orkney writer Ernest Marwick knew someone descended from a selky whose hand had a 'greenish-white tegument fully a sixteenth of an inch thick which was cracked in places and had a strong fishy odour.'

Donald MacDougall, North Uist, was recorded by Angus John MacDonald for the School of Scottish Studies, telling the story of how the MacCodrums acquired their selkie blood.

One of the family had been beach-combing and was sitting by a rock for a rest, when a group of seals came swimming towards the shore. They hauled themselves up on to the sand and slipped off their skins, revealing themselves as beautiful women.

They returned to the sea, playing and swimming in the tide, and MacCodrum could not take his eyes off one who, to him, was the loveliest of them all. Even the skin she had taken off was more beautiful than the others.

He came out from behind the rock and seized it, causing great consternation as the girls rushed to retrieve their skins, put them on and disappear into the sea.

Only the one girl was left and she wept and pleaded with him to give her back the skin. He refused and took her home, the skin firmly grasped in his hand. When he got home he hid it in the rafters of the barn.

The seal woman had no choice but to marry him and she turned out a very good wife and mother to their children. The years passed until one day one of the girls came on the seal skin hidden in the barn. She told her mother about the strange object at bedtime and that was the last time the woman was ever seen. She had taken the skin, slipped it on, and returned to her own people.

Mr MacDougall added that sometimes, in the evenings, a seal used to sit on a reef crying, a fish in its mouth. It was thought by those who saw and heard it that it was MacCodrum's wife looking for the children she had left behind.

This classic tale, with variations, is found in the Hebrides and other seagoing communities such as Orkney, Shetland and Caithness. It is similar to tales of mermaids told elsewhere in this book.

Look into a seal's eyes, especially those of a great grey Atlantic seal, and it is not difficult to see how people came to invest these creatures with human characteristics, to believe that they were half human. Another belief was that they are fallen angels. These soulful eyes have aroused guilt in many a hunter and must often have stayed the hand of a killer. A sense of guilt permeates many of our seal stories.

A good example tells how a John o' Groats seal hunter stabbed a seal with his knife. The animal escaped and swam off with the knife still embedded in its body. Shortly afterwards a stranger came to see the man and told him he knew someone who wanted to buy seal skins. He offered to take the man on his horse to meet the potential customer.

The stranger rode the horse to a precipice overlooking the sea and plunged into the water below. In the depths of the ocean he led the man to a seal desperately ill from a stab wound. With horror the man recognised his own knife. The injured seal was the stranger's father and now he asked the man to stroke the wound with his hand. He did so and it instantly healed.

The man was then escorted home to John o' Groats, having promised faithfully never to harm another seal.

Its pleading eyes are not the seal's only endearing characteristic. There is its curiosity, the interest it seems to take in our activities. It is a common and at times unsettling experience to become aware that a head is bobbing in the water, its gaze fixed on what we are up to.

They seem to love to hear human singing and music and can sometimes be lured to the shore by it. I can remember persuading my wife to sing a folksong to attract seals towards the shore on Flotta, Orkney (I knew my own singing would be no good!). I understand that seals themselves are no mean singers and that there is an almost human quality to the sounds they make deep in their sea caves. I have heard recordings of this and it is a remarkable noise. We found afterwards, by the way, that 'Roan' in Roan Head, the site of our Flotta experiment, means 'seals'.

Appropriately enough, it was on Flotta that, a number of years ago, a fine version was collected of the tragic ballad 'The Great (or Grey) Selkie of Sule Skerry'. Here 'Sule' means 'solan' or gannet, and the skerry, a rocky islet west of Orkney, is a traditional haunt of grey Atlantic seals.

The ballad tells of a young woman in Norway who is seduced by a stranger and gives birth to a child. The stranger has deserted her but he returns and reveals that he is a selkie (other terms are 'silkie' and 'selchie'):

> 'I am a man upon the land,
> I am a selkie in the sea,
> And when I'm far from every strand,
> My dwelling it is Sule Skerry.'

He offers to marry her but, horrified, the girl refuses so he tells her he will come back in seven years and bring money to pay his son's nursing fees.

Sure enough, seven years later he reappears and gives her money. He again presses her to wed him but the girl still refuses. He hangs a gold chain round the child's neck and makes a prophecy: the child will one day join him but they both will meet their deaths, for:

'And thoo will get a gunner good,
And a gey good gunner it will be,
And he'll gae oot on a May morning
And shoot your son and the grey selkie.'

And so it happens, breaking the girl's heart in three pieces.

Shellycoat

A lively spirit or bogle that lived in Border and other waters. The Hermitage and the Ettrick are two of the rivers they haunted and where they played mischief. There seems to have been no evil in their ways but they took great delight in confusing people.

On a dark night, two travellers were approaching the Ettrick when they heard a sad voice wailing 'Lost! Lost!' They followed the cries which led them upstream, on and on throughout the night.

As dawn broke they found themselves up amongst the hill springs at the source of the river. Even there the voice did not stop its pathetic cries but led them on across the top. Only when it began to descend the other side did the men, exhausted, turn to trudge back the long way they had come.

As soon as they did so they heard the voice break into peals of glee and they realised they had been tricked by Shellycoat.

Shellycoats were found elsewhere in the Lowlands and along the east coast. They seem to have lived a solitary life and travellers only knew of the presence of a shellycoat by the rattle of the shells that hung about him and gave him his name.

There was a well known shellycoat associated with a certain rock on the shore of Leith. Local boys brave enough used to run round the rock three times chanting:

'Shellycoat, Shellycoat, gang awa hame,
I cry na' your mercy, I fear na' your name!'

135

Tangie

A type of sea horse found in the waters off the Northern Isles. It would be sighted riding on the tops of the waves apparently enjoying rough weather. Young girls were warned to watch out for one if walking on the shore lest it sweep in on a breaker, snatch her and carry her off to its marine lair.

The Trows

When I stayed for a time, over 50 years ago, in a house on a small Orkney island, I was told firmly there was no need ever to lock the door.

Now there was a very sensible reason for this: the island was crime-free; theft and burglary were unknown. I have wondered since, however, if the advice did not also hark back to the trows, and the old beliefs associated with them. It was well known, in more superstitious times, that these strange little grey-clad creatures objected strongly to finding doors locked against them. It was asking for trouble to lock even a cupboard or a kist.

Belief in trows, it is assumed, was brought to Orkney and Shetland by the Norwegian invaders of the eighth and ninth centuries. The newcomers would have little doubt that the trows (or trolls) who haunted their own hills and valleys would have their equals here. In their minds, they peopled the knolls and rocky places with small shaggy beings and spread their stories about them until they became part of Orkney and Shetland life.

Trows shared the fairies' love of music and, like them, were always on the look out for a fiddler to play or teach them tunes. Too often the luckless fiddler would find, after what he thought a short spell in a trow cavern, he had been there a period of years.

However, it was possible to avoid this misfortune. Tom Tulloch told of a fiddler called Anderson, who met up with a trow annually to play out the Auld Yule. No harm befell him, because he always refused to eat or drink any of the tempting things his host offered him.

Some fiddlers exchanged tunes with the trows while others picked them up by overhearing the musicians in their subterranean homes. You had to be careful doing this, however. At least one man, a Papa

Stour fiddler, was duly punished. He had listened intently to a tune coming from inside a green mound. As he tiptoed away, he whistled the air softly to himself so that he would remember it. Suddenly his ears were boxed vigorously by unseen hands, giving him such a fright he straightaway forgot the tune!

On the same Shetland island, a woman used to watch every Yule night as a company of trows danced on the grass at a spot near the shore. Trows were as fond of dancing as they were of music-making, though their dance steps were strangely awkward, as if they had a limp.

On Fetlar, three concentric circles of stones are said to have been trows who were still dancing when the sun rose. Trows caught out in the open after sunrise had to remain above ground all day till sunset before they could re-enter their homes. The dancing trows must have been punished for their carelessness by being turned to stone. Two stones higher than the others were said to be the fiddler and his wife.

If trows had confined their activities to music and dance, the islanders would have co-existed with them happily enough. What frightened people, and put them against them, was the belief that the trows were frequently kidnappers. Like the fairies of Scotland they were suspected of abducting newborn children, nursing mothers and midwives.

When old folk became confused, developing what we now call Alzheimer's disease, their families said they had been taken 'in the hill' by the trows and blamed them for the condition.

There is no doubt that the trows, once they were introduced to Orkney and Shetland, became very real to the islanders. Their one-time presence is recorded in numerous place-names, from the Trowie Glen on Hoy, Orkney, to names containing 'troll' in Shetland. Last century Ernest Marwick found several natives of Stronsay, Orkney, who could tell him the names of individual trows of the past, Eerlick, Bollick, Keelbrue, and others.

Jessie Saxby collected names in Shetland and recorded last remnants of belief in the *kunal* or king trows, lonely and melancholy creatures who had to have a human mate as there were no female *kunals*. As soon as a child was born to the union the woman died and the *kunals* were not permitted to marry again, hence their gloomy disposition.

These were not the only unusual breed of trows; there is evidence that there were others. The main division seems to have been between trows that lived underground and the ones that lived in the sea. Little has come down about the latter. There were also said to be some who haunted mill streams and shared brownie characteristics.

If there are no trows in the islands now, the church and its clergy can, perhaps, be given the credit—or the blame, according to your viewpoint. The Protestant reformers dealt harshly with such 'nonsense'. A clergyman who visited Shetland in 1838 wrote that 'as experimental and vital godliness increases, these superstitions will be entirely banished.' He quoted a laird as saying that Methodist preachers were 'driving away all the trows and bogues and fairies.'

A Free Church minister, Dr Jamie Ingram, himself entered the folklore of Shetland through his onslaughts on it. A little old trow woman is said to have been left behind when the trows of Yell left the island to escape Ingram's fulminations. They settled in the Faroes where I hope they were left in peace.

But have all the trows really gone from these northern islands? In *The Folklore of Orkney and Shetland*, Ernest Marwick quotes a letter from a Bedfordshire man who was stationed on Hoy, Orkney, during the Second World War. He said that he had been fighting his way along the cliff-top one stormy winter's day when he was astonished to find himself surrounded by about a dozen wild, dancing figures.

'These creatures were small in stature, but they did not have long noses nor did they appear kindly in demeanour. They possessed round faces, sallow in complexion, with long, dark, bedraggled hair.

'As they danced about, seeming to throw themselves over the cliff edge, I felt that I was a witness to some ritual dance of a tribe of primitive men.'

The incident lasted about three minutes and left an indelible impression. What is one to make of the story? A vivid imagination? A vision from the past?

I mentioned tales of fiddlers—and others—being lured underground into trow homes, emerging many years later thinking they had spent only a few hours or a night. This is an international folk theme and is commonly associated with fairies across Scotland as well as in other countries.

It is one of these ironic tricks of fate in literature that a story on this theme, 'Rip van Winkle', caught the public imagination so powerfully that Rip has become a household name though similar adventures were being related long before Washington Irving sat down to write his version.

Irving's source for the story is attributed to Germany and he was American, but his grandfather was from Shetland, where countless Rip van Winkles have stepped blinking into the daylight unaware of the shock awaiting them when they go home.

Urisks

'Lubberly' is a word often used to describe the urisk and in my dictionary a 'lubber' is an 'awkward clumsy fellow' or a 'lazy sturdy' one. 'Abbey lubbers' seem to have been evil sprites who moved into monasteries with the express intention of leading the monks astray, but they were more an English manifestation than a Scottish one. Either our monks were immune to temptations, or they had already succumbed and needed no help from outsiders!

There is, anyway, no suggestion that urisks (or *uraisgs*) led or lured folk into wrongdoing. They were solitary creatures who spent the summer months in remote Highland corries, living in caves, by streams or behind waterfalls.

They were seldom seen, for few people ventured deep into the heart of the mountains. Only now and then a shepherd, perhaps looking for lost sheep, would come back with a story of having sighted a urisk sitting on a large rock, watching him from a distance.

Writing in 1900, J. G. Campbell says that 'not many years ago' a group of boys saw what they took to be a urisk seated on a large boulder in the early evening, the time they were most often to be seen. No doubt the boys beat a hasty retreat for although the urisk was quite harmless, he cut a fearsome figure. Imagine a large grey creature, half man, half goat, with shaggy hair, long teeth and large claws. Not an attractive sight.

Despite his outward appearance, there was something a little pathetic about urisks, for at times the loneliness of their situation grew too much for them and they craved company. A lone traveller would become aware of footsteps behind him in the dark and, turning, would see a hairy monster lumbering after him. All the urisk sought was a little companionship but of course he was never to get it.

It is my belief that the famous Big Grey Man of Ben MacDhui is, or was, a lonely urisk. 'Big Grey Man' describes him perfectly and the behaviour of the creature on MacDhui, following the climber in the dark or thick mist, is typical of a urisk: too shy to make up on the climber, but seeking closeness for company.

When the summer was over and the first chill winds reached the high corries, the urisk would leave his den and make his way to lower ground, often following a mountain burn until he came to the haunts of man. There he would seek out winter quarters in a dry barn or warm hidden corner of an old house or mill.

Urisk

She found the Urisk enjoying the warmth of the fire…

Ugly though he was, it was considered good fortune if a urisk chose to pass the winter under your roof. In return for being left undisturbed he would make himself useful, minding the cattle and doing odd jobs about the place. Then, when the spring came, he would quietly lumber away back to the hills.

It is not surprising that most Gaelic place-names associated with urisks are in lonely parts of the Highlands. One of the tribe must have lived in Gleann Uraisg, at Killninver, Argyll; another left his name on a corrie and pass in the Cuillins of Skye.

The 'Urisk's Waterfall', near Tyndrum, was believed locally to be the winter home of a urisk which spent the summer months high on Ben Doran. Another, which summered on Ben Loy, wintered on the farm of Socoth, Glen Orchy.

At Moraig Waterfall in the district, there used to be pointed out the stone on which it sat dangling its legs and trying, for some reason, to lessen the rush of water.

Two urisks haunted waterfalls on the Lednock burn above Comrie. One, it was said, lured folk in and devoured them, but this is so out of character I wonder if it was some other creature. A local woman claimed she walked into her house one winter's day, having been out to the byre, and found the urisk sitting enjoying the warmth of the fire.

She pretended not to see him but bustled about her work and then went to poke the coals. She picked up a shovel, gathered up the hot cinders, and flung them over the poor thing's feet. The urisk gave a great howl and left in a hurry, never to cross her or anyone else's door again.

Women can be merciless. Another urisk lived on the Carwhin Burn, near Lawers, Perthshire. He was known as Sligeachan and he had a young son who was forever deaving a crofter's wife, asking to be told her name. She refused to say, telling him over and over, 'I am myself, nobody but myself.'

At last one day when the urisk kept asking and asking, her temper snapped. She seized a pan of hot water from off the fire and flung it over the creature's legs. The urisk rushed from the house and ran to his father yelling in pain.

'Who did this to you?' demanded Sligeachan.

'Myself! Nobody but Myself!' wailed his son.

Sligeachan gave him a good thrashing and told him never to be so foolish again. The young urisk had learned his lesson and never bothered the crofter's wife again.

It has to be noted that 'Me Myself' or 'Me Masel' is a widespread story though this is the only version I have seen in which it is applied to an urisk.

Sir Walter Scott, in his *Letters on Demonology*, tells of a urisk in a mill near the foot of Loch Lomond. He calls them 'ourisks' and likens them to the mythical Pan. There was, he says, a tradition that Rob Roy once disguised his men in goatskins 'to resemble the ourisk or Highland satyr.'

Ben Venue in the Trossachs holds a special place in urisk lore. There is a story that an Earl of Menteith persuaded a number of urisks to help build a small headland on the Lake of Menteith. In reward he gifted them a deep corrie on Ben Venue, high above Loch Katrine. It became known, in Gaelic, as 'the Corrie of the Urisks', and according to the Rev. Patrick Graham of Aberfoyle, writing in 1806, a large cave there became a gathering place for these usually solitary creatures.

He writes: 'They were supposed to be dispersed over the Highlands, each owning his own wild recess, but the solemn stated meetings of the order were regularly held in this cave on Ben Venue.'

That must have been a sight indeed.

Wag-at-the-Wa

'His general appearance was that of a grisly old man, with short, crooked legs, while a long tail assisted him in keeping his seat on the crook.'

This is William Henderson's description* of a little Border creature, and the crook was the hook over the fire on which hung the cooking pot.

Wag-at-the-Wa seems to have been thoroughly domesticated, enjoying the company of the household particularly when there was laughter and fun. He loved to watch children at play and would sit chuckling merrily on his cosy perch.

He usually wore a red cap and blue breeches but sometimes donned a drab grey mantle and an old night-cap pulled down over one side of his face because the poor soul suffered chronic toothache.

Like the brownie, to whom he would appear to be related, he was very fastidious. If the house was untidy or dirty the servants got no peace until they had cleaned and sorted it.

He did not mind the family drinking home-brewed ale but if anything stronger was being consumed he would cough noisily to show his disapproval.

*Folk-lore of the Northern Counties (1879).

If he was absent from his seat over the fire, there was an easy way to summon Wag-at-the-Wa. You simply swung the pot-hook and he would appear on it, grinning cheerfully.

An endearing character to have around.

Warlocks and Wizards

First, a look at the two words above. 'Warlock' is now rarely used, its meaning vague in the public mind. 'A sort of warlord?' a friend suggested when I asked him to define it. In fact, not war but witchcraft was his business. Witchery and magic. Warlocks were never as numerous as witches, but were found here and there, dabbling in the black art, or at least believed by their neighbours to do so.

Some of these men were called warlocks and some wizards, which is one of those names, like 'fairies' and 'witches' commandeered by the Victorian illustrators of children's books. They painted wizards with colourful coats, high pointed hats and brandishing a wand. All very exciting, but pure invention.

Warlocks were, in the main, ordinary men living in the community but practicing a bit of quiet witchcraft from time to time.

The name wizard, on the other hand, was usually applied to men higher up the social scale, figures of learning who were suspected of sorcery. In the Middle Ages it was often the fate of the scholar, the inventor or scientist to be feared and distrusted. His superior knowledge, his experiments and library of books aroused deep suspicion. He had to be engaged on the Devil's work.

A whole mythology grew up around Michael Scott, a twelfth century laird's son from Balwearie, Fife, who studied at Oxford and then set out on the grand tour of Continental universities, blazing a trail with his brilliance as a scholar.

He was a mathematician, a philosopher and a linguist, but it was his study of astronomy/astrology which started the rumours back in Scotland. Among other exploits, he was said to have flown to Rome on a witch's back and, through his cunning, extracted a precious secret from the Pope. When he died, he is believed to have been buried at Melrose with his book of spells and magic alongside.

Thomas the Rhymer, the Laird of Ercildoune (Earlston), also entered folklore on account of his intellect and a gift for prophecy, said to have been acquired during his seven years spent with the fairies.

The modern Scot is still distrustful of anyone from his town or village who leaves home and achieves dazzling success. They don't even have to leave home. Success within their own community can make them unpopular and the victim of rumours, though nowadays the rumours do not involve the Devil or witchcraft. But the result is, sadly, the same.

A laird of Skene, Aberdeenshire, in the seventeenth century, was believed to be a wizard. It was said he had no shadow, having lost it to the De'il. The pattern is familiar: he was of superior intelligence and had travelled widely. At Skene, people claimed to have seen him passing in a coach drawn by jet-black horses without harness. By his side were his familiars, a jackdaw, a hawk and a magpie.

He had also been observed searching in the countryside for herbs and other plants. It was assumed they were for his potions. When an unbaptised baby died and was buried, they said that Skene had disinterred the body for his own purposes.

Every wizard was believed to have his book of magic, his most precious possession, which no one else must see without permission. The Wizard of Reay lived in Sutherland and he once entrusted his book to a servant, telling him to take it to a neighbour who also dabbled in sorcery. He gave the servant strict instructions on no account to open the book on the journey.

The servant set off briskly enough, but took a rest on the way and, tempted, started to leaf through the pages. At once he was surrounded by hundreds of little men all shouting, 'Work! Give us work!'

The servant racked his brains and, in desperation for some task to give them, told them to take all the heather round about and make it into rope.

In no time the job was done and the little men were again clamouring for work. The servant had a brainwave: he ordered them to go to the nearby Bay of Tongue and twist the sand into rope. Away the men rushed, but they found the task utterly beyond them and, furious at being given an impossible task, they left the district and never served the Wizard of Reay again.

This wizard was, more properly, Donald Mackay, Lord Reay, and he had travelled and studied abroad. When he came home to Tongue House, the story spread that he had been studying under Satan in Italy. There are other tales about him including at least one other version concerning the book and the ropes of sand.

It seems generally agreed that, even after his little helpers had deserted him, he still retained unique powers. He could, for instance, control the weather with just a wave of his hand, a useful gift on that bleak north coast. In local lore he is associated with the Smoo Cave, Durness, where the hoof prints of his horse may be seen near the entrance.

Attempts have been made, from time to time, to track down a wizard's book of magic, his collection of spells, charms, potions and other magical knowledge. The so-called *Red Book of Appin* (which contains the Devil's own handwriting) may still be in private hands in Argyll, while another, the *Book of the Black Art*, is believed to lie buried in an Orkney garden.

Torridon was the home of the Wizard of the North, a man called MacLeod originally from Skye. A jocular fellow, he loved to play tricks on people, including his own mother. Typical was the time when she lifted the lid of a pot in which she was boiling a cockerel for dinner. Up popped the cock crowing loudly and flapping its wings!

According to the writer Brenda Macrow, for long a resident in Torridon, MacLeod went to America and died there. This was, she said, writing in the early 1950s, within living memory. That, perhaps, is why he seems to have had none of the style of the great wizards of the past and was more of a practical joker.

Much has been written about Kenneth Mackenzie, the Brahan Seer, his prophecies and his death by burning at Fortrose on the Black Isle. J. G. Campbell tells us that Mackenzie had been instructed at 'Satan's black school' and that fellow pupils were a Cameron of Locheil and MacDonald of Keppoch.

If most wizards possessed style, even panache, and could literally work wonders, the powers of warlocks varied. Some, like witches, could change shape. One who lived near Abergeldie, Deeside, was thrown into prison along with a witch with whom he had been consorting. The witch escaped from her cell and the warlock offered to recapture her in exchange for his freedom.

He went in search of the woman and saw a hare which he knew to be her. He changed into a greyhound and gave chase but she then became a mouse and hid in a hole in a dyke. Nothing daunted, he turned into a weasel, slipped into the hole and brought her out.

Later that day, both back in human form, he handed her over to the authorities. He was pardoned and she was burned at the stake.

Major Thomas Weir, commander of Edinburgh's City Guard in the seventeenth century, was suspected of being in league with the Devil and, with his sister, confessed to numerous crimes. Both were put to death.

Captain Macpherson, known as the Black Officer of Ballychroan, died in spectacular fashion at a Badenoch hunting lodge when the building was struck by a thunderbolt or whirlwind. He had been overheard the night before arguing with a mystery stranger, believed to have been his master, the Devil.

If you had a warlock for a neighbour you had to be on your guard. A woman in the Carse of Gowrie lived close to a man called Mungo who used to call on her to ask the time.

One night he came in with his hands behind his back. Suddenly he whipped a bridle over her head, said some words and she turned into a mare. He jumped on her back and she found herself flying through the air. They landed in Bordeaux in France and he tethered her to a post. She had to wait there till he came back and rode her home.

In the morning she awoke exhausted. Never again did she let Warlock Mungo over her doorstep.

Belief in warlocks and wizards lingered in some parts of Scotland into the first half of last century. F. Marian McNeill in her book *The Silver Bough* (1956) says she was shown two green balls that had been the property of a Highland exponent of the Black Art. The balls had, she was assured, been 'worked' by him with dire effects between the two World Wars.

Water Bulls

The Picts held the bull in high esteem. They carved him in all his magnificence on their stones. Their great fort at Burghhead on the Moray coast was protected by an unknown number of bull-stones, on each of which was inscribed a ferocious bull with glaring eyes and angry, lowered head. He was a symbol of power, potency and strength.

In contrast the water-bull of our folklore is shy, gentle and inoffensive. It lived in hill tarns and was seldom seen, for it came out only at night. It was not big and impressive like the Pictish bull but, according to one observer, 'a little ugly beast, not much more than the size of a stirk.' Another witness described it as small and black with a velvety, soft appearance.

It led a lonely life, deep in its dark pool, so perhaps it is not surprising that when it came out it often sought the company of the nearest herd of cattle. A crofter would know his herd had been visited by a water bull when his cows produced undersized calves with short, deformed ears. The bulls, as far as could be seen, had no ears at all.

For crofters the arrival of one of these calves was a bitter disappointment. They never grew to full size and were of little market value. Since the bull would come under cover of darkness there was little the crofter could do to prevent it happening though sometimes he was given warning when he heard, after sundown, the distinctive sound of the water bull. This seems to have been a very strange noise resembling, of all things, the crowing of a cock.

There is a tradition that a water bull was killed with a bow and arrow at a lochan on St Kilda but it was generally held that the only way of slaying one was with a silver bullet or coin. A normal bullet would have no effect.

Although seldom seen or heard, water bulls were believed to be numerous, inhabiting waters on the moors and hills all over the Highlands. There is one instance of a bull that turned dangerous. It lived in a pool near Kirkmichael, Perthshire, and was infuriated when a fisherman, by mistake, struck it with his landing net.

From then on, according to R. MacDonald Robertson, the bull lurked among the reeds and boulders by the Cultalonie pool on the river Ardle, ready to spring out on the unwary passer-by.

> Aince he tossed Chick Stewart's dug,
> Gied him sic a clour;
> Then he charged a fisherman,
> An' made him rin like stour.

It wreaked havoc among the local cattle herds, its many calves being not only stunted and ugly but so fierce they were impossible to tame, as were the progeny that followed them.

Curiously there is a tradition that a bull fought a battle with the Devil on a hillside near Kirkmichael. In 1994 the late Tom Ogilvie showed me a stretch of exposed rock where the encounter is said to have taken place. The rock is deeply pitted with what look like hoof prints and visible signs of a struggle.

What the outcome of the battle was Tom could not tell me and I don't know if the Devil's adversary was the wild water bull of Cultalonie or a different, perhaps earlier, bull.

Water Cows

A man living on an unidentified island told the collector J. F. Campbell that he had often seen a water bull grazing amongst his cattle near a lochside but 'No one has ever seen a water cow.'

Perhaps not on his island, but sightings have been reported from elsewhere. A whole herd of them once came ashore on a farm on South Harris. They were fine-looking beasts, so when they showed signs of going back into the sea local people stood between them and the shore and drove them back to the pastures with any weapons they could find. Here, as in other places, the best method was to throw handfuls of sand or earth between the beasts and the strand. Earth taken from a burial-ground was thought to be the most effective deterrent.

Not all the Harris cows stayed but some did, interbreeding with local herds to provide this corner of Harris with superior stock.

According to J. G. Campbell, who related this story, the animals from the sea looked like ordinary but good quality Highland cattle. One would have expected them to have the half-ears of a water bull's progeny but he makes no reference to this. Alexander Carmichael, however, says that some sea cattle were 'notch-eared' and that the ears were always red in colour. He makes the interesting point that the old Caledonian white cattle had red ears.

Some reports claim that the sea cattle did not all look the same but ranged in colour, brown, black, red, and even brindled or speckled. They appear to have been peaceable beasts, like most water bulls, and adapted well to living on land and grazing on pasture instead of the ocean bed seaweed that was their normal fodder.

Other places where they were said to have come ashore were in Skye, Gairloch, Berneray and Tiree. It was on Tiree that a farm worker, Dugald Campbell, once had a strange experience with what was believed to be a water cow. He was watching the farm herd one evening when a small red cow appeared among them. The herd turned on it and it fled from its attackers. Dugald followed and saw it run straight towards a rock face. To his amazement it vanished into it, closely followed by one of its pursuers. If Dugald had not been there the whole herd would have disappeared. Neither the red cow nor the farm beast was seen again.

It has to be remembered that many people believed water cows to be fairy animals herded by their owners on the seabed.

There are also traditions of water cows living far from the salt spray in inland waters. Loch Tay, in the hills of Perthshire, was one of their abodes and it was said that the dun-coloured herd could sometimes be seen on the slopes of Ben Lawers. From time to time local folk observed them moving down to the loch shore and lowing loudly. It was believed they were calling for the water bull and, sure enough, these occasions were always followed by a crop of new calves.

Not everything in our folklore can be 'explained' but it is not difficult to understand how the birth of an unexpected calf could give rise in a crofter's mind to thoughts of a bull out of nowhere. A strange cow or cows in his herd would sow suspicions, particularly if they had odd physical characteristics. It is in man's nature to search for and demand explanations and if there is no reasonable one on offer, an unlikely one will be even better. In this respect I don't think we are any different today.

However, were I confronted now by a peasant from three centuries ago, I am sure I would be told very forcibly that water bulls and cows *did* exist and that I was a fool to argue anything else.

Water Horses and Kelpies

A little boy and seven little girls went for a wander one fine Sunday afternoon near Aberfeldy, Perthshire. They came to a lochan and were delighted to see, grazing near its brink, a beautiful pony. It looked so docile and friendly they ran over to it. When one of the girls climbed on to its back it took no notice but just went on quietly munching.

It stood quite still as a second girl climbed up behind the first. The other girls gathered round and, one by one, laughing and joking, they pulled themselves up on to the pony's back. 'Come on!' they shouted to the boy but he hung back. The pony seemed friendly and harmless but he had noticed that, as each girl climbed up, its back seemed to grow longer to make room for her.

Frightened, he turned and ran in amongst some rocks. All the girls were on the pony's back now and it raised it head and stared over at him. 'Come on, little scabby-head,' it called. 'Get on my back!'

The boy retreated further into the rocks and the pony rushed over trying to get at him. The girls were screaming now and would have jumped off if they could, but they found their hands were stuck to the animal's back. They could only sit there as it tried to reach the boy who scrambled out of reach.

Finding it could not follow him, the pony tossed its head, swung round, and headed for the lochan. It plunged into the black waters with an almighty splash and the last thing the boy saw was the girls' terrified faces as they sank out of sight.

Next morning there were seven livers floating on the surface of the pool. Nothing else of the girls was ever found.

What the children had encountered that day was a water horse, one of the commonest and most dangerous of Scotland's supernatural creatures. Every loch, big and small, seemed to have one and if all the stories are to be believed they lured countless adults and youngsters to their deaths.

In Gaelic they were the *each uisge*, a name that was breathed with dread all over the Highlands. A. D. Cunningham, in his *Tales of Rannoch*, points out that Loch Eigheach means the Horse Loch and that this bleak stretch of water near Rannoch Station was the abode of a much-feared water horse.

It was, he says, 'fatally charming', with seductive eyes and silky grey coat. It would be found stepping daintily by the loch shore and not only children but adults fell victim to its wiles and climbed on to its back. The result was always the same. With a 'fiend-like yell of triumph' the horse would gallop into the loch to devour its prey at the bottom.

The *each uisge* or water horse was a different creature to the kelpie and much more dangerous. The two have often been confused and many writers have muddied the waters through not realising the difference. The best way to distinguish between them is to remember that the water horse was found in Highland lochs and in the sea while kelpies favoured mainly Lowland rivers and streams. They loved running water, the faster the better.

We will look at kelpies later in this chapter but first, more accounts of water horses. The young heir to the Laird of Kincardine, Strathspey, was once playing with friends on the shore of Loch Pityoulish when they spotted a lovely black horse grazing nearby. Running over to it they were amazed to see that its saddle, bridle and reins were made of the finest silver.

They all seized hold of its reins and at once the horse started galloping towards the loch. To their horror the boys found they could not release the reins—it was as if their hands were glued to them.

The young heir was fortunate—only one of his fingers was curled round them. With his other hand he dug into his pocket, pulled out a knife and cut off his finger. He fell to the ground and looked up just in time to see the horse disappear with his friends below the loch.

Water Horses

In Gaelic they were the each uisge, *a name that was
breathed with dread all over the Highlands…*

151

Orkney and Shetland both have water horse lore. On Rousay, in Orkney, one is said to have come out of the Loch of Kitchen to graze with local horses on the hill. One version of the tale says the horse did not allow anyone near it, but in another version it behaves in true water horse fashion and carries its captives into the loch.

A Skye water horse was said to have, not a nuzzle but a bird's bill. There are traces here surely of the ancient flying horse myth, and there was a belief, recorded by Seton Gordon, that the water horse sometimes appeared as a bird 'like a great northern diver, with the exception of the white upon its neck and breast.'

One man who saw it, said Gordon, described its bill as hooked at the end like an eagle's. Its feet had enormous claws and it left footprints larger than an elephant's.

If that sounds terrifying, the most sinister characteristic of the water horse was its ability to adopt human shape. Its intent was always evil. Many a Highland lass was wooed by an attractive stranger who turned out to be a water horse intent on carrying her to his lair and eating her.

Often the girl realised the truth when, seated by a loch or seashore, the young man placed his head on her lap and invited her to comb his hair. Among his curls she found sand, reeds or seaweed. In some cases, though terrified, she lulled him to sleep and then slipped out of her skirt or, with her scissors, cut her clothes round his head and so made her escape.

In other cases the girl noticed his horse's hooves, hidden until then. There are examples of this tale from Barra, Mull, Durness and many other places. J. G. Campbell points out how similar in detail the stories are: 'Sometimes the young woman is sitting on the turf wall forming the end of the house when the water horse, in the shape of a handsome young man, comes her way; sometimes she is one of a band of women assembled at the summer shieling—the rest are killed and she makes her escape. She detects the character of the youth by the water weeds or the sand in his hair. Many of the stories add that the young man (or water horse) came for her on a subsequent Sunday after dinner, or the church...'

In one account I have heard, the relationship had been going on for some time and the girl suspected nothing. Then one day, when her lover was visiting her home, she accidentally spilled boiling water over his foot. To her horror he whinnied in pain as a horse would do. She hid her suspicions but that night she told her brothers.

'When is he coming back to see you?' they asked.

She told them and when the young man again approached the

house they were lying in wait. They sprang out and attacked him with their dirks and as they rained blows at him he screamed and kicked like a horse. When they stopped, it was not a man that lay there but a stallion.

The following morning, when the brothers returned with a cart to remove the beast, there was nothing at the spot but a pool of slime. In other tales of the successful killing of a water horse the dead creature invariably turns to what looks like slime or jellyfish.

There are reports of lochs being dragged or even drained in order to rid them of a water horse. One loch that was dragged with a net was in the Sleat of Skye in 1870. Some heavy object got caught up in the net, but the men involved in the operation lost their nerve and fled so they never knew if they had caught the horse or not.

Just a few years earlier, the Beastie Loch, near Mellon Udrigle, Wester Ross, had been the scene of an attempt at destroying a dangerous *each uisge*. Local folk had petitioned the owner to drain the loch. When this proved too difficult, barrels of unslaked lime were poured into the deepest section of the water. Whether the horse was destroyed by this or whether it escaped and moved to a new home was never established but it was not seen in the neighbourhood again.

Despite its ferocity it was possible to capture a water horse and put it to work. Fasten a cap to its head, or the kind of neck-shackle worn then by a cow, and it was at once as docile as any working horse.

By one of these means some farmers were able to tame a water horse and got good service from them. There was, though, always the danger of the cap or the shackle slipping off. As soon as it did, the horse would bolt for the loch from which it had come, often carrying at least one victim with it. In some instances it dragged a whole string of working horses after it. Their livers rising to the surface told of their fate.

There was another method of depriving the *each uisge* of its power. A farmer once found a beautiful bridle lying in the heather. He carried it home and hung it up in the stable. Next morning a strange horse cantered up to the stable door. It was glossy black with a white star on its forehead.

There was a lot of ploughing to be done so the farmer told his servants to make use of the horse until its owner claimed it. They yoked it to the plough and it proved to be a splendid worker, steady, patient and strong. The ploughing had never been done so quickly or so well. The farmer began to hope nobody would come and claim it.

One day he had to go to the market in town. He decided to ride there on his fine new horse. As he went into the stable, a gleam in the shadows caught his eye. Ah, yes, the bridle he had picked up on the moor. He took it down and fingered it. What a grand bridle it was! It would look well on his handsome horse. He would be the envy of all his friends. Slipping it over the horse's head he rode off proudly, aware of the fine show he made. He never arrived at the market and neither he nor the horse was ever seen again.

A water horse that loses its bridle is deprived of its powers. The bridles had magical properties and without it the animal was reduced to behaving like a normal horse.

The most intriguing story of a water horse bridle that came into human hands is the one concerning James MacGregor of Dulnain Bridge, Strathspey. The original tale has grown legs through its numerous retellings, but briefly this is what was said to have happened.

A water horse had been terrorising the country folk, appearing by the side of Lochindorb, Spynie or Loch Ness and luring innocent wayfarers to their deaths. MacGregor grew more and more angry about this and began making long journeys in search of the creature.

He caught up with it at last on the Slochd, then a wild and lonely spot in the mountains. The horse, saddled and bridled, stood quietly grazing, thinking it had another easy victim in sight. MacGregor took it by surprise. He walked up to it, drew his sword, and brought it down with all his might on the horse's head.

The creature's jaw was injured but, worse than that, its bridle was severed and fell off. MacGregor picked it up, folded it and stuffed it in his pocket.

He was about to strike the animal a second blow when, to his amazement, it spoke to him, appealing for the return of its bridle. At first he refused and then, sensing the animal's desperation, he demanded to know what made the bridle so precious.

The horse told him that if he looked through certain holes in it he would see the fairies, witches and devils that were flying in the air invisible to man.

This made MacGregor all the more determined that he would keep the bridle and he told the horse so. It ranted and raged in fury but, without the bridle, was powerless against MacGregor's sword.

Nevertheless it followed close behind him all the way home and when they came to MacGregor's house it ran in front of him, blocking the doorway. MacGregor slipped round the back and shouted to his wife to come to the window. He then threw her the bridle and returned to the horse, telling it the bridle was now safely inside.

He walked boldly past the horse and through the door knowing it was safe to do so because he always kept a rowan cross fixed above the entrance. The horse could only turn away defeated.

This version is, I think, the purest I have seen. It is taken from *Superstitions of the Highlanders* by W. Grant Stewart who was told it by Grigor Willox MacGregor, a descendant of the man who stole the bridle (James MacGregor was his grand-uncle).

The bridle, or at least part of it, came down to Grigor Willox who was himself a remarkable character known to his neighbours as 'Willox the Wizard' or 'Warlock Willox'. The name Willox had been adopted by some of the MacGregors when the clan was proscribed.

He lived in Glen Avon where he showed the bridle to the folklorist Sir Thomas Dick Lauder and two friends around 1880. It is recorded that they were puzzled by its appearance. Made of brass and leather it looked like no bridle they had ever seen. This may have been simply because it was incomplete—W. Grant Stewart's account seems to suggest that only part of it was cut from the horse's head.

On the day 'Willox the Wizard' showed his three visitors the bridle he also produced a stone which he told them was given to his grandfather by a mermaid. I have made enquiries to try and trace these strange relics, so far without success.

Although the bridle in that last story has been described by several writers as a 'kelpie's bridle', the creature that wore it was clearly a water horse. The latter was, as we have seen, a Highland phenomenon, denizen of loch and pool, sometimes the sea. The kelpie's home was the rivers and burns of the Lowlands.

Kelpies did not graze on the bank with the intention of luring innocents on to their back. They did not, as a rule, eat human flesh. There was therefore not the same degree of fear of the kelpie; he was regarded more as a nuisance, a mischievous troublemaker.

Still, there is real dread behind the lines of Violent Jacobs' poem 'The Kelpie' in which she puts herself in the shoes of a boy who has to pass the abode of a kelpie on his way home from school. As an Angus woman Jacobs was well aware of the many tales of kelpies in the waters of that county. These are the thoughts she puts in the laddie's head:

> I'm feared o' the road ayont the glen,
> I'm sweir to pass the place
> Whaur the water's rinnin', for a' fowk ken
> There's a kelpie sits at the fit o' the den,
> And there's them that's seen his face.

But whiles he watches an' whiles he hides
And whiles, gin na wind manes,
Ye can hear him roarin' frae whaur he bides
An' the soond o' him splashin' agin' the sides
O' the rocks an' the muckle stanes.

When the mune gaes doon at the arn-tree's back
In a wee, wee weary licht,
My bedclaes up to my lugs I tak,
For I mind the swirl o' the water black
An' the cry i' the fearsome nicht.

And lang an' fell is yon road to me
As I come frae the schule;
I daurna think what I'm like to see
When dark fa's airly on buss an' tree
At Martinmas and Yule.

It would have been unnerving, even for an adult, to see a kelpie surface in a stream or pool and to hear his roar. Compared with the quiet and elegant water horse, your kelpie was a rumbustious beast. Typical behaviour was wallowing noisily, plunging and rising again with much splashing and snorting.

The one that inhabited the Boat Pool on the Isla near Meigle in Perthshire was said to delight in rushing from the Isla into its tributary, the Dean Water. It was always at its most boisterous when the rivers were in spate. It got the blame when, one stormy night, the Isla ferry boat was upset with loss of life. After a bridge was built the kelpie seems to have departed. Perhaps it resented this new obstacle.

Like the water horse, a kelpie could be captured and put to work on a farm. Still in the Meigle district, a local farmer was believed by his neighbours to have one in his stable. A passer-by swore he overheard it bemoaning its fate:

'Sair back and sair banes,
Carryin' auld Balmyre's stanes.'

Not so far away, the Laird of Murphy also had one which made similar complaint about the work it had to do. This tradition is referred to in a vigorous, idiosyncratic Scots poem by the Rev. Jamieson, author of the *Dictionary of the Scottish Language* (1808 and 1825).

In his poem 'Water Kelpie', the creature rises from the waters of the South Esk near the castle of Inverquharity. The man who sees it gives a fearsome description of its appearance and then the kelpie speaks, first reprimanding him for having the temerity to confront him. It recalls its hard life with Murphy:

> 'Quhan Murphy's laird his biggin rear'd,
> I carryit aw the stanes;
> And mony a chiell has heard me squeal
> For sair-brizz'd [bruised] back and banes.'

It describes how, now it is free again, it rejoices in frightening people with its screams and nickerings, and relates with relish that its name is used to threaten young children:

> 'My name itsell wirks like a spell,
> And quiet the house can keep;
> Qhan greits the wean, the nurse in vain,
> Thoch tyke-tyriit, [tired as a dog] tries to sleep.
> But gin sche say, "Lie still, ye skrae,
> There's Water Kelpie's chap, [knock]"
> It's fleyit to wink, and in a blink
> It sleeps as sound's a tap [top]'.

With that the kelpie gives a 'horrid goul' before striking the water with his tail three times and then sinking out of sight. The three slaps on the water were a characteristic 'farewell' kelpie gesture.

Although Jamieson was not Angus-born, he lived in Forfar for many years and took a keen interest in the folklore of the area as well as the language.

If kelpies were not as dangerous as water horses they were still an object of real fear, filling a sort of 'bogeyman' role. There was a belief in some parts that they were capable of taking human shape and they were accused, when they did this, of jumping up behind someone on horseback and gripping them so painfully hard that the rider could not turn to see who or what was there. A thoroughly unnerving experience.

And they could be a bad enemy to make. One Angus version of the Murphy story has it that the Laird captured his kelpie by throwing a pair of branks over its head (you could also do it by slipping the bit between its teeth). He used the beast to carry huge loads of stones for the building of his new castle, working him day after day with hardly any rest.

When at last the building was finished he led the animal to the waterside, took off the branks and set him free. Before the kelpie dived in, it shouted:

> 'The Laird o' Murphy'll never thrive
> As lang's the kelpie is alive!'

The Grahams of Murphy did not thrive but became reduced in circumstances and died out.

Jamieson's verse about the use of the kelpie as a threat to children provides one clue to the reason for the persistence of water horse and kelpie lore into modern times. Children warned that the water kelpie would come for them if they did not go to sleep would picture the creature and remember it all their lives.

Parents also used the kelpie when warning children against going too near burns, pools, rivers and lochs. What better way of making sure your child would give danger spots a wide berth?

But further back than that, of course, there looms a river god who demanded sacrifices, sometimes human, to placate him/her, and so ensure good fishing and calm, benign waters.

It is a little ironic that a Scottish publisher, when giving a name to a series of storybooks for children a few years ago, should have chosen a word that struck fear into the hearts of their great-grandparents when they were young.

However, it is well known that children love to be a little bit frightened, and anyway, how many 'Kelpie' readers of today know that if they are down by a burn, they should watch they don't get splashed by the animal lurking under the water?

Yet traces of the kelpie may still be seen. Not so long ago I knew a man who was collecting photographs of 'kelpie marks', the marks of their hooves left on old stone bridges in Angus and the Mearns.

Water Wraiths

You never knew what lay in wait for you when you crossed a river ford. There were a number of creatures that might be lurking there and one of them was this wraith or spirit.

Hugh Miller said he knew of many fords reputed to have been the haunt of a wraith and he describes one on the river Conan as 'a tall woman dressed in green, but distinguished chiefly by her withered, meagre countenance, ever distorted by a malignant scowl.'

He went on, 'She used to start out of the river, before the terrified traveller, to point at him, as in derision, with her skinny finger, or to beckon him invitingly on.'

Miller was shown the tree to which a 'poor Highlander' had clung when attacked by the wraith one dark night. His friend had tried to rescue him but the wraith had dragged the helpless man into the current and drowned him.

There is a story of one at the Linn of Lynturk, near Alford, Aberdeenshire. The last time she struck was when the Laird of Kincraigie was making his way home after dining with the Laird of Tulloch.

The Wild Shackle

When bridges were still few and far between, natural fords across rivers and streams were vital to the traveller. They held their own dangers, however, and one of these was the *buarach-bhoi*.

The rider would feel his horse pulled under the water and all its struggles to escape were of no avail. Its unseen attacker was a long, eel-like creature, the wild shackle, which had wound itself tightly round the horse's legs. Horse and rider would be dragged into the nearest deep pool and held until they drowned. The shackle then drank their blood at leisure.

Those who had glimpsed the shackle said it had nine holes in its head and back and that the blood it sucked could be seen oozing from them.

The shackle was believed to lurk along the waters on the west coast of Argyll, in Badenoch and Loch Tummel.

Witches

*Witches are the warst kind of devils, they mak use of cats
to ride upon, or kail kebbers [stalks] and besoms, and sail
over seas in cockleshells, and 'witch lads and lasses, and
disable bridegrooms.*
A Fife native, *Ancient and Modern Buckhaven.*

The witch trials of the sixteenth and seventeenth centuries are one of the blackest chapters in Scotland's history. It has been estimated that well over 1,000 women were put to death and we will never know how many more were victims of harassment, ill-treatment and various degrees of brutality.

On local maps, 'Witch's (or Witches') Knowe' indicates the site of a burning, often more than one; and on rivers and streams 'Witch's Pool' tells where women were plunged into the water. Some survived, others drowned or were to die later as a result of the ordeal.

These were real people. They may have been accused of doing the Devil's work, or serving him as their Master, and many, in their 'confessions', said they did, but they were flesh and blood women often picked upon and persecuted simply because they were old, or odd, solitary often, and a bit of a mystery.

They suffered because belief in witchcraft was deep and widespread. Anyone—man or woman—suspected of indulging in it was considered a threat, a danger to the community. The fear could be very real, fuelled by tales told of terrible old women, monsters of evil with supernatural powers. With their spells, it was said, they could destroy your health, kill your livestock, steal your possessions, damage your crops, sink your ship or summon up storms.

Even if you found them out there was often little you could do to defend yourself. They could evade you by changing size or shape, turning into a bird, a cat, a horse, a mouse or other creature. In their own shape they could fly through the air and sail on the water in a sieve.

No wonder that, believing all this, ordinary folk were frightened, quick to suspect their neighbour when things went wrong and if she gave the least grounds for suspicion.

However, there were also 'friendly' witches, women of goodwill who were prepared to use their powers to help you. Instead of a threat they were regarded as valuable to the community and people would consult them for charms, spells, potions and cures. So long as you treated her with proper respect, the 'wise woman' could help you with all sorts of problems. She was a doctor, nurse, vet, agricultural adviser, social worker and counsellor all in one. For her it was a way of earning a crust of bread, a little meal, a glass of ale. So long as things went well, her neighbours were not likely to turn against her.

Her doings are not our concern here. The witches in the villages were one thing, the witches of the folktales another. That was almost certainly not how most seventeenth-century Scots saw it but we must make the distinction, while keeping in mind that the tales we find entertaining were at one time a grim warning, striking genuine fear in the minds of listeners.

Did the Witch of Laggan exist? This well-known story (told under 'Cats' in this book) may have sprung from a true incident. Perhaps there was a hunter who was benighted in a bothy with his dogs. Perhaps a cat shared their warmth. Perhaps that same night a woman fell ill.

Our folklore is full of old women who suffer an injury similar to that inflicted on a bird or animal at the same time. Such incidents may well have occurred, ill-timed coincidences for the innocents involved.

The very sighting of a hare amongst a farmer's cows was enough to arouse suspicion. It could be a witch sucking their milk. Shoot the hare and somewhere in the district an old woman was likely to die.

Many districts, especially in the Highlands, are identified with their own particular witch and her exploits. Here are just a few of these legendary figures.

A one-eyed giant witch made her home in a natural enclosure of huge boulders on the Ross of Mull. She was huge herself and it was said the Hebrides were formed when soil and stones fell from her creel as she waded in the sea.

Every 100 years she restored herself to youth by walking into the waters of Loch Ba at the foot of Ben More. She went in as an old woman and came out a young girl. However, for the transformation to work she had to reach the loch in the early morning before any bird or animal had uttered a sound. There came a year when, more feeble than usual, she was too late. A dog barked and she crumbled to dust.

The Witch of Badenoch is only one of the sisterhood who, flying through the night sky with an apron of large stones, let one fall to the ground. It stands where it fell in Strathardle. Some versions of this say that she had flown from the Isle of Man.

Another witch was responsible for dropping boulders on either side of the Kyle of Durness and there are many more such traditions.

Round our coasts there were 'storm witches' who could raise or calm the wind with their spells. Tarbat Ness, between the Moray and Dornoch Firths, was the home of Stine Bheag o' Tarbat, who could be prevailed upon to provide good weather for fishermen. On one occasion a skipper had asked her for a favourable wind in exchange for two bottles of spirits. He failed to send her the bottles and they were still aboard when the boat sailed. A storm arose, threatening craft and crew with destruction. At its height two ravens swooped down and carried off the bottles. After that the storm subsided.

On another occasion she reluctantly promised a crew a safe voyage so long as they did not remove a bunch of straw she had placed in the mouth of their water-stoup.

The weather proved so calm and fine that, when they were well on their way, a crew member took out the straw and immediately the sky darkened and a gale arose, blowing them back the way they had come.

It required another visit to Stine Bheag, and many apologies, before they set out again. She had put fresh straw in the spout of the stoup and this time they were not foolish enough to remove it and they sailed in safety.

There was a storm witch at Scourie, Sutherland, called Morag, who earned a good living selling favourable winds to seafarers. Her method of ensuring calm seas was to boil a kettle while muttering a spell. To raise a wind she stood outside her cottage and whistled, staring in the direction from which the wind was to come.

Mhoir Bhein lived on the west coast of Caithness and was blamed for sinking ships and other crimes. Some local lads strangled her with a halter. They were tried for murder, but a sympathetic court acquitted them. A similar violent death befell Scota Bess on Stronsay, Orkney. She was beaten to death with flails that had been washed in holy water. Orkney and Shetland had numerous storm witches, sometimes friends, sometimes foes to the superstitious fishermen.

Kintail had not one witch but three and each had a magic hat. If they put it on their head and said something like 'Here's off to London!' they were instantly there. A man who overheard them found a fourth hat and tried it. He landed in a London alehouse. With the three witches he enjoyed a convivial time, so convivial that he did not notice the witches, one by one, putting on their hats and saying 'Here's back to Kintail!'

He came to his senses when he realised they were gone and a waiter was at his side demanding payment for all he and they had drunk. When he admitted he had no money he was dragged off to prison and condemned to death. On the scaffold he remembered the hat in his pocket. As his last wish he asked to be allowed to wear it. He put it on, repeated the magic words, and was home in Kintail, the rope still around his neck.

This tale, popular today at storytelling sessions, represents the lighter side of witch belief.

Returning to the darker side, it is evident that one could incur the wrath of a witch quite innocently. In Galloway the Witch of Glenluce, Maggie Osborne, was once trodden upon when she was a black beetle crawling on the ground. A long time later she caused an avalanche of snow to fall on the cottage of the shepherd who had stood on her, killing him and his wife.

The townsfolk of Crieff still remember Kate McNiven, burned at the stake near the town. They have a soft spot for her because, wrongdoer though she may have been, she showed a streak of gratitude at the end.

The tradition is that, as the flames licked around her, a local laird, Graham of Inchbrakie, rode up and tried to persuade the crowd to free her. Kate bit a blue bead from her necklace and spat it towards him, telling him to keep it and it would ensure good fortune for his family in the years to come. Inchbrakie took it and kept it in a safe place and the Grahams flourished from then on.

Traces of witch belief were still around last century. I was told of one living in a lonely cottage in Aberdeenshire. I was also told by a traveller woman that, walking one day in her local High Street, she came face to face with a woman who glared at her and then shrivelled up and shot into a crevice in the building at the side of the pavement. She was convinced she had met a witch.

There is an old tradition that a Norwegian witch, Dona, was responsible for burning all the ancient forests of Inverness-shire and Ross-shire. She was sent over to do this by her father, the King of Norway, who was concerned that there was no demand for Norwegian timber because Scotland had plenty of her own. By the time the Highlanders had hunted her down and killed her all the old woodlands had been destroyed. So it is not our fault that huge stretches of the Highlands are treeless and bare!

This, it will be seen, is a field enormously rich in folklore. We have been able, in this short chapter, only to hint at the quantity of tales, the depths of belief. There cannot be a corner of Scotland that does not, or did not, have its witch stories. The reader may wish to pursue research locally and there are books devoted entirely to this subject.

I have not touched on the safeguards people used in order to protect themselves and their possessions against witchcraft and what was called the Evil Eye. A great variety of practical measures were employed and in the deeply religious Highlands and Islands there were many prayers and incantations of which this is an example:

> I make to thee the charm of Mary,
> The most perfect charm that is in the world,
> Against small eye, against large eye,
> Against the eye of swift voracious women,
> Against the eye of swift rapacious women,
> Against the eye of swift sluttish women.

If a child fell ill or a horse went lame or some other misfortune befell a household, it was often suspected that a witch's use of the Evil Eye was behind the calamity. There was usually someone in the neighbourhood who had the *eolas*, the gift for putting things right, and he or she would be consulted. They had their own individual ways of doing it.

People dreaded praise as this was believed, paradoxically, to be a means of inflicting harm. Praise of a person, an animal or a crop, would strike dread and foreboding. F. Marian McNeill in *The Silver Bough* tells of a woman and her daughter who were crossing the Kessock Ferry to Inverness when a known witch bent down and said to the little girl, 'What a pretty little mouth you've got!' At once, the girl's mouth twisted to one side and stayed like that until, a month later, a woman with the *eolas* put it right.

Woman of the Water

A shepherd looking for a lost sheep in a rarely visited corner of the hills might overhear the strange singing of this female creature, the *bainisg*. If he listened carefully he might find the song had a satirical edge. Few people ever heard her, however, for she lived in the most remote recesses, so the words were usually lost on the wind.

Worms

In the parochen of Lintown, within the Sherrifdom of Roxburgh, there happened to breed a monster, in form of a serpent or worme...
Seventeenth-century manuscript quoted by Sir Walter Scott in *Minstrelsy of the Scottish Border*.

Worms...it's not a very fearsome name—not to our ears now—but when one of them took up residence in a district there was universal terror. They usually lived in a hole or cave, lying hidden by day and emerging by night to devour cattle, sheep and any person unwise enough to cross their path.

They were like giant snakes with powerful evil breath, though in more modern times they grew closer to the popular conception of dragons. In colour they were often white or grey though the famous Linton Worm, according to the manuscript quoted above, was 'similar in form and colour to our common muir adders'.

It seems purely by accident that the worm at Linton is remembered locally while countless others are forgotten. Perhaps its memory has been kept alive by the carved stone above the door of the local church, depicting a knight in battle with the creature (I will ignore the theory that the story was invented to explain the stone!).

Linton lies near the Kale Water south-east of Kelso and close to the village of Kirk Yetholm, not so long ago the home of the Border gypsies' 'royal family'.

The worm lived in a hollow on the side of Linton Hill and from this hole or den it crawled out at nights to hunt down its prey. To protect their animals farmers moved them to safety further away, but the worm just made longer journeys to find them. All the time it was growing bigger and stronger and on fine days it could be seen lying sunning itself coiled round a hill which is still known as Wormiston.

Several attempts were made to kill the worm or at least frighten it away, but these had no effect. Its thick skin was sound protection against spears, arrows and stones.

News of the havoc the monster was causing reached the ears of Somerville of Lariston, a young man whose family had lands in the district. He was living out of Scotland at the time but he decided to return to see what could be done.

Some say he first tried attacking the worm with his lance, others that he was more circumspect and crept close enough to inspect it in its lair. Whichever is right, he went away and devised a plan. When he returned it was with a piece of peat impaled on the tip of his lance. At the last moment his servant set fire to the peat. Lariston then spurred his horse and rode headlong towards the beast. When it opened its mouth, he thrust the lance down the gaping throat. The weapon broke but the peat did its work and the worm burned to death.

The tympanum over the church door is said to have been paid for by local folk to commemorate Lariston's daring deed. He was also honoured with a knighthood and appointed Royal Falconer.

The method of destroying the Linton Worm by means of a burning peat thrust into its stomach is similar to the one used by Orkney's Assipattle when he killed the mester stoorworm. It occurs in other tales as well. A local hero, Hector Gunn, disposed of a worm in the valley of the river Cassley in Sutherland by pushing his spear down its throat. The peat on the end of it had been plunged in boiling pitch. This worm is remembered by Toll na Cnoimh, the Worm's Hole, and Cnoc na Cnoimh, the Worm's Hill, round which it coiled itself as the Linton Worm did round Wormiston.

The worm's habit of curling itself round a circular hill is reported from elsewhere, for example, the Mote of Dalry, in Galloway. Sheep and other animals make circular paths around hills, one above the other in tiers, and it is not difficult to see these as having been created by a long coiled snake.

Another method of killing a worm is recorded by Seton Gordon in his book *Hebridean Memories*. He tells of a worm that terrorised Glen More on the Isle of Mull. The glen had become almost deserted because of it but at last a saviour sailed into Loch Scridain at Glen More's western end.

Anchoring in the bay, he laid a strong cable between his ship and the shore. A number of barrels were attached to it, and they and the cable were studded with sharp iron spikes.

He then went ashore and rode to the worm's lair. Along the route he tethered several horses, and when the worm pursued him he galloped back from one horse to next, leaving each exhausted mount to be killed by the worm.

When he reached Loch Scridain his crew were waiting to row him to his vessel. The worm could not swim but it saw the cable and began to follow by crawling along it. Soon it found itself trapped on the spikes and the more it struggled the deeper and more severe were its wounds. The waters became stained red with its blood and when it was too weak to struggle any more the crew finished it off.

Seton Gordon calls this creature a serpent or dragon and, in the Gaelic, a *beither*, but there is no doubt it was one of the race of giant worms. He draws attention to Beinn Bheither, the Hill of the Beast, above Ballachulish, and suggests that the *beither* of that hill and the one in Glen More 'may be one and the same monster.'

I have to disagree. The worm of Beinn Bheither (in English, Ben Vair) was killed in a similar fashion but it was a different beast. It was, unusually, a female and it lived in a prominent hollow on Vair, Corrie Lia, from which it made forays in search of victims.

It was a man called Tearlach Sgiobair, Charles the Skipper, who is credited with luring it to its death. Anchoring off shore, he constructed a similar fatal 'bridge' of barrels bristling with spikes. He then lit a fire on his boat and started cooking chunks of meat. The worm followed the delicious smell and, like the one in Loch Scridain, cut itself to death.

This was not quite the end of the story. The worm had left a young one hidden up in Corrie Lia and in time there was a whole nestful of baby worms. The mother moved them, for safety and warmth, into a corn-stack at the foot of the hill. She was up in the corrie when the farmer discovered them and immediately took a burning brand to the stack.

Up in the corrie the mother heard the agonized cries of her brood and rushed to their rescue. She was too late and, in her grief, she lay down on a big flat rock and lashed it with her tail until she died.

A similar version of the first part of this story is told of a 'loathly worm' on Islay, which died on spiked barrels in Loch Indaal having devoured seven horses on the way.

The worm at the Mote of Dalry also died from spikes or knives but they were attached to the armour of its attacker, Michael Fleming, whom it swallowed whole. He cut his way out after it was dead.

These traditional tales of giant worms, serpents and dragons have very deep roots. They are old stories but nothing like as old as the body of beliefs out of which they grew. The tales told here have to be seen as misheard, misunderstood, impure interpretations from an earlier culture. And although well embedded in Scottish soil they do not stand in isolation but are shared worldwide. The serpent, the dragon and worm occupy a significant place in world folklore.

To see how far back they go in man's consciousness in this country, you have only to look at our treasury of Pictish carved stones. Amongst the many figures and symbols are serpents, snakes and allied creatures.

On the earliest class 1 stones of probably the seventh century, there are at least 14 snakes or serpents. Why are they there? The writer Elizabeth Sutherland has studied the Picts and their art. In her book *In Search of the Picts* she writes:

> One of the mystical beasts of Scotland, the snake is a creature of the earth both wise and dangerous, a symbol not only of healing and fertility but also of death and rebirth. Its spiralling body represents the journey to the Otherworld where it sleeps until it emerges in early spring from its hole in the ground and sheds its old skin to appear new-born.

Put another way, it is a symbol of eternity. Such a creature was not one to offend but to propitiate. From that it was not too long a journey to fear, distrust and, eventually, loathing.

Alexander Carmichael collected a Gaelic rhyme associated with Bride, goddess of marriage and childbirth, whose festival fell in February.

> Today is the day of Bride,
> The serpent shall come from the hole.
> I will not molest the serpent,
> Nor will the serpent molest me.

This implies a rare day of truce and that, ordinarily, the one would attack the other. So by the time that rhyme was made, there was respect for the serpent, awe even, but, I would also suggest, dread and hostility.

It was from the juices of a great white worm that one of the most celebrated wizards was said to have derived his powers and wisdom. The story is that Michael Scott, as a young man, encountered a notorious worm on the Pass of Drumochter. There were two friends with him who turned away at the sight of the beast. Scott drew his sword and, after a long battle, slew it.

His friends returned and they cut the worm in three and carried the parts on to an inn, possibly at Dalwhinnie, where they were to spend the night. Their landlady at once pressed them to accept free board and lodgings if they would give her the animal's middle portion. The three readily accepted but Scott was curious to see what the woman would do with the slice of worm.

He found she had made it into broth which was boiling on the kitchen fire. He tasted it and at once his mind was filled with knowledge, spells, and all sorts of magical things of untold value.

Because he realised he had stolen all this from the innkeeper, he left the inn at once while it was still night and before she would have the chance to kill him.

This is not the only story of someone acquiring wisdom and special gifts through tasting the brew made from a white serpent or snake. St Fillan learned his healing arts from one taste on his thumb, as did a member of the old Ramsay family of Bamff, Alyth, in Perthshire, who became a celebrated man of medicine.

A young Laird from Broughdearg, Glenshee, is said to have had the same good fortune, while the famous family of Highland doctors named Beaton may have owed their skills to the first of the line tasting the magical brew.

The same story is told of a native of Tongue named Farquhar and, incidentally, a Sutherland white worm may have been the very first wheel. It was said to wind itself into a ring or hoop and then roll over the moors at a tremendous pace. It killed several people before it was itself destroyed.

Though the circumstances differ from story to story, there is a general pattern. A young man meets a stranger who asks him to catch and kill a white serpent at a certain spot. The stranger then instructs him to cook it but on no account to taste it.

The man does taste it, either accidentally or deliberately, and at once realises the gifts that are now his. Knowing he has 'stolen' these from the stranger and that his life is now in peril he escapes and embarks on a successful career.

The abodes of the white snakes are often by a stream or under a hazel bush. The well-known mineral well at Pananich, Ballater, was said to be the home of one of these creatures, but don't let that put you off drinking the water; it may not taste all that nice but it is very good for you!

Wulver

A lone creature who lived in a hill cave on the Isle of Unst, Shetland. He walked like a man but had a brown hairy body and a wolf's head. Islanders often saw him catching fish from a rock which became known as the Wulver's Stane and he often left gifts of fish on the windowsills of the island's old folk. A kindly and benevolent creature with which to round off our collection.

Some Sources Consulted

Hannah Aitken, *A Forgotten Heritage* (Edinburgh, 1973)

Katharine M. Briggs, *The Personnel of Fairyland* (Oxford, 1953)
  A Dictionary of British Folk-tales (London, 1970-71)
  A Dictionary of Fairies (London, 1976)

Janet Bord, *Fairies: Real Encounters with Little People* (London, 1997)

A. J. Bruford and D. A. MacDonald, *Scottish Traditional Tales* (Edinburgh 1974)

J. F. Campbell, *Popular Tales of the West Highlands* (Edinburgh 1860)

John Gregorson Campbell, *Superstitions of the Highlands and Islands of Scotland* (Glasgow, 1900)

Alexander Carmichael, *Carmina Gadelica* (Edinburgh, 1900-71)

Robert Chambers, *Popular Rhymes of Scotland* (Edinburgh, 1826)

R. H. Cromek, *Remains of Nithsdale and Galloway Song* (London, 1810)

John Currie, *Ancient Things in Angus* (Arbroath, 1821)

A. D. Cunningham, *Tales of Rannoch* (Perth, 1989)

Tim Dinsdale, *Loch Ness Monster* (London, 1976)

John H. Dixon, *Pitlochry Past and Present* (Pitlochry, 1925)

Sir George Douglas, *Scottish Fairy and Folk Tales* (London, 1893)

W. Y. Evans-Wentz, *The Fairy Faith in Celtic Countries* (New York, 1910)

Robert Scott Fittis, *Sketches of the Olden Times in Scotland* (Perth, 1878)

William Forsyth, *In the Shadow of Cairngorm* (1900 and 1999)

Duncan Fraser, *Guide to the Glens of Angus and Mearns* (Montrose, 1953)

Affleck Gray, *Legends of the Cairngorms* (Edinburgh, 1987)
  The Big Grey Man of Ben MacDhui (Moffat, 1989)

Walter Gregor, *Folk-lore of the North-east of Scotland* (London, 1881)

Ron Halliday, *The A-Z of Paranormal Scotland* (Edinburgh, 2000)

E. S. Hartland, *The Science of Fairy Tales* (London, 1891)

Lizanne Henderson and Edward J. Cowan, *Scottish Fairy Belief* (East Linton, 2001)

Seton Gordon, *Hebridean Memories* (London, 1923)

R. T. Gould, *The Loch Ness Monster and Others* (London, 1934)

Patrick Graham, *Sketches of Perthshire* (London, 1812)

William Henderson, *Notes on the Folk Lore of the Northern Counties of England and the Borders* (London, 1866)

F. W. Holiday, *The Great Orm of Loch Ness* (London, 1968)

Robert Kirk, *The Secret Common-wealth* (Cambridge, 1976)

Marion Lochhead, *Magic and Witchcraft of the Borders* (London, 1984)

Neil McCallum, *It's an Old Scottish Custom* (London, 1951)

Alasdair Alpin MacGregor, *The Peat-fire Flame* (London, 1947)

Donald A. Mackenzie, *Scottish Wonder Tales from Myth and Legend* (London, 1917)

   Scottish Folk Lore and Folk Life (London, 1935)

   Tales from the Moors and the Mountains (London, 1931)

Angus MacLellan and J. L. Campbell, *Stories from South Uist* (Edinburgh, 1997)

F. Marian McNeill, *The Silver Bough* (Glasgow, 1959)

Hugh Miller, *Scenes and Legends of the North of Scotland* (Edinburgh, 1835)

   The Old Red Sandstone (Edinburgh, 1841)

   My Schools and Schoolmasters (Edinburgh, 1852)

John Macpherson, *Tales from Barra* (Edinburgh, 1992)

Brenda G. Macrow, *Torridon Highlands* (London, 1953)

Ernest Marwick, *An Orkney Anthology* (Edinburgh, 1991)

   The Folklore of Orkney and Shetland (Edinburgh, 2000)

Norah and William Montgomerie, *The Well at the World's End* (London, 1975)

Tom Muir, *The Mermaid Bride and Other Orkney Folk Tales* (Kirkwall, 1998)

James Napier, *Folk Lore in the West of Scotland* (Wakefield, 1976)

Timothy Neat, *When I Was Young: The Islands* (Edinburgh, 2000)

James R. Nicolson, *Shetland Folklore* (London, 1981)

Nancy and W. Towrie Cutt, *The Hogboon of Hell and Other Strange Orkney Tales* (London, 1979)

Neil Phillip, *The Penguin Book of Scottish Folktales* (London, 1995)

Diane Purkiss, *Troublesome Things* (London, 2000)

R. MacDonald Robertson, *Selected Highland Folktales* (Newton Abbot, 1961)

   More Highland Folktales (Edinburgh, 1964)

Anne Ross, *The Folklore of the Scottish Highlands* (London, 1976)

Jessie M. E. Saxby, *Shetland Traditional Lore* (Edinburgh, 1932)

Sir Walter Scott, *Minstrelsy of the Scottish Border* (Edinburgh, 1802-3)

   Letters on Demonology and Witchcraft (London, 1884)

Eve Blantyre Simpson, *Folk Lore in Lowland Scotland* (Wakefield, 1976)

171

Antony Mackenzie Smith, *Glenshee: Glen of the Fairies* (East Linton, 2000)

Lewis Spence, *British Fairy Origins* (London, 1946)

W. Grant Stewart, *Popular Superstitions and Festive Amusements of the Highlanders of Scotland* (London, 1851)

Elizabeth Sutherland, *In Search of the Picts* (London, 1994)

Alan Temperley, *Tales of the North Coast* (London, 1977)

   Tales of Galloway (London, 1979)

Francis Thompson, *The Supernatural Highlands* (London, 1976)